THE EMBODIMENT OF EVIL

Something stood there—something darker than the night. I knew in that instant that every word the maid'd told me had been true. A flash of lightning ripped across the sky outside, and I saw the Waster clearly silhouetted against its sudden light.

He was shaped like a man, but stood almost eight feet high, towering like a monolith above us. Coals of red fire smoldered in his eyes. He was too big to come through the door—but he had no need to enter. He picked me up with a hand that was hard as iron and, as my fists struck futile blows against his massive chest, hurled me across the room. I landed with a jarring crash.

Helplessly, I watched him take up the Grey Rose and turn from the threshold. Her eyes were wide with terror, her scream silent.

Then a darkness came washing over me and I knew no more.

CHARLES de LINT

The HARP of the GREY ROSE

AVON BOOKS ◆ NEW YORK

A portion of this novel previously appeared in *Swords Against Darkness IV*, edited by Andrew J. Offut (Zebra, 1979), under the title "The Fame of the Grey Rose."

AVON BOOKS
A division of
The Hearst Corporation
105 Madison Avenue
New York, New York 10016

Copyright © 1985 by Charles de Lint
Cover art by Darrell Sweet
Published by arrangement with the author
Library of Congress Catalog Card Number: 90-93397
ISBN: 0-380-76202-1

First Avon Books Printing: February 1991

AVON TRADEMARK REG. U.S. PAT. OFF. AND IN OTHER COUNTRIES, MARCA REGISTRADA, HECHO EN U.S.A.

Printed in the U.S.A.

RA 10 9 8 7 6 5 4 3 2 1

for my
grandmother
Oma Kamé

and

dedicated
to the
memory
of my
father
Frederic Charles
(1919–1967)

Has it flown away
The cuckoo that called
Waking me at midnight?
Yet its song seems
Still by my pillow.

—Fujiwara Shunzei
(Toshinari)

Contents

The fateful slumber floats and flows
About the tangle of the rose;
But lo! the fated hand and heart
To rend the slumberous curse apart!

—William Morris

THE GREY ROSE

Secret roads there are,
entwined like a clutch of reeds
made silver by the moon
—the tinker's road, the hunter's road,
the hidden way the Harpers go;
but more secret still
are the ways the elder folk once trod.
Gentle and merry,
haunted of old,
they wind deeper still.

—from the SONGWEAVER'S JOURNEYBOOK

ONCE A YEAR AT MIDSUMMER, TESS'S BROTHER FINAN CAME to stay with us for a day or three. They were both Kelledys, tinkers from Lillowen originally. But while the road was still Finan's home Tess had quit the travelling life before I was born. She'd settled into a small cottage on the edge of the West Downs in Eldwolde where she played the part of witch-wife to the folk of Wran Cheaping and, for the past fifteen years, fostermother to myself.

She was a big-boned woman, old enough to be my grand-mother and taller than me by a good three inches, though I stood just under six feet. Her hair was the grey of a sun-bleached stone, her features lean and her eyes a piercing blue—"A witch's eyes, sure enough," the villagers called them. I was never sure what part of her cures and far-seeing was simply good commonsense and what was owed to that "wee touch of the old blood" that she claimed ran in her mother's side of the family, bypassing the sons in favour of the daughters.

Knowing her as well as I did, I had to admit—when she was mixing up her herb simples or merely gazing far-eyed into the fire—that there was something fey about her. There was a certain look in her eyes that never touched her brother's.

She was ten years Finan's senior—a fact she liked to play up when they argued.

"You'd do well to listen to your elders," she'd tell him, a long bony finger stabbing the air for emphasis. "Remember who it was that changed your swaddling when Da' was on the road and Mum too busy to pay any mind to your wailing. Broom and heather! I knew a thing or two before ever you were howling out your lungs, and if I don't know more now, you tell me—who does?"

Finan would grin then and give me a wink.

He was a tall, handsome man, black-haired but greying at the temples, smooth-shaven and dark-eyed, with a gold loop in each earlobe and his clothes a shock of colour you could see a mile off on the downs—all reds and yellows like an armload of pimpernels and dandelions gathered in a bunch and set down on a rock. He gave me a shirt once—bell-heather pink with a collar ruffle—but I'd yet to wear it out of sight of the cottage. It was hard enough that the folk of Wran Cheaping thought of me as the witch's foster son, without my parading about like a jack-a-dandy. There were whispers and wary smiles a-plenty behind my back. No need to add laughter to them.

This summer Finan arrived a day early—in time for the week's end market—and he and I rode into the village where he sold three of his tinkerblades for twice as many silver pieces and mended a pot or two for a handful of coppers. There were sausages from the market and fresh greens from the garden for dinner that night, washed down with a skin of wine that Finan produced from his seemingly bottomless pack. Afterward we let the fire die down and sat talking by the glow of a single fat candle that did its valiant best to light the whole of the small cottage from its spot on the mantel.

The cottage was all one room, with a low bed, with a small chest at its foot in each of two corners, a large stone hearth from which hung an array of tinwork, cast-iron pots and pans, and wooden utensils; and a long, low table by the door where Tess cut and bundled her herb simples. A small shelf of books stood in a third corner—a rare treasure in a land where few could read and fewer still cared to. Throughout the cottage, wherever there was space on the rafters, hung dried bunches of herbs, flowers, and the like for teas, medicines, and simples. Stacked in the fourth corner were dried willow withies that we soaked in a large tub to make pliable before we did our basketwork.

Two chairs completed the furnishings. Tess's was a rocker, while mine was a sturdy oak affair with legs that I'd tried to carve into the semblance of a brecaln's feet. They'd come out looking not so much like a hill cat's paws as some strange cross between a furred bird's feet and who knew what. Finan had my chair tonight while I sat on a pillow by the hearth.

"Should've seen the lad," he teased, and I saw what was coming. I'd already heard it on the ride back from the market. "Gawking about like he'd never been to the village before. He had his eyes on one lass—let me tell you. If I hadn't caught them and popped them back into his head, I'm sure he'd still be there, scrabbling about in the dirt looking for them."

Tess shot me a considering look, and I knew what was brewing behind those bird-bright eyes of hers. She was ever pushing me to make friends in the village, but I found it hard. Few had time for the witch's fosterling, and I had little in common with any of them. It wasn't that I thought myself better; we viewed the world through different eyes, and it set me apart. They met me with a curious mixture of mockery and fear—the fear that Tess had taught me a spell or two.

"Was she pretty?" Tess asked.

Finan wagged his hand in the air and arched his brows.

"Pretty enough," he said, "in a peculiar sort of way."

Again, I had to wonder if he'd seen the same maid I had.

She was a stranger to Wran Cheaping, as far as I knew. Since I lacked a name for her, in my own mind I called her the Grey Rose for the blossom she wore in her rust-brown hair. That rose was the colour of twilight, as grey as the mists upon the West Downs. I swore its petals were still damp with morning dew, for all that the day's end was nearly upon us when I saw her.

Farmer Howen's sons were examining Finan's tinkerblades when she swept by, her mantle rustling like windblown leaves. Their backs were to her, but I was looking beyond them, trying not to listen to their cautious jibes, so that I saw her when they did not.

"Fair gives me a chill," Jon, the elder, was saying, "standing so near one who deals with the fairy folk."

His brother Sewell smirked. They were cut from the same cloth, these two big, brawny farm lads with hair like straw and dung-brown eyes.

"Best watch your tongue," Sewell said, "or he'll turn you into a toad, and you'll eat nothing but flies."

Finan gave them both a hard look, but I paid neither of them any mind. I'd heard it all before. It made me sad as well as angry, as always. Nothing I could say would change their minds. Well, let them have their magic and legend and superstition. I knew better.

I watched the maid I had named the Grey Rose move through the market. For all that no one else seemed to give her more than a glance, she'd bound me with a spell. Her mantle was oak-leaf green, and under it she wore a rust-coloured smock and a cream-white blouse. Stars appeared to glisten in her dusky eyes, so clear and bright, and there was an air about her like a breath of autumn—a sweet and heady scent. Though she wasn't tall, something about her lent her the appearance of height, and she walked with a loose, easy stride. Here she bought a sack of grains, there a handful of fresh sprouts and greens, and carried it all in a wicker basket on her arm.

I wondered where she was from and why no other gaze

followed her as mine did. She set my heart a-singing, and I longed to speak with her, but I was too aware of my rough woolens and shabby cloak. I was always shy—and what had I to speak of with one like her? She seemed highborn . . . I suppose it was, although the only noble folk I had experience with were in the tales Tess had told me.

As she reached the far side of the market, she stole a glance my way, and her gaze caught mine in such a way that we seemed to share a secret that only we two could understand. She smiled; I cast my gaze to the ground, my heart drumming. I could feel my neck redden under my collar. When I had looked up once more she had been gone; and all I had to look upon were the plain, broad faces of Howen's sons.

"She was beautiful," I said, giving Finan a warning look.

He shrugged as if helpless. A smile tugged at the corners of his mouth, but he said nothing.

"What was her name, Cerin?" Tess asked.

"I . . . I don't know."

She made a *tching* sound with her tongue, and I could see the cogs in her mind whirling as she planned the matchmaking.

"I never seen her before," I offered.

"There are ways to find folk," she declared.

A fey look came into her eyes. At times like that I was always uneasy. I liked the idea of magic better than being confronted with it.

"Leave it be," I said, shaking my head. "Please."

I might never see the maid again, but I didn't want the memory of her tied up with either Tess's herb charms or her brother's jokes. I think Tess read that in my face, for she pursed her lips, sighed, then turned to Finan and asked him of his trip from Lillowen. I stayed to listen for a while, but I found it hard to concentrate. Since that moment in the market my thoughts had never strayed far from the maid of the Grey Rose and, reminded of her once again—even in such a way as Finan's teasing—I was hard put to think of anything else.

At length I fetched my harp from beside my bed and went out into the night to sit beside the well. There was a smoothed stone there that I'd found out on the downs two summers ago and spent a few days half rolling and half dragging to its present location. I liked to sit there at night sometimes, playing my harp.

It was a rudely carved instrument, not the work of a skilled craftsman, for I'd laboriously fashioned it myself. The supports and soundbox were cut from weather-worn barnwood, and it was strung with bronze-wound strings that Finan had given me to replace the original cow-gut ones I'd begged from Ralen Tagh, who had a meat stall in the market. Yet for all its rustic looks, it had a pleasing enough tone; and I could coax tunes from it to fill the long hours I spent on my own. The case—I'd sewed in myself—was made of goatskin.

I sat with it on my lap for a while, feeling the night's stillness settle in me. There was a light wind blowing in from the downs, carrying with it the smell of heather, and the stars wheeled in their constellations above, both distant and close.

I began to tune the harp, but neither the night's quiet nor the task at hand could ease the trouble in my heart. That one smile from the lips of the Grey Rose had awakened a longing in me that would not be stilled. Not so much for her, for I knew little enough of women. Besides, what would one such as her want with the likes of me? No, it was a discontent she reawoke—one that was never far from me. It had nothing to do with Tess, for I loved her as if she was my own mother, but it was more her fault than the girl's, for Tess had filled my head with tales of the world beyond these downs that I longed to see with my own eyes. Every year when Finan came, those feelings grew stronger, and yet . . . I was afraid to go, as well.

When the harp was tuned, I let my fingers play what they would. They strayed across the strings while I let my thoughts ramble, until I found I was playing the opening bars to a cradle song Tess used to sing to me. When I thought of my parents—I was only two years old when the sickness took them and left me an orphan—it was her face that came into my mind's eye. What I knew of them was only what Tess had told me.

My mother had been Eithne Gwynn, a Harper of the old school, revered and respected until she was exiled from the Harperhall in Wistlore for wedding a gwandryas, one of the wandering nomads of the Grassfields of Kohr. It was from her that I got my knack for tunes and the like, while my father's wild blood was responsible for a feyness that Tess said I had, though any such had yet to manifest itself—if it was present at all. Some might argue that it was my father's blood that set me apart from my peers in Wran Cheaping, but I thought not. It was nothing so romantic. I was simply too aware that there was a world beyond, while they preferred to ignore it.

Tess had known both my parents. Eithne she described as a tall woman, with brown hair more red than my own, and the same green-gold eyes. She had been such a skilled Harper that the mantle of Masterharper would have fallen to her when the old Masterharper Curran Wemyse passed on, had she not met and wed Windalane. Tess said he was a lean man, with skin tough as leather, dark from the wind and the sun and more at home in the saddle than on foot. He was as wild as the Grassfields themselves.

She tended them both when they came down with the sickness and took me in as a fosterling when they died. It was a bad time, Tess told me. For six months the plague raged through Eldwolde and down into the Trembling Lands. Then it was gone as suddenly as it had come. It had taken a sixth of the village folk, except in the most outlying regions—and the hardest struck of all were those not native to the area—travelling folk such as tinkers, merchants . . . and Harpers. Fifteen years later, it was still known as the Black Winter.

As a child, I wasn't lonely—for I had nothing to compare my life with Tess against. My whole world was the cottage and its gardens and the walks we took on the downs or to the Golden Wood where Tess collected the herbs and plants she didn't grow herself. But, as I grew older, the differences between my life and that lived by those in the village and the neighboring farms became more evident. By this time I had resolved to master the minstrel craft, as my mother had, and earn my living with the harp rather than with a hoe or following the herds.

It was Tess who showed me how to fashion a harp. My mother's had been burned along with the rest of my parents' belongings to forestall the spread of the sickness. I had dreams of making a name for myself with the instrument—of travelling to distant Wistlore where the Harpers, Loremasters, Wyslings, and other wizardly folk were said to hold court. I wanted to show them what had become of Eithne Gwynn's son. Then I would return to Wran Cheaping with gold in my pocket and the title Harper before my name so that the villagers could see what had become of the witch's fosterling.

I meant to show them all. And perhaps, if that maid of the Grey Rose lived here still, I'd go a-courting her with a fine harp strapped to my shoulder and tales worth the telling to delight her ears.

I laughed softly to myself at such fancies. I'd yet to gather the courage to set the first foot on the road. But still. . . . Did we all not need our dreams?

My fingers trailed quiet melodies on the harp until weariness came over me. I played one last tune and returned to the cottage to find Tess and Finan both asleep—she on her bed and he wrapped in a cloak before the hearth. I stored my harp safely away and readied my own bed, falling asleep to dream of a maid with red-brown hair and dusky eyes the colour of a twilight rose.

THE NEXT DAY FINAN HELPED ME PUT A NEW ROOF ON THE goats' shed on the south side of the cottage. I had cut the branches we'd need a few weeks earlier, and we spent the morning taking the old roof off and weaving a new framework. After a noon meal of cheese curds and freshly baked bread, we laid the turf, holding it in place with weighted ropes.

"That should keep them dry another year or two," Finan said as we stood back to admire our handiwork. "Tess said you had a bad winter down here."

I nodded. "Early coming and late going."

We took turns washing up at the well; then we made ourselves comfortable on the wooden bench in front of the cottage with our backs against the stone wall and our feet stretched out in front of us. After a while I fetched some tea. When I returned, Finan had a sheathed tinkerblade on his knee. He was playing with the leather-bound hilt and nodded a thanks when I passed him his mug.

"Couldn't help but notice," he said, "at the market yesterday—those boys. . . ."

"John and Sewell Howen," I said with a shrug. "They mean no real harm."

"I saw one or two others give you an odd look as well."

I sipped my tea, but said nothing. What was there to say? Things between the villagers and me stood no different now than they ever had.

"You're what now? Seventeen?" Finan asked. When I nodded, he went on. "It's time you had a friend or two, don't you think?"

I sighed, sure now that Tess had put him up to this talk.

"We've nothing in common," I said.

"How are you so different? You've lived round here so long you might as well be a native. With only Tess for company, you must get lonely."

For a long moment I stared out across the downs.

"In here," I replied at length, tapping my chest. "The difference lies in here. And I'd rather Tess's company seven days of the week than theirs for an hour. . . . They look on a forest, Finan, and see nothing but lumber and firewood. They look on the hills and think only of grazing, or how the soil can be turned for their crops. Women are for bedding and raising their children. Music is something they think of only when they're drunk. The old tales are for children."

"But they're still your neighbors, Cerin. They're not such odd folk."

"No. It's folk like you and Tess and me that are odd, and I'd rather leave it so. Tell me, Finan. Would you settle down in Wran Cheaping and live as they do?"

The tinker smiled. "Me? What for?"

"Just so."

Finan thought for a moment, then nodded, accepting my logic. He said nothing for a while, then handed me the blade that lay across his knees.

"Take this," he said.

I looked from it to him and smiled. "What would I do with it?"

Tinkerblades are short swords or long knives—depending on your outlook. They have fourteen-inch blades, usually set into briar handles with leather grips wrapped about. I took the weapon and turned it in my hands. I knew little enough about such things, though like any boy I'd cut myself a staff and spent more than one afternoon whacking it against tree trunks or using it to shear the tops from weeds that in my imagination were gremlins and dragons and who knows what.

"You needn't do anything with it," Finan explained. "Only wear it. You're old enough to be considered a man now. With a blade strapped on your belt, the jibes won't come so quick, I'm thinking."

I shook my head and handed it back.

"I think not, Finan. I'd as like cut my hand off with it. But I thank you."

He wouldn't take the blade. "Hang it by your bed, then," he said. "I made it for you. It's a real blade, Cerin—the kind we make for ourselves, not the sort we sell. Time'll come when you'll set out on the road. Be good to have a blade at your belt then."

He smiled at the far-off look that came into my eyes.

"You've been thinking about it more than once, haven't you?"

I nodded. "But there's Tess. . . ."

"You forget your worries about her, Cerin. It's only her own stubbornness that keeps her sitting here in the middle of the downs rather than coming back to Lillowen and living out her life like a proper tinker would when she'd done with the road. I don't know what passes through that poor excuse of a mind of hers sometimes—truly I don't."

I began to protest, but he cut me off.

"Na, na. Don't *you* leap to her defense. I'll tell you why she stays here. It's not the air or a love for the country. Oh, no. It's for those same queer looks that you get when you go to the village. Mark my words. She thrives on the very idea of being the old wise woman living out on the downs—a little strange, touched with a certain feyness. Ballan! When we were children she used to put on me mum's old grey shawl and sit about practicing that eerie stare of hers. . . ." He shook his head, then grinned. "But she makes a grand witch-wife, now doesn't she? I mean, she has the look—there's no mistaking it."

I laughed with him. And if she could have heard him talking. . . .

"Don't let it be her that keeps you back," Finan said. "She loves you—and never doubt it—but there always comes a time with folk such as us when the road calls too strongly, and we must be off and away down it or never again be content."

"Sometimes. . . ." I looked at him. "Sometimes I want to go so badly it hurts, but then . . . it frightens me to think of that world out there and me in it. Here I know who I am and what I am. Out there. . . ."

"We all have misgivings from time to time. The road can be lonely, Cerin, true enough. And dangerous, too. But there's nothing like it for meeting folks and making true friends. You spend a month or two on the road with a fellow—broom and heather! You'll either be the best of friends or at each other's throat." He paused, sipped his tea. "You can come with me if you like. My packs are light this year, and we could easily divide their weight between the two horses. . . ."

I thought of it, as I had every year since I turned twelve, but then the image of the Grey Rose came into my mind, and, foolish though it might be, I knew I had to see her at least once again, talk to her perhaps . . . though what I'd say. . . .

Finan must have seen something of my thoughts in my face.

"Thinking of that maid, are you?"

"I can't stop."

"She the first as made you feel this way?"

What way? I was going to ask, but I already knew.

There was more that was curious about me than the way I thought or whatever it was that my parents' blood stirred in me. Under Tess's tutelage I had learned to read and write. I had learned a hundred ballads and tunes and old tales. I knew more of the histories of the lands beyond Eldwolde's borders than the folk of Wran Cheaping knew of their own small village. And yet, with all that learning cluttering my mind, I was still an innocent. I knew nothing firsthand about the workings of the world, or even about such a simple thing as what took place between a man and a woman who loved each other—only what I'd learned in books and songs.

And, when I thought of the Grey Rose, what stirred in me was something I could not readily explain. It was like the beginning of a ballad, or unlooked-for moonlight on an overcast night. It was more than her beauty. It was that look we shared. It was . . . I knew not what.

"There was something about her," I said at last, but I could no more frame the words than I could explain to myself what I felt.

Finan shrugged. "There's some might look at you and see nothing but a downs lad, while another might look far enough to see the Harper hid inside. As for your maid—I was teasing, but only in part. I found something disquieting about her, a touch of the same feyness that makes the villagers keep their distance from my sister and you. And because she's unknown to me. . . . That sense of disquiet disturbed me."

"Few paid her any attention," I said, "either wary or admiring."

"I know," Finan said softly. "As if there were some glamour about her that only you could see through. . . ."

He had all my attention then, but Tess chose that moment to call us for our supper. The moment when I could question him about it again never arose throughout the rest of his visit.

We went inside, and I hung my new tinkerblade on the

wall behind my bed. That night we all had a little too much of Finan's wine, and long past bedtime we were sitting out in front of the cottage, bellowing the chorus of some song that none of us could remember the verses to, waking the goats with our noise, then shocking them into silence as we lifted our voices above their bleating. In the morning we all slept late, waking with heads that felt too thick for the small space between our temples.

FINAN DIDN'T REPEAT HIS OFFER BEFORE HE LEFT. I THINK he knew that, for all my yearnings, it was still not the time for me to take the road. He rode off alone, leading his pack horse, and our lives returned to their regular routine. The morning after he left I finished my chores early and, with my harp over my shoulder, I made for the Golden Wood that lies just north of Wran Cheaping. I meant to make a day of it. There was a loaf of bread and a slab of cheese in my wallet and a lightness in my heart as I said my goodbyes to Tess and set out.

"Mind you bring us back some mushrooms," she called after me.

"I will."

"And some cress—if you're going by the stream."

"All right."

"And some clover—red, mind you. Do you have a sack?"

I didn't, so I returned for the one she was holding in her hand.

"Don't get lost," she said with a mock frown, and gave me a push. "Now be off with you—I've work to do."

By the time I reached the Wood's shade, the sun was bright overhead, though there was still an hour before the noon. I wandered for a while under the summer-rich boughs of the beech and elm, then pushed my way through stands of thin maple and silver birch until I reached the banks of Clossey Water. The stream's clear, bubbling water was too inviting to resist. Stripping and throwing my clothes to the ground, I made a path through the cattails and watercress and plunged in.

I lolled about in the water until my fingers and toes turned white, then clambered up the bank and sat in the sun until I was dry. I dreamt lazily of the world beyond the West Downs and of magic things. There was supposed to be muryan living in the downs—little brown folk with horned brows and grey cloaks—and erlkin were said to make their homes in the dark glades deep within the Golden Wood itself. I longed to meet an erl or any sort of magical being but had to content myself with a pair of chattering squirrels in the trees by the stream.

After a while I got dressed, and, after storing some cress in Tess's sack, I fared deeper into the wood. For almost two hours I walked, my head full of dreamy thoughts, until I came to a dale filled with orchids and red campions, light blue columbines and other wild flowers, all shimmering in the deep grass as if this were some fairy glade. As I stepped from the trees, a hawfinch rose chittering before me and winged quickly into the canopy of the oak and elm that roofed the dell. There were mushrooms growing in abundance, and I picked enough to eat later with my cheese and bread as well as filling Tess's sack.

When I had had enough, I sat down and tuned my harp. Soon I was deep into a new tune, losing myself in the wealth of harmonies I could imagine within its measures. Here the tumbling, breathy timbre of a flute could add a frill; there the lift and lilt of a fiddle's tone could strengthen the flow.

This was for the maid of the Grey Rose, I decided as the tune took a firm hold of me. I hummed it to myself until words came to mind—ill shaped by a true Harper's standards, perhaps, but fair-sounding enough to me.

> Perchance the dream has grown o'erbold
>   to wend the paths of day,
> yet fair you are, and fairer still,
>   and love I may not stay.
> O I will call you Friend,
>   as oaken leaf to oak does cling
>   and oft' the moon her golden ring,
> O I will call you Friend.

> *Yet I would cast no bond o'er you,*
> *and I would lay no snare;*
> *let lip kiss lip and hand meet hand*
> *and mingled be our hair.*
> *And I will call you Friend,*
> *as oaken leaf. . . .*

Imagine my surprise when I heard another voice, low and sweet, join my own in the refrain. I stopped in mid-tune and looked up to find the selfsame maid of my new song standing in front of me. She was wearing a short white kirtle that outlined the shape of breast and hip and contrasted sharply with the sun-brown of her skin.

I scrambled to my feet, hot with embarrassment, my harp falling to the grass with a discordant ring.

"Wh-what are you doing here?" I asked.

I wished I hadn't spoken as I stumbled over the words.

A low chuckle escaped her throat, and she smiled.

"Why, I'm picking mushrooms for my supper, Harper," she replied, brushing a willful lock of rust-colored hair from her cheek. "That was a brave tune you were playing. What is it called?"

For a moment I thought she was mocking me, my only thought was to flee the glen. But her face held no guile, and her words were so generous that I gathered my courage.

"It's a . . . new tune," I said. "When it was finished I was going to name it for you . . . for the Grey Rose."

I could feel my cheeks go red as I spoke. The maid lifted a hand to the blossom in her hair, then smiled again. Gracefully she settled herself in the grass, her slim legs tucked under her kirtle.

"You honour me, Harper," she said. "Will you play it through for me again?"

Numbly, I nodded in agreement and sat down across from her. I picked up my harp and nervously strummed the opening chords until, haltingly and with many false starts, I began the tune again. I was too shy to sing the words I'd sung earlier, but I tried to play the air with the best of my skill. When I

came to a complex sequence of notes, I suddenly forgot my
shyness. The tune took hold of me once more, and I played
with an assurance and confidence unknown to me—except
when I was alone in some secluded wood or field. Even with
Tess, my playing was usually subdued.

She hummed the air with me, and my fingers fairly flew
over the strings. Her voice set me all a-tremble, but all too
soon the moment passed and the last strains of our music
faded into the afternoon air. She sighed.

"How are you named, Harper?"

There was something about her voice—an accent or the
way she shaped her words—that told me she wasn't from
Eldwolde. I thought of erlkin again, and a delightful shiver
went through me.

"My name's Cerin. But I'm not a Harper."

She looked at me quizzically.

"You've not the look of one, that's true enough. You've a
husbandman's raiment, and your hands are callused from
more than harping, yet who's to say what a Harper should
look like? You've a touch as light and fair as any I've ever
heard." She stood suddenly. "I thought to eat early. There's
barley-bowl and fresh mushrooms waiting for us, if you'd
care to share a meal with me."

I nodded, my heartbeat quickening.

"What shall I call you?" I asked.

She smiled and touched the bloom in her hair again.

"Grey Rose is a fair name," she said.

I waited for her to say more, but when she spoke, it was
only to ask, "Shall we go?"

I gathered up my harp, my wallet, and Tess's sack to follow
her through the woods to her home. She moved with an erlkin's grace and, though she wasn't tall—as I mentioned
before, for the top of her head reached only to my shoulder—
still when she walked beside me I felt that I had to look up
to see her face.

We came at last to another glade bounded by gnarled ash
trees and thickets of birch and young oak. There was a cottage in the middle, built of stone and draped with vines, with

a garden of wildflowers at the front and a well to one side. While she went inside to fetch refreshments, I stood looking about myself, marvelling. I'd been here before—early in the spring—and though this cottage had been here, at that time it hadn't had a roof and the glade itself had been overgrown with weeds and brush.

I remembered Finan's disquiet, and some echo of it stirred in me. Who was she, this maid of the Grey Rose, who took the name I gave her rather than telling me her own and lived in the middle of the wood all alone? I puzzled at the mystery. But when she came outside, balancing a tray laden with two mugs of steaming tea and a platter of fresh-baked bannocks, I soon forgot the riddle, exchanging it for the food and her company.

That afternoon and the evening that followed passed like time spent in a dream. We dined on simple fare and talked long into the night, and that discontent she had awakened in me in the market found its focus. Whatever mysteries she hid behind her smiling eyes and easy conversation no longer worried me. I felt as if we were old friends who hadn't seen each other for a while and were now come together again, and I yearned for her as any man might yearn for a maid who warmed his heart.

We sang some songs that evening—tunes that I'd written or learned from Tess, and others, strange wistful ballads and airs that the maid taught me. It wasn't till after I'd set my harp aside and we'd sat for a while in a companionable silence that she told me something of her past, and then her words were couched in such vagueness that, rather than settling my worries, it fired them again.

"I am from a place that is near, yet far from here," she said.

I thought of the Middle Kingdom that the old tales said lay side by side with the fields of men—close as a thought, distant as a year's journey. Much as I loved the legends, I couldn't believe them, though sometimes my Harper's heart ached to be a part of it all—the stuff of magic. The maid regarded me a moment, then glanced away, her gaze following the play of shadows on the walls of the cottage. The room was a third the size of Tess's cottage and was plainly furnished. There was little in the way of personal effects, and the only light was the dim glow of the hearth. What furnishings there were—a bed in the corner, a table and two chairs near the hearth, a small cabinet under the rear window—I remembered from my previous visit. The only difference was that the broken leg on one of the chairs was mended, and all the wood was polished to a fine glow.

"There is a geas upon me," she continued, "that drives me like a leaf before the wind—through many lands. There is a shade of the dark that follows me and strives to undo all my deeds and make me its own. Long roads have I wended, Cerin, until at the waxing of the Dyad Moon I came to this wood, weary from wandering and yearning to rest a spell. But not for long . . . no, never for long. . . ."

Her voice trailed off, and she lapsed into a thoughtful silence. What she said confused me but made me anxious for her sake. Whispers of old tales and ballads crept into my mind. I saw all the forces of darkness raised against her and myself her only protector. I was about to offer her my help, for what it was worth, when she smiled suddenly and turned the conversation to other matters until my anxieties for her fled, and I had to smile at myself for letting my imagination get the better of me.

There was a mystery about the maid of the Grey Rose—that I couldn't deny. But just as I let my own fancies of becoming a Harper sustain me, I was sure she had her own reasons for cloaking herself in mystery. Loneliness is always easier to bear when one can convince oneself that being alone is just a step along the way to a greater destiny. And my new friend, I realized, was as lonely in her own way as I was. More so, perhaps, for she had no one else while I at least had Tess.

I vowed to myself not to pry, to be only the friend to her that I would have her be to me. When I arrived at that decision, a weight seemed suddenly to lift from me. I realized then that the riddle of who she was and why she was here had troubled me more than I'd thought. Now that it was eased, I was hard put to explain why. When I looked at her with the firelight playing on her features and hair, I saw a maid—no more. Fey she was, but only in the way that a woman is when a man's heart yearns for her.

The Mead Moon was high when I rose reluctantly to make my way home. The maid accompanied me to her threshold and touched my arm as I stepped outside.

"Will you come again, Cerin?" she asked.

I said I would, readily enough.

My step was light as I walked through the darkened Golden Wood, and I paid no mind to the chill in the night wind that came off the West Downs. The afterglow of the Grey Rose's company kept me warm. The cottage door creaked on its hinges as I slipped inside and tiptoed to my bed. I had put away my harp and turned to leave the sack of mushrooms and cress on Tess's worktable when I saw that she was awake and watching me in the dark.

"Out late," she remarked.

There were still coals glowing warm on the hearth. I laid a twig against them and blew lightly on it. When it caught, I used the flame to light a candle, then went to sit on the edge of Tess's bed.

"Met her in the wood, did you?" she asked.

I nodded, wondering if it was plain on my face, or if she knew through methods of her own.

"So what's her name?" Tess asked, sitting up.

"The Grey Rose."

Tess smiled. "And are you her Brown-haired Harper?"

"It's not like that . . ." I began, but she laid her thin hand on my own and squeezed it gently.

"I know," she said. "I'm happy for you, Cerin. It's time you met a girl—Ballan knows, you're a fine-looking lad with a kind heart. Now tell me, does she like you as well?"

"She asked if I'd come to see her again."

"Ah," Tess said, and a contented look came into her eyes. "Best you get some sleep now, Cerin."

"I will."

"Sweet dreams," she said.

I smiled as I leaned forward to kiss her goodnight. Blowing out the candle, I went to my own bed. I thought I would lie awake half the night, but no sooner did my head touch the pillow than sleep stole over me, deep and sudden.

THE MEAD MOON GAVE WAY TO THE WORT MOON, WHICH in turn gave way to the first moon of the autumn, the Barley, and so the summer passed. I worked with Tess in the garden and about the cottage, readied wood for the winter months. We made the baskets that the farmers bought to stock their produce in—a tinker's weave was always in demand—and completed the herb simples and packets that Trader Haberlin bought from us each year around Samhain and, in turn, sold in the Southern Kingdoms as he made his way home for the winter. The villagers came by from time to time for cures and medicines, and we bought a new goat from Farmer Howen when old Gara died at the end of the summer. We named the new goat Ruane after a cousin of Tess's.

In the evenings I wrote tunes for the Grey Rose, or added airs to the tales she told me—sometimes setting them to rhyme. At least twice a week I made my way to her cottage in the Golden Wood to spend an afternoon or evening with her. The time passed all too quickly in quiet talk and the sharing of songs and, if we never lay together as lovers, the friendship that blossomed between us eased my loneliness, leaving me well content.

Sometimes at night, I lay awake thinking of her. Then I'd dream of her in my arms, her head against my shoulder, her body pressing against mine, until I'd need an hour's walk on the downs to still the drumming of my heart. On the following day when I walked to her cottage, I'd be determined to advance the cause of my love, yet somehow, once we were together, the urgency would fade. I'd be content with her company and think to myself: it will come . . . in its own time. . . .

And a change did come, with the Blood Moon, but not the change I'd looked for.

One day in early autumn I walked from home with a new tune at my fingers and my heart filled with the wonder of the season. The harvests were all gathered—from the farmers' fields and from the small garden that Tess and I tended—and the whole world hummed with the coming of the year's end. Seas of rust and gold, brown and singing red, swept across the downs. The Golden Wood was so bright that I almost had to turn my eyes from it.

Underfoot, bright melyonen bloomed violet amongst the fallen leaves and nuts. The bushes hung heavy with berries—thick splashes of colour against the increasingly somber attire of the undergrowth. My heart was light, and I hummed merrily to myself as I stepped along. A quickening confidence had blossomed in me along with the maturing of the barley and corn in their fields, and I harvested that sense of self-worth more eagerly than the farmers did their crops.

That was my gift from the Grey Rose. She taught me that to be myself was enough, that what I was meant more than anything others would make of me.

When I reached the glade where her cottage stood, I paused in midstep and the lightness of my heart washed away. The difference was hard to define, but I sensed a subtle change in the glade that was more than just the turning of the seasons. It was as if a darkness brooded in the shadows of the trees, waiting for just the right moment to sidle forth. . . .

I hurried across the glade. The door to the cottage stood ajar. When I peered inside, I saw the Grey Rose sitting disconsolately at her table, a half-packed journeysack on the floor beside her. I crossed the threshold.

"What's happened?" I asked.

But I already knew. From the looks of things she was making ready to leave. She'd spoken of it before, but I'd never paid much attention. I had convinced myself that such a time would never truly come.

She looked up at the sound of my voice and attempted a brave smile.

"Ah, Cerin, I must away. I've tarried here too long. Though time seems to pass slowly in this wood, it speeds by nevertheless. I have a geas that is overdue in its fulfilling, and I fear I've not the strength to flee it any longer. My bane will soon come a-knocking on my door.''

"What do you mean?''

She was silent and sat as if she hadn't heard me speak. My thoughts returned to the first evening we'd spent together and the curious things she'd said then that she was repeating now. We hadn't spoken of them since. I tried to still the thudding of my heart to no avail.

"Let me help you.''

"I fear you can't, dear friend.'' She sighed and took my hand. "Sit you down, Cerin, and I will tell you the tale of my life and the sorry end it comes to.''

I was still taken with her quaint manner of speech, but today her words filled me with foreboding. It seemed that the time for the mystery's unravelling had come. Curious as I once had been, I wished now that this time had never come.

"Have you heard tell of the Cradle of the Kings?'' she asked.

I nodded. "Tess's told me of it. It was a great city in the old days, though now it lies in ruins not too far from here. She said that it was once more revered than Wistlore. Bright lords ruled it and searched out the wisdoms of the world from its tall towers. It lay just above the western entrance to Holme's Way—on the edge of the Perilous Mountains—and fell in some great war. Now nothing remains but fallen towers and the ghosts of the dead. She had another name for it as well. . . .''

"Banlore,'' the maid said.

"That was it.'' I paused, trying to read in her features what was wrong. "But was does that place have to do with you?''

"I am hand-fasted to one therein. His name is Yarac Stone-slayer, and he is a Waster—a child of the Daketh, the Dark Gods. He it is that I must wed.''

I was horror-struck at her words. I opened my mouth to speak, but she tightened her grip on my hand.

"No. List first to my tale, Cerin, before you voice your protests. It was long ago I pledged my hand to him. In return for that vow, I gained the promise that no harm would come to the Hill Lords—those who reigned in the Trembling Lands at the end of the Elder Days.

"There was war between the Hillfolk and Yarac—a cruel war that seemed to rage for longer than long is. The Hill Lords were pitiful in number, for all that their hearts were brave and true. They would have fallen soon had we not this offer to make to the Waster. I am of the Hill Lord's kin, you see, though my mother was of an older folk still. It was by my will that this bargain was made—hateful though it proved for me.

"On the eve of our wedding—while I stood at the Daketh's unholy altar in Banlore with Yarac—he sent a plague of were-riders and yargs into the Trembling Lands. They slew almost all the surviving Hill Lords. Yarac never dreamed that I would learn of it until it was too late—until my body was his, my power his. But word came nevertheless. I flew from Banlore, and he pursued me.

"On the hills near those evil ruins, Yarac met with me and the remnants of the Hill Lords. The battle raged for a day and a night, until all but I were slain. I escaped when the last of the Hillfolk died—and I flee yet. . . ."

I shook my head in bewilderment. I knew the tales of the Wasters, but thought them only tales. And as for the war of the Hill Lords. . . . There *had* been a war in the Trembling Lands, one that had touched even the West Downs and the Golden Wood, but that had been in ages past. There'd been no strife of that magnitude in these lands in living memory, yet she spoke of it as if it had happened yesterday. For that she would have to be . . . centuries old. It couldn't be. The undying lived only in tales. . . .

My scalp prickled, and a cold sweat of fear touched me.

"Who are you?" I asked.

I was afraid to hear her answer.

"To you," she said with a sad smile, "I would e'er be the Grey Rose."

That was no answer. I was about to say as much when she continued with her tale.

"My people have an ability to imbue certain objects with a part of ourselves. When we keep something long enough, it becomes a part of us. Such as this bloom." She touched the rose in her hair. "It lives because I live. Freely given, to a lover or a friend, that love sustains us as if the gift were never given. As if we still wore it. But otherwise. . . ."

She looked away for a moment, then back, her grey eyes catching my gaze with their sorrow.

"I had a heartstone that I wore at my neck—a small gem of no great value, save that it had become a part of me. Three years ago it was stolen and now . . . now Yarac has it. I can feel him inside me now, and there is no escaping him. He follows me with his thoughts and. . . . It is as if he'd stolen my shadow. I have a hollowness inside me, a weakening of my strengths, for now he owns a part of me. He has leagued himself with others of the Dark, and tonight . . . I know he will come for me. There is nothing I can do to stop him.

"No matter where I flee, he can follow, for the heartstone binds us. We are the last, Cerin. We are all that remains of that ancient struggle. They are all gone . . . the Hillfolk, the were-beasts, the yargs . . . all gone save he and I . . . and now he has this power over me. . . ."

She shook her head slowly and fell into a brooding silence.

"How . . . how can such things be true? These things happen only in song—in legend!"

She looked at me with a strange light in her dusky eyes.

"You and I," she said, "we've played with the ballads of old tales. But, Cerin, I know that many . . . so many of them are true. There is old magic—true magic as real as you and me. Eldwolde borders the lands of men in the south—but northward. . . . There are stranger things than you can imagine in the northlands, dear friend. They are not all like Yarac, they are not all evil. The mountains protect you from them—for few dare their heights. Eastward, the Great Waste is yet another barrier. But if you were to fare beyond them . . . there is still living magic in the north, Cerin."

I could only stare at her, my mind awhirl. My parents came from the north—my mother from Wistlore, my father from the Grassfields. And what of Lillowen, Tess's home-land? It lay beyond the Perilous Mountains as well. The Grey Rose's mien was so serious. I trusted her with my heart; I knew she didn't lie. But believing her meant I knew even less of the world than I'd thought. If the ballads and tales were real. . . .

I felt as if the world had shifted under my feet. I thought of the stories that Finan told of his travels, and the parts that I was sure he'd added just to make them sound better—trading with tall erlkin, meeting with a band of brown-skinned muryan on the hills at dusk, spells and enchantments. The way Tess nodded her head when I wouldn't believe the work-ing of a charm, or what she'd seen in the flicker of a fire's flames.

The idea was hard to accept. But if it were true . . . And then I thought of what the maid had told me, of this Yarac and his broken pledge.

"I'll help you," I promised. "I don't know how, but I'll stop him."

"Bravely spoken, Cerin, but it would be better if you were not here when he comes. To face him could mean your death, and I would not have that on my hands."

"I won't leave."

She sighed, and I sighed with her. She knew I wouldn't go, that it was no good in asking. We sat at the table together, and the day slowly wore by. I still wasn't sure what exactly it was that we waited for, but I was determined to protect her as best I could. A Waster . . . I shook my head, and the chill I felt had nothing to do with the coming of night.

As the shadows grew long in the cottage, the Grey Rose stood to light a candle from the hearth. Wearily she finished packing her journeysack with the air of one simply going through the motions.

"We could go away," I said. "We could travel somewhere he can't follow."

"There is no place where he won't follow. He calls me, pulls me near. I have no will to flee again."

She finished her packing and sat down once more to gaze

out the open door at the darkening glade. It hurt me to see her so. Her eyes were haunted, her features drawn with strain. Even the rose in her hair appeared unwell, the petals drooping.

Quietly I arose and closed the door, dropping an oak bar the width of my thigh across it. Returning to the table, I saw tears glistening in her eyes.

"Cerin, Cerin," she said. "I would not have you die. Flee now—I beg you. You can't know what you will be facing. This is no tale to be told before a roaring fire with mugs of hot tea in hand and a harp plucked softly behind the telling. I say again, there is more to the world than the ways of mankind. In the ancient forests and on the dark moors the old ways are not forgotten. There legends live, breathing the same air as might you and I. There are erlkin in those forests—as there once were in this wood—muryan on the moors, dwarves in the mountains. And where there are beings that follow the Light, there are the minions of the Dark as well.

"Yarac Stone-slayer is real, Cerin. If you bide here with me, he will slay you as easily as he could crush a stone."

"That may be," I said. "But still I'll stay. We are friends. How could I leave you to face this alone?"

"You must. This is no man that comes for me tonight, but a monster."

"My mother was a Harper and my father was a gwandryas from Kohr. My kin are from those same magical northlands, and while I lack whatever magics they might've had, I've still my own mortal strengths to raise in your defense."

I wished then that I had Finan's gift in my fist. A tinker-blade might well give pause to the monster the maid feared. How would it know that I lacked the skill to use it effectively?

The darkness grew while we spoke.

"You lack no magics," the Grey Rose said.

Her voice was so low that I wasn't sure I'd heard her. I turned to ask her what she meant, but then we heard the wind rising outside the cottage, rattling a loose shutter and tearing at the autumn-dried vines. I could feel my courage dry up and blow away with that wind, but I refused to let my fear rule me. A look of despair touched the maid's eyes when she saw I wouldn't go.

It was almost fully dark now. The wind was like a thing alive, howling about the cottage. Nothing but an autumn storm, I thought—a common enough thing for this time of year. The moon would rise soon, invisible behind the banks of black clouds that rode the sky. It was the Blood Moon— the first true moon of autumn. As the wind continued to howl, I wondered at the ill omen of its name.

Suddenly the Grey Rose stood, so abruptly that her chair clattered to the floor behind her.

"He calls," she cried in a hoarse voice. "Oh, Cerin. He calls and I am afraid."

I stood beside her, straining to sense what she heard, but all that came to my ears was the raging of the wind. She groaned and took a step toward the door. I put out a hand to stop her. No sooner had I touched her arm to draw her back than the door burst apart, whipping shards of wood about us.

I turned just in time and shielded her as best I could, staggering as a heavy weight struck my shoulders. The candle blew out as the wind tore into the cottage, but I had no need of its light to see the Grey Rose moving toward the door where the intruder waited.

"No!" I cried as I saw him.

Something stood there—something darker than the night. I knew in that instant that every word the maid'd told me had been true. Pushing her aside, I caught up a chair with both hands and leapt at the figure, putting all my strength into the blow. The chair splintered into kindling against the huge form, and my hands went numb. Something struck my shoulder—a hand twice the size of my own—and I was flung to the floor, the wind screaming in my ears. A flash of lightning ripped across the sky outside, and I saw the Waster clearly silhouetted against its sudden light.

He was shaped like man, but stood almost eight feet high, towering like a monolith above us. Coals of red fire smouldered in his eyes. He was too big to come through the door— but he had no need to enter. He picked me up with a hand that was hard as iron and, as my fists struck futile blows against his massive chest, hurled me across the room. I landed with a jarring crash, the breath struck from me. A pain stitched in my chest, and I thought I'd broken a rib.

I tried to get up, but found I couldn't. Helplessly, I watched him take up the Grey Rose and turn from the threshold. Her eyes were wild with terror, her scream silent. Raging, I dragged myself across the litter-strewn floor, too shaken to stand. It took forever to reach the door.

Weakly, I clutched at the door frame and pulled myself to my knees. I glared out into the ensorcelled night, a bitter taste in my mouth. The wind shook the trees into frenzy. A sheet of rain erupted from above, and I could see no further than my hand. But before the torrent fell, I'd seen that the glade was empty. Both the maid of the Grey Rose and her abductor were gone.

Tears stung my eyes as my failure struck home. Slowly I sank to the floor and laid my cheek against the stone while the storm raged on, unabated. A darkness came washing over me and I knew no more.

HICKATHRIFT TRUMMEL

This is the way I will go:
underhill, a-barrowed.
I will be bones
in that place of stone.
I will be a wind
that howls on the hills at dusk.
I will be the tears
in a Harper's eyes
when he sings of who I was.
I will be a ghost
—a shape without a crown,
a name without a form.
I will be gone.

—"Alken's Song"
from the SONGWEAVER'S JOURNEYBOOK

I REGAINED MY SENSES JUST BEFORE THE MOON SET.

The glen, and the forest beyond, were as silent as a held breath. My clothing was soaked from the rain that had fallen while I had lain unconscious. I shivered—as much from shock as from the cold—and ached from a hundred bruises, although I could feel no broken bones. Cautiously, I stood and made my way from the door, swaying with each step. My chest hurt when I breathed too deeply. But the shock of the Waster's reality hurt as much as the blows, and I was surprised. I had been so confident before. Now . . . I found the candle on the floor where it had blown from the table and lit it from a coal in the hearth. Righting the Grey Rose's chair, I dragged it to the table and slumped in it, trying to gather my thoughts.

29

I closed my eyes for a moment and woke with a start to find that I'd slept away the remainder of the night. In the bright morning light, the stump of the burned-down candle seemed to watch me, mocking me for my failure. Oh, I'd been full of brave words last night, but I'd accomplished nothing. Now the Grey Rose was gone, stolen away by the Waster and . . .

I had to follow them.

There was no question in my mind. I knew where I must go. The maid'd told me of the Cradle of the Kings—the ruined city that was now called Banlore. That was where the monster would've taken her, so there I must go as well as if I was to rescue her. But first, I needed knowledge. I must know the Waster's weaknesses—if he had any. I must discover how he could be destroyed, for there was no other way that I could see that the maid might be rescued.

I thought of his size, the sheer bulk of him, and how he hadn't even staggered under my blows while he'd thrown me effortlessly across the room. He was everything the old tales said a Waster was and . . . I could almost remember how it was that the heroes in those tales had defeated the creatures, but as soon as I reached for the memory, it flitted away, out of reach.

Tess would know.

I drew myself from the table and hobbled to the door. There, I leaned against the twisted remnants of its frame to draw a deep breath of the crisp autumn air into my lungs. My chest hurt, and I was forced to breathe more shallowly as I made for the woodpile on the far side of the cottage.

I searched through the unchopped wood and kindling for a length of wood that might serve me as a cane. After much prying and scrabbling, I found a thick rowan staff that I tried to break into a suitable length. Either my strength was more depleted from my encounter than I'd thought or the wood was especially resilient, but I couldn't break it.

I glared at it, as if an angry look would serve where my hands couldn't, then smiled. It would serve me admirably as a staff just as it was. So, leaning heavily on its white wood,

I made my way home, slowly and steadily. By the time I reached our cottage, the better part of the day was gone.

"Broom and heather!" Tess cried as I staggered in through the door. "What's happened to you?"

I was too exhausted to answer. I stood on shaking legs with a headache thundering between my temples, my vision blurring. Tess helped me to my bed, muttering all the while about staying up half the night worrying about me, and where was my harp, and Ballan, look at these bruises. . . . She had my clothes off and was working salves into my wounds, while I tried to tell her what had happened.

She laid a finger against my lips and *tched* softly.

"Don't talk now," she said. "There'll be time enough to tell me later."

I fell into an exhausted stupor under her ministrations. At some point I slept again and didn't wake until the next morning.

IT WAS A WEEK BEFORE MY STRENGTH RETURNED ENOUGH that I could even begin to think of hazarding the journey to Banlore. Tess was sure I'd cracked at least one rib, and the morning after I made my way back to the cottage, half my body was covered with yellow and black bruises. I fretted as I lay in the bed, my thoughts always on the maid of the Grey Rose. At the worst, I thought, she was dead. Then I thought of her with the monster in that ruined city—perhaps she'd be better off dead.

Tess fed me broth that morning and helped me sit up in bed. I told her all that'd befallen me, and she accepted the story with far more grace than I had when I was finished.

"I feel so weak," I said when I was finished.

"Lucky you're not dead," Tess remarked.

She made me drink a bitter tea and fussed over me, complaining all the while, but with a look of concern plain in her eyes.

"I've told you more than once," she said, "that there's more to the world than what lies in these downs. There are queer folk abroad—especially in the north. Some are good, but some are like the Waster. Ballan! You were mad to think you could stand up to one such as him.''

''I have to follow her.''

Tess studied me, and a look of sadness came into her eyes.

''I know. Best let me do a far-seeing for you before you go hobbling off after them.''

I was to protest but stopped myself before I spoke. After what I'd been told and what I'd seen with my own two eyes, it was time I opened my mind to the magics that lay all around. An ageless maid and ancient wars . . . a Waster and the ruins of a haunted city . . . and even my foster mother . . . The Middle Kingdom lay closer than I'd thought, and there was more to the old tales than make-believe. When I thought of how I'd longed for magic, to be the hero in some tale of wonder . . . I could only shake my head, realizing that I hadn't known what it was I was asking.

The red eyes of the Waster rose in my mind's eye, and I could almost hear the storm winds once more. I shivered and tried to push the memory away, only to see that last wild-eyed look on the maid's face. . . .

''A far-seeing would be good,'' I said.

Tess grinned, but there was little humour in her features.

''It's hard, isn't it—to have it all thrust on you like this?''

I nodded.

''We'll wait till you're stronger,'' she said, ''and see what the fire tells us about the road you must take—and about how a Waster is slain.''

BY THE END OF THE WEEK I WAS MUCH STRONGER AND DE-termined to go. That night we went out onto the downs and laid a fire with seasoned hazel wood on a hilltop guarded by a tall grey standing stone.

''Hazel hoards knowledge,'' Tess said, ''like the salmon in its pool.''

She dropped a coal from a small clay pot into the kindling and soon the fire was crackling and spitting sparks. A wind came up low on the downs. The firelight flickered eerily in Tess's eyes. I laid my staff on the ground and crouched across the fire from her, a chill travelling up my spine. For the first time in all the years I'd know her, I was afraid. She looked at me, and it was as if a stranger gazed from her eyes.

"Wasters," she murmured.

Her voice was no longer that of my fostermother's. It was low and remote, like the wind on the downs.

"They're kin to the Dark Old Ones, they are—wicked creatures with nothing but a black void where men have a heart. . . ."

She stared into the flames and nodded at what she saw. I looked as well, but could see nothing. The chill that had touched me grew deeper.

"Heartsure in your belt . . . and a deft thrust with a dead king's sword . . . a sword of shadows. . . ."

She began to hum, and I recognized the tune. The first few lines of the ballad came to mind. I spoke them softly.

> Tall was Coran, Kilden's son,
> in days of old, in days of song;
> bright the shadow, bright the blade,
> blood of Heartsure, there inlaid. . . .

Tess nodded at the words.

"But mind," she said, and now her voice was her own.

She looked up from the fire and, while the firelight still flickered in their depths, the stranger no longer looked through her eyes.

"Mind you have the dead one's blessing," she cautioned, "or you'll reap more sorrow than ever a Harper's son might bear."

I shook my head. "But . . . a dead King's sword? I don't even know where to begin to look for one."

"In a barrow," Tess said.

I shivered. "Where?"

"Didn't your Grey Rose tell you about the battle fought outside Banlore and the Hill Lords that died that day?"

I nodded.

"Heartsure you can find in the foothills—gold blooms, tiny

as forget-me-nots, that grow in the form of heart-shaped bells.''

"And. . . ."

(Bright the shadow, bright the blade . . .)

". . . the sword of shadows?" I asked.

Tess sighed, and she looked very old in the fire's light.

"Cerin," she said softly. "That I don't know. The fire shows only bits and snatches. Hazelwood's for far-seeing, but the song it usually sings is 'When you seek me, I am not to be found. . . .' If I looked for another, the flames would show me more. But when I look for myself, or one close to me, it shows little.

"It seems to me you must do as Coran did in the old song when he went to rescue his Jessine from the Wormbone Serpent, and that's to seek a weapon in a king's barrow."

We sat in silence while the fire died down to coals and the winds blew up from the downs. When we finally made our way home, I leaned on my staff and Tess leaned on me, but when I lay in my bed, sleep eluded me. I worried at riddles of dead kings' swords and barrows. I thought of Kilden's son, Coran, and the Serpent. But mostly I thought of the Grey Rose, and my eyes were wet with tears for her when I finally did sleep.

TESS WAS UP BEFORE ME. SHE HAD A MUG OF HOT TEA READY and a platter of corncakes and berries for my breakfast. By the door stood one of Finan's old journeypacks that she'd readied for me. A water sack that still needed filling hung from it, and my staff leaned against the wall above it. Tess's eyes were ringed with dark circles. I knew I looked no better, for I'd slept little. We sat, and she watched me eat. Then, all too soon, it was time to go.

I'd never meant it to be like this, I thought as I filled the water sack at the well. When I finally took to the road, I'd meant to go like Finan did, with a light step and looking for adventures—but not looking too hard. The travel itself would have been adventure enough. Now a pall hung over the morn-

ing, and I looked about the small holding with the thought
that I might never see it again. Or Tess. . . .

She stood waiting for me by the door, dressed all in grey
and brown, a sorrowful look in her eyes that she did her best
to hide. We embraced, and it was I who wept first. She
dabbed at my eyes with the end of her sleeve while the tears
rolled down her own cheeks.

"I'll come back," I said.

She nodded. *If I survived* . . . The words hung unspoken
between us.

"Cerin," she said, "look for friends along your way—and
look for them in strange guises. But remember, as well, that
the sweetest face can hold treachery, and there can be evil
even in the councils of the wise."

"Did you *see* this . . . ?"

She shook her head. "Tinker's wisdom," she replied. "No
more. Best you be going now. The day grows no longer, and
you've a fair piece to travel."

I nodded.

"Maybe I'll go back to Lillowen," she said. "You might
look for me there if you don't find me here."

"Banlore's not so far."

"That's true. But if you make it as far as the ruined city,
your road'll take you farther still. And this is something I
have *seen.*"

She kissed me once on each cheek and again on the mouth,
then handed me my staff.

"Use the Kelledy name if you meet up with tinkers. Otherwise, follow your own wisdom. Now go with my blessing,
son of my heart, if not the son of my flesh."

Leaving that holding was the hardest thing I'd ever done—
not for what lay ahead of me, but for what I left behind. We
embraced a last time, and I set off for the Golden Wood again
with a heavy heart and tears stinging my eyes. It took me
longer than usual to reach the maid's cottage, but I was pacing myself. While my hurts were mostly healed, I knew I'd
a long way to go, and I was still somewhat short of breath.

I planned to stop at the cottage just long enough to fetch

my harp, but once I was there, I sat for a while at the table, more wearied of heart than of body. The maid's journeysack lay where it had fallen, and I went through it, setting aside the spoiled food. The white shift that she'd worn that first day in the forest I rolled up and put into my own pack. There was little else I could bring with me—a comb, a copper bracelet.

As I was leaving, I saw something by the door and bent to pick it up. It was the grey rose she'd always worn. It must have fallen from her hair when she'd struggled in the Waster's arms. The rose was still a-bloom—though not nearly as healthy as I remembered it. I felt a strange tingle touch my spine as I held it—more magic, but a magic that was fading.

As I examined the rose, I wondered if its feeble vitality meant that the maid was still alive. That thought gave me strength and lightened my heart for the first time in days. I placed the blossom inside my tunic where it lay cool against my skin, and taking up my journeysack, I shouldered it with my harp. So burdened, with my staff in hand, I turned my steps westward for the Perilous Mountains and the days to come.

THAT NIGHT I CAMPED IN THE WEST DOWNS AND WATCHED the twilight settle over the gaunt foothills that I had to travel through tomorrow. The silence was deep—broken only once by the hunting cry of a brecaln. The sound was eerie, and I drew my cloak closer about me. I ate a cold meal of smoked ham and bread while the dusk settled over the land and watched the stars appear in the sky—first one, then another, as if some celestial chambermaid was lighting them for her lord. Before moonrise, I wrapped myself in my cloak and fell into a dreamless sleep that lasted until dawn.

In the morning I lay awake for the first few minutes, wondering where I was and why my bed was so hard, before it all came back to me in a rush. I was stiff, both from my hurts and from the rough bed, but not so tired that I couldn't build a small fire. My breakfast consisted of toasted cornbread and tea. I boiled the water in a large tin mug that Tess had given me and dropped in a sprinkle of tea leaves when the water was bubbling to a froth. She'd also given me a small cast-iron cookpot and a pair of wooden spoons, and I had Finan's tinkerblade strapped to my belt.

When I'd finished my tea, I covered the fire with dirt and set out. As the morning went by, the gorse- and heather-topped hills gave way to a rough and wild land, pocked with granite outcrops and patches of shale that made for uneven footing. I used my staff for balance and was pleased to find that my stamina had increased enough that I needed to take only a noon break before camping again for the night.

The sky grew overcast in the later afternoon, but the rain held off, for which I was thankful. I camped near the opening to Holme's Way, the pass I must take through the mountains to reach Banlore. The foothills of the mountains began their clambering rise here, soaring to heights that towered above my camp. Only the hardiest weeds and brush grew in the patches of soil that were clumped in rills and folds of solid rock, and I was hard put to find fuel for my fire.

I awoke the next morning to a thin drizzle and started up the pass, wet and miserable. In the middle of the morning I thought I heard thunder and stepped up my pace. Finan'd told me about the sudden floods that a mountain storm could cause. I thought of looking for shelter, then paused to listen more closely. The sound I heard took on a clearer meaning—that of horses' hooves clattering on the rock floor of the pass and echoing against its heights.

Despite what Tess'd said about looking for friends along the way, prudence told me to find shelter first and see what manner of men these were before making my presence known to them. I looked about and worried, for only the sheer walls of the canyon met my gaze, and they were too high and steep to scale. Then I saw an opening in the wall some three hundred paces to my right. Taking a firm grip of harp, staff, and journeysack, I ran for it. I had just reached the mouth—it led into a cave, I discovered—when I slipped on some loose rocks and fell in a tangle.

My breath was knocked out, but I still had sense enough

to gather my belongings and scramble the last few yards. Once I was safely hidden, I stored my harp and pack and turned to peer cautiously out, hoping for a view of the oncoming riders so that I could decide whether or not to show myself. I held my staff with white knuckles as five riders came thundering around a turn in the pass.

The drizzle had let up, but the sky remained overcast. Still, even in that dull light, their mail seemed bright and glittering. I could see that they were well-weaponed—with swords, spears, and two great axes—and as they approached I saw that each rode with the easy familiarity of a trained horseman and carried his weapons as if he knew how to use them. Their faces looked grim, unshaven. Their cloaks were patched and their hair thick and matted. Only the weapons and mail appeared to be well taken care of.

It might be wrong to judge a man by his appearance—after all, I looked like a ruffian myself—but I thought I wouldn't be far off in assuming that these were outlaws or brigands of one sort or another. I was congratulating myself on my good sense at hiding from them when disaster struck.

You did well to hide yourself from the likes of them, manling.

I went sick with dread as that gruff voice resounded inside my head. I twisted about, my eyes wide with shock as I stared at the huge humped form that had addressed me from the depths of the cave. Then, like a fool, I stood and backed away, only to stumble again. This time I fell out of the opening and into plain view of the approaching riders.

I cursed myself for a blunderer, but it was already too late. The riders had seen me, while from the cave shuffled the figure I'd seen inside. It was a bear. A bear that spoke with mindspeech. I shook my head in disbelief. It was almost ten feet tall standing on its hind legs—an immense bulk of grizzled brown fur, topped with a shock of steel-gray hair above its dark eyes.

My staff lay at my hand, and I reached for it before I stood, slowly backing away from the bear. I could hear the riders pulling up behind me. I didn't know which was worse. Perhaps the riders could help me against the beast. On the other hand, the bear hadn't threatened me, and when I remembered what little I'd seen of the riders, I realized that they could well be more of a threat.

One of them called out mockingly and made my decision.

"Ho, brothers! What have we here? A ragged boy and his pet. I wager the boy'll yelp louder with a blade in his gut than the beast."

"Then you've never been bear-baiting," another said. "The damned things bleat worse than pigs."

I turned to face their laughter, my staff raised chest-high and held loosely in my hands—much as I'd seen the boys in Wran Cheaping prepare their quarterstaves for mock combat. But this'd be no play-fight, and the fiercest foe I'd lifted my staff against was the trunk of an old oak tree. I thought of the Grey Rose—what a poor champion I'd made for her.

The men sat easily in their saddles, regarding me with jeering smiles. I shifted uncomfortably, too aware of the bear behind me and what a plain target my back made.

Behind me, manling.

Again that gruff voice rumbled in my mind.

I glanced over my shoulder, then stepped aside as the bear charged past me. The riders' horses moved uneasily until one of the men kicked his heels against his mount's flanks to meet the bear's attack. The beast lifted all fours to his full height just as the rider was almost upon him. One sweep of those terrible paws and the man was thrown from his frenzied steed, his chest caved in. He lay like a broken doll on the rocks, and his horse bolted.

As one, the remaining riders bore down on us, fierce battle cries replacing their laughter.

What happened next took place in a sudden flurry. One moment, there were four warriors storming toward us. The next, two men lay hurt to their deaths, and the others fled, following the lead of the riderless horses. I'd wielded my staff, striking one man a glancing blow. But the bear'd been a whirlwind of action—killing his man, then finishing off the man I'd struck.

As I watched the rapidly dwindling figures, I wondered what they'd hoped to gain from a beast and a poor traveller such as me. If it was only for sport they'd attacked us, then I felt no guilt in the hand I'd had in killing three of them.

I was still breathless from the brief skirmish when I turned to the bear. My heart drummed as I regarded my strange ally. His head cocked as he thoughtfully returned my gaze. The silence grew uncomfortable until at last I gathered my courage.

"My thanks for your help, Master . . . ah . . . bear. . . ."

My voice trailed off. I felt foolish talking to an animal. But there was intelligence in his eyes, and the memory of his voice in my mind was still very clear. I remembered, as well, that I'd learned in the past week that the old tales held more truth than ever I'd thought.

Your thanks are accepted, he said, *though if I hadn't startled you we might well have avoided this danger.*

I blinked as the words came into my mind again. The voice in my mind wasn't an easy thing to accept; neither was the beast in front of me whose voice it was.

As a cub in Auldwen the elders of my tribe named me Trummel, but now I go by the name of Hickathrift. I'm lately come from Wistlore, where I earned the mantle of Loremaster. William Marrow himself inscribed my name in the record scrolls.

I nodded as if I understood. Nowhere had I heard that there were beasts ranked amongst the wise in Wistlore. In old tales. . . . Perhaps this was a Wysling disguised as a bear?

And you? the bear asked me. *You're a Harper by the looks of that instrument—though perhaps not a rich one. Still, when was there a rich Harper, except in the days of Minstrel Ravendear? Those days are long past now, I fear. Mind you, there's Caradoc. . . .*

I listened to him gossip in friendly fashion, and some of the strangeness of the encounter wore away. But when he paused a moment and I told him who I was, I was still half convinced that I'd wake up in my camp outside the pass to find that the whole thing had been only a dream.

Cerin? he repeated. He shook his head thoughtfully.

Remembering Tess's caution, I'd given him no more than my first name, for all that instinct told me I could trust him. *Your name isn't familiar to me*, he added. *Is it listed in the record scrolls of the Harperhall?*

"It wouldn't be."

I found a rock to sit on and tried not to look at the three dead men. I was still trembling at the close call I'd had and having a conversation with a bear wasn't helping matters any. I put my hand inside my tunic and touched the Grey Rose's bloom—and gained a little comfort. Taking a breath, I asked what was foremost on my mind.

"Are you . . . are you really a bear?"

He looked at me, astonishment plain in his ursine features. *What do I look like to you?*

"Like . . . like a bear. It's just that . . . I've never. . . ."

In the lore books they call us mys-hudol, he said, a grin touching his lips. *Our kinship is with the Kindreds, rather than the beasts of the fields and woods. We rarely travel in the south. There, menfolk are too ready to hunt us as if we were beasts—those that don't try to kill us with silver because they think we're were-creatures.*

He spoke with humour, but his eyes didn't smile. I wondered what it was like to have the mind of a man trapped in the shape of an animal—then wondered if that was even the way he saw himself. For some reason, that was the moment that my wonder at our encounter wore away.

("Look for friends along the way," Tess'd told me, "in strange guises. . . .")

Could there be anything stranger than a bear that spoke mind-to-mind with the voice of a man?

Are you from the south?

I nodded, adding: "But I don't hunt bears."

Again a smile touched his features. It was curious how expressive a beast's face could be, I thought, then corrected myself. Mys-hudol, not beast.

Harpers rarely do, he said.

I was determined to say nothing more that would show me

for the simpleton that I felt I had appeared to be. At the same time, I felt a sudden need to raise myself up in his eyes, to make up for the picture I'd painted of myself so far.

"I've never been in the north," I said, "but both my parents came from the lands beyond these mountains. My mother's name was Eithne Gwynn, and she was a Harper. My father was a gwandryas from Kohr. His name was Windalane."

I've heard of them. Their tale is recorded in the lore books in Wistlore—though nothing is said of what became of them. Nor did it mention that they had a child. Hickathrift shot me a considering look. *They weren't well loved when they left Wistlore. Did you know that?*

"Yes."

Someday I meant to go to the Halls of Learning in Wistlore and confront the elders with my parents' exile. What did it matter who a person wed, as long as there was love between the two? Had my parents never been banished, they might never have died of the sickness in Eldwolde. I could have known them—learned my harping at my mother's knee and a warrior's skills from my father. I'd have been able to protect the maid of Grey Rose when the Waster came. . . .

And then I shook my head. The sickness could've taken my parents anywhere. Had things not turned out as they did, I would never have known Tess, or Finan, or even met the maid herself. Never to have known my parents was a sorry thing, as Tess often told me, "The Great Wheel turns, and our lives with it. We are what we are because of the shapes of our lives, and the goods balance the ills. Would you be someone other than who you are, Cerin?"

It was a difficult question to answer, simply because I *was* who I was. I might yearn to be a better musician, or to know this or that skill . . . but to be someone else?

Are you bound for Wistlore? Hickathrift asked, breaking into my thoughts with his gruff mindspeech.

"Perhaps . . ." I said. "In time."

I looked at him and he at me, and, few though my friends had been through the years, I saw something in him that called out to me. It was like that moment in the glade when the Grey Rose appeared in the middle of the song I was writing for her. When the first few moments of awkwardness had passed, I felt as if I'd known her forever.

Tess'd told me to follow my wisdom, and what wisdom I had told me to trust my new companion. So I told him a little of my life, concentrating on the fate of the Grey Rose and the things that Tess'd seen in her seeing-flames. Hickathrift was quiet while I spoke, stopping me only once or twice when my story ran ahead of itself. Then I had to backtrack to explain before I could go on.

I'd like to meet your fostermother, he said when I was done, *as well as this maid you call the Grey Rose. The histories of that war between the Stone-slayer and the Hill Lords of the Trembling Lands tell little—though, by all accounts, it was a dread time. In the north none that I know of has the tale's ending, or knows of your friend's brave sacrifice.*

He paused and glanced at me.

A strange and fortuitous meeting this is, he said after a moment. *My coming south has to do with these selfsame Hill Lords. It came to my mind that, for all that the lore books place them as men, the Hillfolk were kin to the weren, that the old blood of the Wild Folk ran in their veins; but I saw no way to prove such a theory without faring to the Trembling Lands myself.*

"But you said it was dangerous for you."

Hickathrift smiled. *Curiosity is the greatest danger of all. You see, it's my thought that the Kohrian Grasslands—your father's kin—are the descendants of the Hillfolk, but could not prove it without coming south myself to see what relics and remnants I could find.*

"Weren," I asked. "Are they like the muryan—the little people of the moors?"

That is another matter of dispute. The record scrolls number them amongst the Kindreds as the Second Born, or the low erlkin. But the muryan themselves claim kinship to the Wild Folk. They are a secret people who follow old ways and have little to do with either men or erls. Their gods are not the gods of the Kindreds. They give their faith to a Moon-goddess and her consort, a Horned Lord.

"And my father's people?"

The gwandryas of both the Grassfields and the Great Waste hallow the same god and goddess though under differing names. Many of their songs and legends are the same.

I could see now why Hickathrift had become a Loremaster. He obviously loved to talk of the old histories and had a curiosity to match that love. What he said gave me pause. If it was true, then there was a kinship—however distant—between the Grey Rose and myself. I remembered as well what I'd heard, or thought I'd heard, her say.

("You lack no magics. . . .")

If there was weren blood in my father's line, that same blood was in me. Thinned by now, but . . . . The very thought of it both excited and frightened me.

I would like to accompany you on this quest of yours, Hickathrift said, *if you will have my company.*

I looked at him in surprise; I hadn't expected such an offer. With his knowledge and strength to help me the future didn't seem nearly so grim. I said as much, and he laughed, deep and throaty.

Don't think of me too highly, Cerin. I will help you as I can, but neither you nor I have the power to stand against a Waster. You'd still be best off to take your fostermother's advice. . . . Heartsure and a dead king's sword.

"Are there barrows near Banlore?"

I explored one, but only to a small extent. I saw no sword or any weapons. And even if we were to find one, the riddle still remains as to how the flower and blade are to be used as a weapon against the Waster.

I had nothing to add. I knew only Coran's song, and whatever advice there was to be found in it was couched in poetry—ambiguous at best.

But our first worry, Hickathrift said, *is to find this sword. We can only hope that when we've blade and Heartsure together, what we must do with them will become apparent.* He lifted his muzzle to scent the air. Overhead the clouds were gathering thickly again, and the sky grew dark. *The storm will strike in earnest soon,* he added. *I give it another hour. What do you say to leaving this place of death and journeying for that hour? I passed other caves farther up the pass. We can spend the night in one of them and talk of all this some more.*

I had no great urge to get any wetter than the morning's drizzle had left me and agreed readily enough. Before we left, I tried to express my gratitude to my new friend for his offer of help. He shrugged off my thanks, adding:

My reasons for helping you are selfish in part, Cerin. Even if the fate of the Hill Lords didn't intrigue me so, I'd still want to meet this Grey Rose of yours.

"Whatever your reasons," I replied, "I'm still grateful."

He appeared somewhat taken aback by my earnestness.

Time we were going, was all he said, and we left it at that.

We let the brigands lie where they'd fallen. I thought of taking one of their swords with me, but I knew nothing of swordplay and decided that Finan's tinkerblade would serve me better in any case. Gathering up my harp and journey-pack, I followed Hickathrift down the pass.

The rain came just as we reached the caves he'd spoken of. There was dry fuel inside, and I built a fire just far enough back from the opening of the cave that its glow and reflection wouldn't be seen from outside once it got dark, but close enough to let the smoke escape. I shared my food with him and was a little worried at how much he ate; at that rate my provisions wouldn't last more than a few days.

We talked through what was left of the afternoon and long into the night, and slept deeply afterward while the storm howled outside our shelter.

THE NEXT MORNING, WE AWOKE TO FIND THE SUN UP BEFORE us and the sky clear. After a quick meal, we reached the western entrance of Holme's Way by mid-morning without mishap. The opening of the pass was a jumble of strewn boulders. Gnarled thorn trees lifted leafless boughs, and what grass grew, was withered and brown. The ground was rugged, and after we made our way through the pass, Hickathrift cast about for a landmark. Once he found it, he led a winding way through the rough foothills until, with much scrambling on my part, we reached the barrow he'd told me of. It lay half hidden in a small gully, choked with brush and the dried blades of coarse grasses.

The dusk comes, Hickathrift said.

We stood before the dark opening. It was flanked by two tall weathered stones that had strange runes inscribed on their surfaces. My knowledge was limited to what Tess'd taught me, and these runes were unfamiliar. When I asked Hickathrift as to their meaning, he too shook his head.

The runes are familiar enough, but they spell words in a tongue that I have no knowledge of.

A strange sensation stole over me as I looked into the shadowed opening. I'd never given a great deal of thought to ghosts and the like, but with so much else that I'd thought to be only tales now proved true, I was nervous about confronting what might lie in the barrow. As if his own thoughts followed my own, Hickathrift counselled that we wait.

We can try it tomorrow, he said. *There are spirits that inhabit such places when the sun sets, and they do not care to be disturbed.*

I shook my head, for I'd tallied the days since the Grey Rose was abducted, and that count was too high. Her blossom, that I still carried under my tunic next to my skin, had appeared more sickly when I'd looked at it this morning.

"No," I said. "It must be now."

I fell to searching for a length of wood. There was nothing near, so I gathered an armful of the tall dried grass and sat down to twist its rough fibers into a serviceable torch.

"Time's running out," I explained as I worked on it. "I have a feeling that we might be too late already. All I can think of is *her* need."

On your head be it, Hickathrift replied, obviously displeased. *The counsels of the wise are specific in their warnings. If you won't heed them, then you must take the risk alone. Tomorrow I'd have entered with you. But tonight . . .*

*I will stand on guard outside to keep you safe from mortal
foes. But I won't chance a curse of the dead.*

I shrugged, though I wasn't feeling particularly brave myself. Haste might lead me into ruin, but a desperation of sorts
had settled in me, overriding my own fear. I'd failed my Grey
Rose once as it was. I wouldn't chance failure again.

My torch was ready; I lit its end with flint and steel. When
it caught, I turned again to the entrance of the barrow. Leaving my harp, pack, and staff behind, I entered with only the
torch in one hand and Finan's tinkerblade in the other.

Luck go with you, Hickathrift murmured.

Then there was only silence, unbroken except for the scuf-
fle of my boots upon the stone floor and the sound of my
laboured breathing.

The passage narrowed, and I soon felt cloistered. The walls
seemed to press in on me from either side. It wasn't a pleasant feeling, treading this dark confined space with only the
light of a torch made from twisted grasses that was burning
too quickly for my liking. It burned unevenly, its light flickering and sending strange shadows scurrying ahead of me
down the narrow passageway. I thought of returning to make
a few more torches, then realized it wasn't the quick burning
of the torch that worried me so much as my own fading courage.

I pressed on, before my resolve fled completely. Ahead I
could see that the passage was opening up into a wider space
of some sort. When I reached it, my half-burned torch threw
its wan light across a small chamber. I made out Hickathrift's
paw prints etched in the thick dusk and followed them into
another passageway on the far side of the chamber. Soon I
was in yet another corridor. This one was a little wider, but
by now my heart was thumping. The tons of rock above me
did nothing to ease my fears. It was very easy to imagine the
corridor collapsing, trapping me. . . .

An oppression crept in one me so that I glanced nervously
about and looked back over my shoulder at the ceiling to
judge the strength of the rock. Then the passageway came to

an end, and I stood in the heartroom of the barrow—the crypt itself.

My guttering torch showed me a litter of broken rock and the shards of what must once have been weapons and other finery. The stone slab, where the inhabitant of the barrow should have lain, was chipped and empty. Peering closer, I could see a snarl of bones beside it, along with the remnants of age-rotted cloth and rusted armour.

My torch sputtered, and I looked about for something to replenish my dying light. On one wall there was a wooden torch, blackened with tar. I touched it with mine, and the tarred wood took fire readily, illuminating the whole chamber more brightly.

The minutes slipped by as I took stock of what was in the barrow. There were weapons—or at least the heads of axes and spears, their shafts lying broken in a tangle. Of riches there were none. I saw plenty of clay bowls and dishes shaped from stone and rough metal. Some were painted with colours that had faded over the years, though once they must've been fair.

Despair settled over me as I finished my inventory. I didn't see a blade—not a sword or even a dagger. Silence hung leadenly in the stuffy air, and my nerves, which had settled a little when I found the place untenanted, wound tight again. Then I heard a sound.

At first I thought it was Hickathrift come to lend me his help after all. Then I realized the sound had come from the wall that faced the passageway. The torchlight didn't quite dispel the shadows about that wall, and as I stared at them fear came rearing up inside me once more. I turned, meaning to run back to the outside and safety, when a keening wail pierced the chamber, freezing me to the spot.

The keening rose, shrill and eerie, then died. Silence filled the barrow once more, but I couldn't move. I turned slowly to face the wall of shadows, and a voice broke the silence— a voice so loud that the stones of the burial chamber rumbled as it spoke. I covered my ears to lessen the din.

"WHAT DO YE IN MY BARROW?"

My knees shaking, I stared at the shadows.

"ARE YE SO WEARY OF LIFE THAT YE HAVE
COME TO JOIN ME IN THESE COLD HALLS OF THE
DEAD?"

No matter that the torch cast its light about the chamber;
I could see nothing but darkness against the wall. If anything,
the already black shadows enshrouding that side of the barrow grew deeper.

"N-no . . ." I managed at last, my throat tight with fear.

I struggled to overcome my terror and was rewarded. I
took one shaking step back, then another, my gaze glued to
the shadows.

"I . . . I sought only a sword," I said. "There is a geas
upon me and . . . and I need the sword of a dead king to
fulfill it. . . ."

I took a third step back as I spoke.

"A SWORD?" the bodiless voice asked. I caught a hid-
eous chuckle behind its words. "AND WHAT WOULD YE
GIVE ME IN EXCHANGE FOR A SWORD? WHAT DO
YE HOLD MOST PRECIOUS IN ALL THE WORLD BE-
YOND THESE WALLS?"

Dumbfounded, I stopped my backward movement to peer
closer into the darkness.

Was there a sword here? Would this spirit bargain with me
and allow me to leave the barrow with it?

I racked my mind, trying to think of something I possessed
that might please this shade. I had little except for my harp,
my tinkerblade, and the clothes on my back. I knew these
wouldn't be enough. Then I thought of the rose, cool against
my skin inside my tunic. How could I give it up? But to save
the maid. . . .

Slowly I pulled it forth and stepped forward, laying it on
the burial slab.

"I have this," I said.

The torchlight caught its petals, still damp with morning
dew. Though it wasn't nearly as fair as it had been, I marvelled that it still flourished at all.

"WHERE GAT YE THIS?" the voice boomed with anger.

Shadows pulled away from the wall and moved toward me. The force of the shade's anger tore at my senses, and I staggered under its attack. Horrors twisted and lapped at the boundaries of my consciousness. Numb with terror, I tried to form words to explain how the blossom came into my possession, but the ghost wouldn't listen.

"WHERE GAT YE THIS?" it boomed again. "THIS WAS MY DAUGHTER'S OF OLD—ERE THE COMING OF YARAC WASTER, ERE THE WARRING FELL UPON US. LAST WAS I TO FALL, HERE SO CLOSE TO HIS CURSED HOLD—LAST, AND TO NO AVAIL. HOW DARE YE STEAL THIS BLOOM FROM HER AND OFFER IT TO ME? I WILL SLAY THEE, THIEF. HERE IN MY TOMB THAT THE DWARVES WROUGHT FOR ME ERE THEY FLED NORTH—HERE I WILL REND THEE. SPEAK, THIEF! WHERE GAT YE THIS BLOOM?"

The darkness fell on me. I babbled, trying in one rush of words to explain all that had befallen the maid of the Grey Rose and what I meant to do to help her. I fell to my knees as my bones turned to water. I held Finan's blade uselessly in front of me, as if I could fend off the shade's wrath with it.

Instead, the darkness tore inside me, lashing my mind like a terrible wind. I felt unfamiliar thoughts in my own head, probing my mind, weighing unspoken words for their truth. The shade of the dead Hill Lord tore my memories from me; it was not gentle in its silent questioning. I writhed in terror, trying to break free of its hold. But not until the dead king was done did it withdraw from my mind. I fell weakly to the floor.

"YE SPEAK THE TRUTH," the voice of the shade said, each word still thundering in the chamber. "AND I THANK YE FOR WHAT YE WOULD DO FOR THE CHILD OF MY FLESH, OF MY BLOOD. TAKE YE THE ROSE THAT YE MAY RETURN IT TO HER. I WILL GIVE THEE A SWORD—A SWORD THE LIKE OF WHICH HAS NE'ER BEEN SEEN IN THE WORLD SINCE THE LAST OF THE HILL LORDS FELL. BATHE IT IN SMOKE, FRIEND OF

MY DAUGHTER, THE SMOKE OF HEARTSURE BURN-
ING IN A FIRE OF ROWAN WOOD. YELLOW FLOWER
AND WHITE WOOD—SUCH IS A WASTER'S BANE.
HAD I BUT KNOWN IT IN MY OWN TIME, 'TIS HE
WOULD BE LYING HERE IN THIS THRICE-DAMNED
TOMB. AND I . . . I WOULD BE FREE.

"GO, FRIEND OF MY DAUGHTER. LAY HIM LOW.
WITH HIS DEATH, MAYHAP I WILL KEN PEACE AT
LAST. TAKE THE SWORD AND GO!"

My ears were still pounding with the volume of his voice,
and I lay prostrate on the floor. When I realized that the shade
was gone, I rose slowly to my feet, shaking my head numbly.
I found the rose still lying on the slab, picked it up, and thrust
it into my tunic, then searched for the sword that the Hill
King's shade had promised me.

There was none to be found.

I couldn't believe it. I looked again and again, tearing at
the rubble strewn over the floor, but in vain. Not until I gave
up hope of there even being such a blade did I see it—or at
least its shadow, reflected on the wall. With a cry of triumph,
I turned to where the sword that cast the shadow must be.
Again I saw nothing.

Bewildered, I shook my head. Riddles, always riddles. Yet
I knew the solution lay in front of me if I could only see it.
Then I remembered what Tess had far-seen in the hazel fire.

("A dead king's sword . . . a sword of shadows. . . .")

Uncertainly, I approached the wall and put my hand on the
hilt of the shadow-blade to find it solid under my touch. Filled
with wonder, I grasped it and drew my hand back from the
wall. The sword came with it—dark, more an outline of shape
to the eye than a physical presence, but in my hand it had
weight and substance.

Here was magic, I thought with a faint tingle of awe. A
magic as strong as any that the Stone-slayer might wield.

I picked up Finan's tinkerblade from the floor where I'd
dropped it and replaced it in its sheath. Then, bearing the
shadow-blade in my hand, I retraced my steps to where Hickathrift waited for me outside the barrow. I carried no light,

but I neither stumbled nor carried with me the fears that had plagued me when I entered. As I stepped out into the night, Hickathrift stared at the dim outline of the sword in my fist with a look in his eyes as strange as that I knew to be in my own.

You have it! By my ancestors, you have it! I thought you were dead when I heard the sounds from within, and then a bitter cry as if a soul were being torn from its body.

I couldn't recall that scream, though it must've been ripped from my throat when the shade of the dead Hill Lord entered my mind. I told Hickathrift what had happened in the barrow. He nodded his head calmly while I spoke, but I could see the excitement gleaming in his eyes.

A Hill Lord's barrow, he said when I was done. *I should have guessed it by the unfamiliar runes. And he was your Grey Rose's sire as well!*

Now he seemed to regret that he'd stayed behind, and he made me tell the whole tale through once more to fix it firmly in his mind.

Now I will do my part, he said, *and search out a stand of Heartsure while you take some rest. But rowan wood . . . where will we find that in these hills? Your guess is as good as my own. I saw none when I passed through on my own and—*

The thought struck us both at the same time. Rowan wood—my staff was cut from the wood of a rowan. We shared a smile then, the bear and I.

"So now there's a real chance," I said.

Hickathrift nodded, adding: *I only pray that we are not already too late.*

He padded off in search of the Heartsure and I drew the rose from under my tunic. While it lived, I had hope. I replaced it. I couldn't help but marvel at how well my mission had progressed. The satisfaction gave me a peace I had not known for days. Making a pillow of my pack, I fell asleep with the hilt of the shadow-sword clasped firmly in one hand.

TELYNROS

As the moon is silver   in the twilight
and the green fire   burns hill to hill
so roots run deep   and boughs reach high
and the rose itself   is a grey sea of riddles.

For such a harp   could court the summer stars
each of its strings   is a mystery
and each tune played   is a promised wisdom
but the knowing lies   only in the harper's hand.

—"Telynros"
from the SONGWEAVER'S JOURNEYBOOK

AT MIDAFTERNOON OF THE FOLLOWING DAY, WE TOPPED THE last hill and gazed down upon the ruined city of Banlore, once named the Cradle of the Kings. I stood and looked at the broken buildings for a long time. She was there—my Grey Rose. I touched the blossom in my tunic. It lived still, and so did she.

Cerin? Hickathrift called.

I turned at last, the pain unhidden in my eyes. We laid a fire with the broken shards of my rowan staff. With flint and steel I set the kindling smoldering, and we added the fuel once the fire was ready. Hickathrift had gathered the Heartsure while I slept, and, when the fire was burning well, I dropped the golden blossoms, one by one, into its red heart.

Do you see that spire—or at least what remains of one?

Hickathrift pointed a broad paw toward the northernmost part of the city, where it hugged a cliff.

That was the Lord's Tower in the elder days. That is where he will have her. And that is where we must go.

I nodded, then watched the flames as they lapped around the Heartsure blooms. They didn't burn as normal flowers would have; instead, they glowed brightly. Smoke bellowed richly from the fire, and that worried me, in case Yarac had set guards, but we'd decided that whatever magics we'd work, we'd save them until we were inside Banlore. Neither of us cared to wake the power in the shadow-sword too soon.

I held the blade in the smoke; we watched grey runes form along its shadowy length. My throat felt dry, and I swallowed with difficulty.

"What . . . what do they say?" I asked.

Hickathrift shook his head.

I know no more than you. They are written in the tongue of the Hill Lords, and they alone would know their meaning.

I watched the Heartsure blossoms flare and burn finally, holding the sword in their smoke until the last of them was gone and only coals remained of the rowan wood. I withdrew the sword and held it aloft. We gazed at it for a few moments. The sun caught the runes and seemed to turn them to fire, so that the whole of the sword glowed. Each rune was the pure gold of a Heartsure blossom, while the sword kept its shadowy black.

The paradox of dark and light bewildered me until I remembered the song of Kilden's son again.

> *Bright the shadow, bright the blade,*
> *blood of Heartsure there inlaid. . . .*

This was as powerful a weapon as that carried by Coran in the old song. A shadow that was bright . . . the gold blood of a flower. . . .

Caryaln, Hickathrift said suddenly, *the shadow-death. That is what you hold in your hands, Cerin. Knoller carried a blade like that in the yarg wars—as Jasklin did before him and Calwyth did in his own time. The old lore books tell that the first of the caryaln was made by Tyrr Stormbringer, the eldest of the gods, and given to Bearwulf that he might slay the worm on Drummas Peak. But legend has it that only one such weapon survived from the elder days—and it was in the shape of a spear.*

I looked from the weapon I held to his broad face.

"A spear?"

He nodded. *It has been lost for a very long time—so long that there are some who doubt that it ever survived the elder days. I wonder where the Hill Lords got this blade . . . and why they never used it against the Waster in their own war.*

"He didn't know then," I said. "He said as much in his barrow."

Heartsure and rowan. Hickathrift nodded. *Secrets from an old song. . . .*

I laid the blade down and shouldered my harp and pack before taking it up once more. We were ready to start for the ruins below when a long howl broke the still afternoon air. I shivered at the sound and looked about in surprise.

"What?"

An answering cry filled the air, followed by another.

Direwolves! Hickathrift cried. *The Stone-slayer must have set them as guards, and they have our scent. Quickly! We must make a run for the city.*

With the sorcerous blade in my fist, I bolted for the ruins, Hickathrift loping at my side. Howls rent the air again—many of them—and they came now from every direction. Glancing over my shoulder, I saw dark shapes on the hilltop we'd just quit. They stood silhouetted against the sky with their long muzzles lifted in the air. They were larger than I'd imagined wolves to be. New howls rang out all around us, and the creatures on the hilltop left their vantage point and sped toward us.

To my right and left I could discern more of the dark shapes. I could see that they meant to ring us about, and my heart sank. There were at least a score of the beasts running in the pack, and we were only two. I doubted that we could outfight them, but I saw as well that we couldn't reach the dubious safety of the ruins before they were upon us. I stopped my mad flight to stand panting. Hickathrift brought himself up short beside me.

Why do you stop? We must make for the ruins!

"They're too far. I'd rather face them here than have them pull us down from behind while we flee."

Then if they must be faced here, let it be me that holds them. You go on with our quest.

"No. We succeed or fall together."

Fool! His gruff voice was like a storm in my mind. *Think of the maid. Think of your Grey Rose.*

I thought of her—but it was too late. The direwolves closed in, snarling and growling as they charged. The hackles rose along Hickathrift's back, and he met their noise with a low warning rumble that stopped them for a moment. They ringed us now, their mottled grey pelts shifting and spinning in the sun as they moved, making me dizzy and increasing my fear.

But I held the shadow-sword in my fist. I held power.

With that thought foremost in my mind I leapt at the nearest beast, swinging my blade awkwardly. The direwolf dodged my blow with a deft sidling movement. It darted for me as I stumbled, off balance. But before its jaws could close on my throat, Hickathrift's paw sent the creature reeling backward, dead before it hit the ground. Then the rest were upon us, and we fought for our lives.

I'd dropped my harp and journeysack when we stopped to make our stand. As the wolves struck now, I fell back from their attack and put my foot through the soundbox of my harp. It splintered under my weight, and I cried out at the sound. Rude it might've been, but it was all I had. I returned to the fray with renewed fury.

I killed one and wounded another. Hickathrift had slain three more. But their sheer numbers were overwhelming us. Already, Hickathrift's magnificent coat was torn from dozens of cuts—for he was taking the brunt of the attack—and my sword arm was weary, so weary. The blade seemed to fight with a will of its own—I certainly had no skill in its use—but it was my arm that bore it, my muscles that ached. I was unused to such work and soon felt that I couldn't lift the blade any more, let alone wield it.

Then came a lull in the struggle. We stood breathing heavily as the wolves regrouped for another attack. Hickathrift turned to me and mindspoke, the force of his words stinging in my mind like a blow.

Go now! I will hold them off!

I began to shake my head, to say that I wouldn't leave him. He bared his teeth.

Go!

I backed away from him, my heart filled with worry. And yet . . . if we both fell here, who was to rescue the maid from Yarac?

Go! he roared.

Cursing, I spun and ran for the city.

The wolves sent up a howl and made for me, but Hickathrift cut them off, throwing himself upon them. When I reached the edge of the ruins, I turned and saw him borne down under their weight. I stood aghast, the weathered stones lifting about me, and cried my rage. One beast, then another started for me. With tears stinging my eyes, I turned and fled deeper into the ruined city.

It was my reason that bade me to go on, to finish what we'd begun, but my heart cried *stop, go back*. My sorrow rose in an anguished wave, but I knew that if I died there as well, Hickathrift's death would have been for nothing. I *had* to go on, if there were to be any meaning in his sacrifice, but it was hard. We might've been together only a few days, but the bond that had formed between us seemed to span lifetimes.

So I wept, but I sped on. The blade in my hand hummed his death dirge in my mind. A hint of red appeared amongst the shadows and gold runes.

I made for the crumbling tower we'd spied from the hill outside the city, but saw only Hickathrift's features through the mist of my tears. The day began to fail about me, and a wan light suffused the streets. The ruined buildings cast strange shadows across my route. Their dark, weathered stones brooded all around me and whispered their fell secrets, but my sorrow was stronger than my fear.

Once I turned to kill the two direwolves that had followed me into the city, the blade came alive in my hand, and I watched the slaughter, taking no part in it, for all that it was my hand that held the sword.

As I neared the tower, my pace slowed. Although time had passed since I'd first entered the city, the twilight still wrapped the still streets, as if the night were held indefinitely at bay by the half-lit grey of dusk. Under my tunic, the maid's rose grew cold against my skin. The gold runes that ran the length of the shadow-sword's blade were redder still.

My movements became so sluggish that I could hardly put one foot in front of the other. It was as if I was forcing my way through water, or the full drifts of a winter field. Thought tendrils touched the boundaries of my mind. They were like the Hill Lord's, in that they wove in amongst my own—and mocked my sorrow, made little of my ability to see the deed through. But they were different, in that their foulness brought bile up my throat and made me bolster all my inner strength to evade their touch.

On I fared, but slower and more slowly still so that it seemed that I hardly made any headway. The mind-touches grew stronger and more foul, stabbing into my mind with a strength that I could no longer fight. Only the sword pushed me on, tugging me in the direction of the tower, when my own will was failing. Sometimes I fought with such concentration to break free of the mind-touches, that when at last I gained a moment's respite I'd find that I hadn't moved at all. Then I would set one foot laboriously in front of the other and so go on.

I had no way of judging how long my hellish journey took. Throughout it all I held to my sorrow; I did it for the maid and for the brave sacrifice of my friend. Had my quest been for my own gain, I doubt that I'd ever have made it as far.

Throughout my struggle the unnatural twilight soaked the avenues of the ruined city. In some places walls still reared, and I had to find a way around them. Other times I had to clamber over heaps of rubble that blocked my path, for there was no other route. And the mind-touches continually battered away at my consciousness.

After one such struggle, I found myself lying prostrate on the ground. It took all my strength to regain my feet and continue. I thought of Hickathrift and the Grey Rose, and the sword pulled me on. The air was like cobwebs that clung to my face and filled my lungs with a cloying, choking sensation.

I was at the end of my strength when I came at last to the base of the tumbled structure that was all that remained of the Lord's Tower. I stared dumbly at it, then stepped through its ruined portal. A blast of power struck my mind so that I staggered and fell to my knees. I heard a wild, ragged howl and realized it'd come from my own throat. Tears blinded my eyes as I struggled to my feet and fought the evil from me. I lurched on through the doorway and gagged as a foul stench hit my nostrils.

It was dark inside. I moved slowly across the debris-strewn floor, fighting the mind-power each step of the way. The shadow-sword pulled me forward until I came to another door. When I entered, a piercing light flooded the chamber, and I stood blinking in its glare. The light was sickly ochre, as foul to my eyes as the stench was to my nose. I lifted my gaze to where a ravaged dais still stood at the far end of the long room.

They stood there, together: the Grey Rose and her tormentor, Yarac Stone-slayer.

I moved forward, the hilt of the shadow-sword slippery in my sweating palm. The power that had pounded against my mind was gone. The silence was ominous, but more ominous was the fact that nothing hindered my approach. I glanced left and right, seeking danger. But there was no one in the room but we three. I advanced across the room while they stood like images carved from stone, like two playing pieces on a knar board—grey queen and yarg warlord.

When I stood in front of the dais and looked up at them, I wondered. The gaze of the towering Waster was fixed on the blade in my hand. Why didn't he make his move? Had the shadow-sword already stripped him of his power? My heart leapt with a hope that was dashed in the next instant. From beside the Waster's silent bulk, the Grey Rose spoke. I turned to her, then took a step back as I saw the hate in her eyes.

"How dare you follow me?" she demanded, her voice laced with venom. "Did you not think that if I required your aid I would have bided with you? Instead you profane this place with your very presence. You are not welcome here, Harper."

She made a mockery of the word, and her laughter sent a chill of horror down my spine. How could I have been so wrong?

"You'd be a Harper, would you?" she said. "Why not try your tunes on the wolves outside the city? They have need for dinner music, I should think."

Her contempt was too much for me. A rage awoke in my heart that she should speak of Hickathrift in such manner. My fingers tightened on my sword, and I took a step forward. I stood looking up at her, shivering under her withering gaze. I meant to speak but my pain stabbed too deep. I saw the heartstone at her throat; against my skin the rose was like ice. Hell-fires burned in her once-dusky eyes—eyes that'd looked on me with friendship, but no more.

I ignored the Waster then, for I saw that all I'd attempted had been for nothing. There was no need for rescue here. She was the monster's willing bride. Realizing that all we'd shared had been a lie, that my own efforts and Hickathrift's sacrifice had been pointless, I found my voice.

"I loved you," I said, the words rising from my heart. "As a man loves a maid, as a companion loves his friend, I loved you. There was a fane in my heart where you once dwelled, but now its foundations crumble. All that was holy in it, is like a dead thing. I'd thought—"

"Begone!" she cried and pointed toward the door. "Begone, or I will lose my patience and command my mate to slay you. You live now only for what was once between us. But that is no more—it means nothing. Begone!''

I stood trembling, looking from the silent shape of the Waster to the maid I'd thought I'd loved. The heartstone flickered warmly at her throat, but I knew that that warmth was as much a lie as anything that had lain between us. A hundred warring thoughts ran through my mind—that somehow the Waster had bent her to his will, that she was enspelled, that she needed me still—but all it took was one look at those hate-filled eyes to turn my hopes to smoke.

I glanced at the Waster, and turned, the blade heavy in my hands. In my mind's eye I saw Hickathrift fall to the wolves once more; then I saw the maid as she'd been in the market at Wran Cheaping, in the Golden Wood, in her cottage. . . . Lovers' touches had never passed between us, but I could remember a friend's hand on my arm, lips on my cheek in a goodnight kiss. I saw Hickathrift dead, I saw her warmth turned to ice, I saw the gaze of the silent Waster—

And then I knew.

I whirled, and the shadow-sword lifted in my hand.

(If I was wrong. . . .)

I plunged the blade into the maid's breast—

(If I was wrong. . . .)

A scream tore through the chamber—a scream so fearful and pain-filled that the walls began to crumble and fall in upon us. The ochre light flared to a burning brilliance. Stark in its blaze I saw the darkness that was the shadow-sword buried to its hilt in the massive chest of Yarac Stone-slayer.

''No!'' he howled.

The light dimmed, then flared again. I shielded my eyes and staggered forward to pluck the heartstone from the Waster's neck. As he collapsed, the room plunged into darkness. I ducked his toppling form and sped to where I had seen his image when I'd first entered the room. My questing hands found the still body of the Grey Rose.

I lifted her in my arms—she was surprisingly light—and bore her from the tower as the ruin fell in upon itself. The thundering of the falling stones that I dodged echoed the drumming of my heart. My whole mind was in confusion.

I'd defeated the Waster, but I felt no pride in the deed. For all his evil, I felt more as if I'd crushed a maggot under my heel than that I'd rid the world of a horror. It wasn't a deed to sing of, merely something needful that had been done. My losses were too great for me to know any joy. The lies still yammered in my head, for all that I knew them to be lies. The maid was still my friend, and she was safe. But Hickathrift was dead.

Once outside, I found that night had finally come to Banlore. The proud vessel of the moon rode the star-flecked sky overhead. I bore the maid until we were some distance from the tower, then laid her gently on the stones. My hands shook as I tied the heartstone about her neck. I withdrew the rose from my tunic and fixed it in her hair.

Her life was tied to these objects; she'd told me as much. I prayed that they'd heal whatever hurts she'd sustained as the Waster's captive.

Again I took her up and made my way out of the city. We were on the opposite side from where I'd entered . . . from where Hickathrift lay slain. I was torn between a wish to raise a cairn over my friend and the need to tend the maid as I could. I didn't have the strength to carry her any farther, but I couldn't leave her either. In the end, I stayed by her, knowing that Hickathrift would've bade me tend to the living before I paid my respects to the dead.

But my heart was heavy as I stood watch by the maid. A roar came from the city as the Waster's tower finished its collapse, burying the monster. A fine tomb that rubble would make—a tomb he didn't deserve. Tomorrow I'd lay stones over one who'd earned his monument.

THE SUN ROSE FROM BEHIND THE EASTERN HILLS TO FIND ME standing dry-eyed but with my sorrow in no way lessened. I regarded the ruins of Banlore, as I had for most of the night, still trying to find that sense of grandeur that the old songs rang with. I saw no glory in my friend's death. The trade, his life for the Waster's, seemed too dear a price to pay.

And yet . . . Yarac was finished, and the maid was safe. I tried to convince myself that it meant something. Then a low, familiar voice broke into my musing.

"Cerin?"

I turned to see the Grey Rose attempting to sit up and went to her side. She pushed aside my helping hand and stood on her own, albeit shakily. Her eyes were warm as they looked on me, and, taking a deep breath, she stretched her limbs with obvious joy.

"Sweet life," she said, smiling at me. "How did you free me, Cerin? I remember only darkness from the night Yarac took me away. How did you best him?"

I sat down in the grass, and she lowered herself by my side. I told her of all that had befallen me since the night she was taken. My eyes—wept dry, I had thought—brimmed with tears once more when I spoke of Hickathrift and his sacrifice. The maid laid her hand on my arm, and a look came into her eyes that was like the look Tess had when she was far-seeing.

"Not dead," she murmured.

"What?"

I clutched at her hand. Her eyes cleared, and she smiled.

"Your friend," she said. "He still lives—though he is sorely hurt."

I thought my heart would burst. Scrambling to my feet, I pulled her up beside me. She laughed for my joy, and together we ran down the hill and, making a circle around the ruins, came to where he lay.

"Hickathrift!" I cried when I could see him.

I left the maid behind and fairly flew over the remaining distance. I wanted to hug him but forebore because of his wounds. He'd pulled himself up a small hillock, clear of the direwolves' bodies, and there he lay. He was battered and so badly cut that I still feared for his life. His fur was matted with dried blood. Hardly able to lift his head at my approach, he still managed a weak grin at my worried look.

Look around you, Cerin. I didn't fare so badly as some.

He spoke the truth. The slope below his refuge was littered
with the corpses of the direwolves that had attacked us. He'd
slain them all.

At that moment the maid came up beside me. She put a
hand on my arm and leaned against me, and for the first time
I was proud of what we'd accomplished. *Now* it was like an
old ballad! My joy was such that I didn't notice the look that
came into Hickathrift's eyes as he regarded the maid—not
until he spoke to her.

So you are the Grey Rose, he said.

There was a curious quality to his voice that puzzled me.
"I have known that name."

And what other names have you known?

I looked from him to her, sensing the tension that lay between them, but not understanding it. I thought the maid
would answer and I'd know her name at last, but she stood
silently at my side, meeting Hickathrift's gaze without flinch-
ing. A pinprickle of fear went through me. I remembered
that time in the Waster's tower when Yarac had worn her
flesh, and she his. Did Hickathrift see some evil in her that
I was blind to?

I never heard the Hillfolk were so long-lived, he said then.

"I have other kin," she replied, "though few in this time
know anything of the Hillfolk—let alone how long-lived they
were in times of peace."

Yet not even the erlkin live for as many years as you claim.

I knew then what troubled Hickathrift. It was worry for
me—the same worry I'd had when she'd told me her history.
Only the gods lived forever . . . the gods, and the undying
who—legend had it—lived on the flesh of men.

"She isn't what you think," I said.

Hickathrift turned his attention to me, but before he could
speak, the maid said: "You have wounds that need tending.
Loremaster. If you'll trust my remedies, I'll see to them as
I can. Then we can speak of histories and names and the
like."

Hickathrift nodded slowly. I fetched my water sack from
where my pack lay on the battlefield, and, while I built a fire,

the maid cleaned his wounds. She bound the worst of them with strips of cloth torn from the white shift that I'd carried in my pack. When I had water boiling in a tin mug, she took herbs from her pocket and dropped them in.

"Drink," she said to Hickathrift when the brew had cooled enough. "It has healing qualities."

He let her feed him the herb broth and was soon nodding. When he fell asleep, she set the mug down and we gazed at each other. All was right with my world at that moment. Hickathrift lived. The maid was rescued. Yarac was slain. But now there was a doubt in me about the Grey Rose that I couldn't quite frame into words. She was my friend, and I trusted her. But I knew little of her world, while Hickathrift had spent years studying histories and old lore. If he distrusted her . . . I thought then of tales Tess'd told me of the undying rising from their graves, hungry for man-flesh. I looked at my friend and couldn't believe it of her. But I still shivered.

"Finish your tale for me," she said. "When you entered the ruins . . ?"

I nodded, glad of the respite from my own thoughts.

"I remember now," she said when I was done, "though it comes to me as memories from a dream. I saw you come in, and my heart leapt that you should risk all for me. But tell me—how did you know that the form you slew was not mine?"

"The shape of the Waster—it had your eyes, while the maid wore the heartstone he'd stolen from you. I guessed that if it had such a power over you, he wouldn't return it. But something puzzles me. Why didn't he simply kill me and be done with it? Why the guile? How could I best him so easily when you've had to run from him for uncounted years . . . when all the Hill Lords' might couldn't finish him?"

"Was it truly so easy to best him?"

Remembering my nightmare journey through the ruins, I shook my head.

"The High Born of the Daketh fear only one thing, and that is caryaln—the shadow-death" she said. "It's believed that only one of those weapons survived the elder days, and it is in the shape of a spear. Yarac knew of it. He was so confident of his power that he told me where it lies hidden.''

"Hickathrift told me of it.''

"A Loremaster would know,'' she said, "but I doubt he knows where it is hidden.''

She was quiet for a moment, a distant look in her eyes, although she wasn't far-seeing.

"I remember Yarac mocking you,'' she said. "He thought you but an innocent fool—how could you know of the caryaln? And that was his folly, for innocent you are, perhaps, but no fool. He never measured the courage in your heart. And when you appeared in Banlore with the caryaln in your fist, he panicked. He thought to deceive you into leaving so that he could deal with you at a later time.

"Those of the Dark are bold when the power is theirs. But show them strength, and they slink away to hide in the shadows. And there they will wait, for untold years, until you show the first sign of weakness. And then they strike. . . .''

Silence slipped over us once more. For all that the Waster was dead, I could still feel an evil in the ruins behind us. I turned my back to it so that I saw only the maid. The closeness of her and the sweet heady scent that seemed to follow her quickened my pulse. Then I glanced at Hickathrift's sleeping form and remembered his worry.

"Who are you—truly?''

She took my hand.

"Look into my eyes, Cerin. Look if you would know me for what I am. . . .''

Hesitantly, I lifted my gaze to hers and was lost in the swirling depths locked inside their dusky lights. All the shades of grey were there—light and dark mingled in perfect harmony. Images took shape in my mind. I saw a hundred worlds, joined in a webwork of gossamer light, and a tall, red-haired race of beings which walked one of them. I saw their world fail, destroyed in a war of such magnitude that nothing remained. Its very foundations were broken and the rubble cast through those hundred other worlds.

The red-haired folk arose again to walk those worlds. I saw the coming of the erlkin to them, the beast-kin, the tree-folk. I saw mountains delved by sturdy dwarves, tree-halls raised by erlkin, hills hollowed by muryan. And, lastly, the coming of mankind. Then the red-haired folk withdrew from the worlds.

The images spun and wove a pattern in my mind. Tales spilled through me, washed me with their histories—tales that would take years for the telling, for they concerned un-counted worlds.

I dropped my gaze, confused at what I'd seen. Had the past come alive for one endless moment to rush through me?

"My name is Meana," the Grey Rose said. "My father was the Hill Lord whose shade you met. His name was Wendweir an Kasaar, and the erls called him Alken. But my mother was of the Tuathan—the eldest race, save for the weren. If I am undying, it is their blood that makes me so, rather than any partaking of the flesh of the Kindreds."

My mind reeled at what she told me. The Tuathan were gods.

"Why . . . why didn't you tell Hickathrift?"

"He would not believe," she replied. "He trusts his scrolls and records too much, and I am not listed in them."

"I . . . I believe."

"I know. The wild blood of the weren runs in you. How could you not believe?"

I shook my head. "No. I believe because it's you who tell me."

The maid I'd named the Grey Rose smiled sadly. She knew I loved her. The words I'd spoken in the Waster's tower lay between us; they could not be unspoken. I would not want them unspoken.

She sighed and disengaged her hand from mine. Rising with a graceful motion, she offered me her hand and drew me to her side. There was a strength in her arms now that belied her earlier helplessness.

"I have another journey to make, Cerin, and I fear I must leave you once more. While Yarac held me in his power, he told me of the ills that he and his kind have planned for this world. He has freed Damal, the daughter of the Dark One who rules the Daketh. I must bring this knowledge to the Wise Ones of my people so that we can make our own plans to stop her.''

"Let me help you. Haven't I proved my worth?"

"Indeed you have, three times over. But this is a journey that will pass the swifter if I fare on my own. You've not yet learned to walk the ways I know, and swiftness is what is needed now."

"But—"

"Fear not, dear friend. We will meet again—in unlooked for places and perhaps in fairer times. You've proved true to me, Cerin, and you will always have my thanks for what you've done. This I will now foretell—your life will be long, longer than that of most men, because of the weren blood your father passed on to you. In days to come you will become the most renowned of all the Harpers. Today I name you Songweaver. For now, though, I must bid you farewell. We will meet again. . . ."

As she spoke the last words, her form began to shimmer and fade. This sudden show of power made my knees go weak, and I took a step back for all that I yearned to hold her to me. She was more fey than either Finan or Hickathrift had guessed. A daughter of the Tuathan, the Old Gods. They had power beyond any that a man could know. But, goddess or not, I loved her.

"Don't leave!" I cried.

"I must."

"What about Hickathrift?" I asked. "Couldn't you heal him with . . . with your power?"

I thought of his wounds, but I thought as well that if she tended him, she would be near me for that much longer.

"I am not a Healer," she said. Her form was almost gone now, vague and pale in the sunlight. "I have a brother. He is the Healer in my family. Because of my mixed blood my strengths are not so great."

"You can't go. Without you. . . ."

But the words grew tangled in my mind before they ever left my throat. To rescue her, only to lose her again.

"We *will* meet again," she promised in a whisper. "I will leave you a parting token as a promise and a gift for the life you returned to me. Ne'er let the fane within you die, dear friend, for it would grieve me sore."

I bowed my head, for I couldn't look at her gossamer shape as it faded before my eyes.

"I go." Her voice was faint and distant now. "Tell Hickathrift that the Daketh are rising. Already they have their spies in Wistlore, seeking to destroy it from within. The Wyslings must be told. Fare ever well. . . ."

I looked up. Her voice faded, and she was gone.

"Farewell," I said.

My sorrow lay like a heavy hand on me. I found it hard to breathe. My chest was tight, and the empty hillside blurred. I turned slowly to look at Hickathrift and saw, lying beside his sleeping bulk, a leather bag. Slowly I walked toward it, already guessing its contents from its shape.

It was a harp, an instrument such as I'd never seen. The bag was made of otterskin, and as I drew its folds away from the instrument, my heart nearly stood still at its beauty.

There was an age about the wood and its grain, so that it shone darkly in the sunlight. The soundbox was decorated with subtly carved knotwork, while the forepillar and curving neck had all manner of mythical beasts carved into their lengths. All the metalwork—the tuning and rest pins, eyelets and blades—was silver, as was the tuning key that hung from a leather thong. I hung this about my neck, where it lay cool against my skin. The strings were made of a silvery glistening metal that I could not put a name to, while set at the top of the join, where the forepillar met the neck, was a grey rose— a living blossom that had the appearance of being fresh-plucked, with dew still damp on its petals.

I touched a string, and a clear note rang forth, echoing and re-echoing over the hillside; at its sound, the tightness eased inside me. I heard a voice in my mind as the note faded.

Its name is Telynros, the voice said. *The roseharp.*

I held its weight on my lap and listened in vain for the voice to speak on; I knew now that she was truly gone. My sorrow lay inside me, but the immediacy of it had run away like water from a leaf. Whether it was the tuning key, now lying warm against my skin like a talisman, or the harp itself, the maid had put some charm on me so that what I felt was like an old sadness . . . never to be forgotten, but no longer overwhelming.

I lifted my hands to the roseharp's strings, hesitated—then began to play. I remembered Tess's words and knew she'd been right. I'd not be returning so soon to Wran Cheaping. Instead, I'd fare to Wistlore with Hickathrift. I had a world to see and a long road to wend through it. I'd hidden away in the West Downs for too long. And somewhere on that road, I could look to meet the maid of the Grey Rose once more.

The harp rang deep and thrumming under my fingers, and I remembered her promise. I would write her a song that I would play on that day—a song that would draw her to my side so that she'd never leave me. I'd call it "The Fane of the Grey Rose," and its strains would encompass all of her sweet wonder.

I looked down at the instrument I played. For a moment I hesitated, my fingers drawn back from its strings. Telynros. The roseharp. I stared at my hands, scraped and chapped from the rough use they'd always known. Such an instrument . . . how could I be worthy of it? It was meant for a Master-harper, not a self-tutored lad.

And yet . . . the harp called to me—was a part of me already. I was filled with awe at the wonder of it, but I thought of the maid.

(*"Today I name you Songweaver. . . ."*)

In her eyes I was worthy. I had only to believe it myself.

I let my fingers touch the strings once more and played until Hickathrift woke from his sleep.

WE PASSED THE NIGHT HIDDEN IN A SMALL GULLY, OUT OF sight of Banlore, but not far enough away that its evil presence could not be felt. I knew the Waster was dead, but a chill wind blew from the direction of the ruins, and as I sat up that night I could hear dark murmurings and curses on that wind. The maid had said that Yarac had freed a daughter of the Daketh, and I wondered if it was her I sensed in the air.

Hickathrift was utterly spent from the exertion of moving to this hiding place. I prayed that there'd be no need for us to move again—at least not soon—for I feared that he wouldn't survive even the shortest journey. The worst of his wounds had opened again, and fresh blood matted his fur. He tried to hide it from me, but when I saw his condition I insisted we remain here. I still had food in my journeypack, and, taking the water sack, I went in search of a stream or seep, leaving him to lie on the rough bed of gorse that I'd fashioned for him.

Luck was with me, for I came across a small spring not three hundred paces from our campsite. It was a rigorous climb to reach it for it was situated halfway down a rough tumble of rock. The water collected in a basin then flowed over the side and lost itself among the rocks.

I returned with my sack full to wash and rebind his wounds. Then I gave him a drink. He was too weak even to use mind-speech, but I read the thanks in his eyes before he dropped into sleep once more.

We stayed three days in that hideaway. Four or five times a day, I climbed down to our small source of water and brought back enough to clean his wounds and for us to drink. My few wounds were nothing compared to his. I was stiff and sore—for I'd sustained a cut or two in the battle with the direwolves—but it was Hickathrift who'd borne the brunt of their attack.

Our food ran out on the evening of the third day. By then, Hickathrift was somewhat stronger—strong enough that we could plan what we would do in the days to come. We talked of the maid's story, and I told him all. He marvelled at her gift but—as she'd warned me—wasn't so ready to accept her lineage. The one thing we both agreed on was that we should bring her warning to Wistlore.

I can travel soon, Cerin, he told me that night, *albeit slowly. But any travel will help us reach Wistlore the sooner. Some of what the maid told you I find difficult to accept—*

"She had no reason to lie."

But still, he continued, *her warning fills me with foreboding that rings with truth, and the Wyslings must know of it as soon as possible.*

Westward we can't fare, for the Perilous Mountains run straight into the sea. To bypass them, we'd need to swim ten leagues of icy ocean. The ship that left me on Eldwolde's shores won't be back until the spring, or so the captain said. I say we go east, following the foothills until we reach the Great Waste. If we turn north there, it's no more than another month's journey to Wistlore, although it means faring through Drarkun Wood, a chancy place at the best of times.

But if Damal is indeed free, she might well be lodged in that ancient forest. . . .

"Who is Damal?" I asked.

Evil is what she is, he replied. *She was sired by Yurlogh Tyrrbane, the eldest of the Dark Gods. The first undying sprang from her womb.*

"But surely the gods have no interest in our affairs?"

We are their only affair. The choice we make in our living—what we make of our lives, the good or ill we do—is what sustains them. The more evil there is in the world, the stronger the Daketh become. The more good, the more Tuathan's power increases.

I shook my head. It seemed to me that the gods should have better things to concern themselves with than meddling in the affairs of men or any of the Kindreds.

"You make it sound as if they walk the world even now, watching us, weighing our worth."

I'd never been easy with the villagers' concept of vengeful spying gods. Ballan, the god of the tinkers, was of the Tuathan, but he rarely meddled in their affairs—if Tess and Finan were to be believed. While they called on his name when things went ill, Tess, at least, turned more to the Moon-goddess Arn for her prayers, she who was the Mother of the World. Arn was claimed by Tuathan and weren alike for she was a goddess of the harvest—of peace and growing things.

What of your maid? Hickathrift asked. *Meana of the Grey Rose whose name is unrecorded in the history scrolls?*

"You think she judged me?"

Hickathrift glanced at the roseharp and nodded.

Judged you and found you worthy, it seems.

"But she was trapped by the Waster. . . ."

Just so. Do you think one of the Tuathan could be held so?

"She said she was kin to them, not a goddess."

I knew the argument was futile even as I spoke. I'd seen her power, and the roseharp was witness to it. It remained as indisputable evidence that there was more to her than to one born of mortal parents.

Hickathrift sighed.

It does us no good to argue, Cerin, he said finally. *Mortal or not, I no longer fear that she is evil.*

I nodded, accepting that.

Instead we should think of our journey. I've a friend who dwells on the edge of Drarkun Wood, this side of the Winding Clay. His name is Calman, and he will tell us if the forest is safe to travel through—or at least as safe as ever it is.

We might have differences in some matters—for all Hickathrift's superior learning—but I was more than willing to let him plan our route. What knowledge I had of the lands beyond the West Downs was only hearsay.

He fell asleep soon after and the next morning sent me out in search of galsa and Heartsure. The tubers of the galsa plant make good eating—or at least so he insisted, and we needed food—while Heartsure has ever been a hallowed plant. Tea made from its dried buds and leaves was heartening and a sure cure against weariness and many diseases. Its use as a weapon against the Dark was only one of its properties.

I had little trouble finding the Heartsure. Its bright gold flowers stood out like beacons against the stark grey of the rocks and weathered brush. Galsa I was unfamiliar with, and

I spent many hours searching out the small diamond-shaped leaves that heralded the long tuber. With some difficulty, I worked the clinging roots from the soil until, by midafternoon, I had a sackful to bring back to the camp.

That night I took Telynros from its otterskin case and tuned it. That was the first time I'd played it while Hickathrift was awake. Night and day I'd sat by him, watching over him, leaving only to fetch water for his wounds and our thirst, food for our hunger. When he slept, I stole a few moments of playing before sleep claimed me as well.

But tonight he'd asked me to play, and I was willing. He was no longer on the threshold of death; although he was still weak, his eyes were clear and bright. He fretted with impatience at his body's slow recovery and needed something to take his mind from it.

I was nervous, playing for him, but once I ran my fingers across the strings and felt an answering stirring deep inside me, I let the roseharp's sweet tone carry me away with its beauty. I was still in awe of the instrument, but not enough to forbear playing it. My heart filled with memories of the Grey Rose. Summer days in the Golden Wood flitted through me, evenings in her cottage, longings and yearnings. Again I felt the sweet press of her body against mine as I carried her from the ruins.

Meana. I whispered her name to myself, wove it into the music.

("We will meet again . . . we will meet again. . . .")

The roseharp seemed to sing that phrase in harmony to the music I drew from its strings. I glanced at Hickathrift, wondering if he heard it too, curious as to what he thought of my playing and the tone of this wondrous instrument, but the worry-lines on his furred brow were smoothed and his eyes shut. Sleep held him fast.

I smiled, my fingers never straying from the strings, never letting the air falter. I played for the night now, for myself and Meana, the Grey Rose.

It was long after midnight when I returned the harp to its case and went to my own bed. That night the chill wind that had blown each evening from the direction of the ruined city ceased, and the air was quiet. My dreams were untroubled, and I was well rested when I awoke the next morning.

Another few days, and we would set out at the slow pace we'd decided upon. I thought of Tess, missing her and wondering how she'd known that I'd go on. Tinkers understood the call of the road, I supposed. And this road . . . I longed for the journey to begin, for, somewhere in the days to come, I looked for Meana's promise to be fulfilled—we would meet again.

CALMAN STONESTREAM

Blood to blood
the gift flows.
From the grave-fire,
from the raised stones,
from underhill,
from the Summer Country
—the voices of our kin
still reach
to weave a pattern
in the flesh we wear.

—from the SONGWEAVER'S JOURNEYBOOK

THE JOURNEY FROM BANLORE'S RUINS TO THE EDGE OF THE Great Waste took us the better part of two months. Day by day Hickathrift's strength returned. By the end of the second month he was almost as strong as he'd ever been, and we began to make better time.

Those weeks on the road proved my foster-uncle Finan's words true, for the initial friendship that had sprung up between the mys-hudol Loremaster and myself grew into such a bond that all the gathered might of the Dark could never have broken it. We spoke little on the road, but at night around our small campfire we often talked into the night.

I learned of Hickathrift's youth in Auldwen, how the elders of his tribe had taken him aside when they saw his affinity for knowledge—what they called ''root-ways''—and the maintaining of the old histories. At length they sent him to Wistlore, for they saw in him one who could forge a bridge between the simpler histories of Auldwen and those of the wide world that lay beyond its borders.

One day I'll return, he told me. *For with all the knowledge I acquire, I see that the simpler a pattern appears the more complex it truly is. With what I know now, I find myself needing to speak up to my tribal elders once more—to view Auldwen's histories through eyes that have studied the records scrolls in Wistlore. I can sense resonances in them that I was never aware of before—and these I would share with the elders. It was for this they sent me out into the world—I see that now.*

We spoke of Wistlore—of the Harperhall and the Libraries; of the gwandryas, both my father's people and those of the Great Wastes; of erlkin and tinkerfolk and the dwarves who claimed direct lineage from Truil, the Tuathan Lord of Stone. Rarely did we speak of the Grey Rose, though she was much on my mind. But most nights I played her gift, and we did speak of the harp.

Roseharp, Hickathrift said once. *Did your fostermother, or the maid herself, ever speak to you of Young Innes—the Lord of the Wild Roses?*

I shook my head.

It was he who gave the Harpers their three magics—those of laughter, tears, and sleep.

I ran my hand down the carved forepillar of the roseharp. "You think this was his?

No. But he played a harp of roses—or so the tales have it. His instrument was carved from a rosebush and large as an oak, and its strings were the wound hairs of Celeste, the Weaver of Dreams. He gathered them at night from the riverbank where by day she washed and combed her hair. For the love of her he made his harp and his music.

"And did he win her?"

Hickathrift shook his head. *The tale says that he seeks her still. Your instrument's name brought the story to mind. Telynros, the roseharp. I wonder . . . Every rose has its thorn. . . .*

"There's no evil in this instrument—or in the maid."

He shrugged but said nothing. We'd agreed not to argue about the maid any more. But as I thought of his tale of Young Innes I felt the prick of a thorn in my heart. The only thorn in this rose was that the maid was gone. I said as much, and Hickathrift shrugged again. Only I could know how sharply that thorn pierced.

A gift like this harp, he began again, trying to change the subject, *in the old tales such gifts were catalysts and awoke feyness in their players so that they could walk in the* Middle Kingdom *or see the weren run across the hills where others saw only the wind touching the heather. Minstrel Ravendear had an enchanted harp with a white raven carved into its head. With it he could call up shadow-dancers that would playact the ballads as he sung them. It worked, I've been told, as a focus for his own powers—much like a Wysling might use a staff or a name to set a spell.*

I smiled. "The only things I can call up are tunes, Hickathrift."

But I thought of my father's blood and what Meana had told me.

("You lack no magics. . . .")

I shivered and touched the grey rose that bloomed in the head of my own instrument. Perhaps I could call the maid up. . . . No. What did I do each night but play for her, call to her? She'd not returned although two months had gone by since I'd last seen her. We'd retraced our path through Holme's Way during that time, following the foothills of the Perilous Mountains through the West Downs. We travelled far north of Wran Cheaping and skirted the Golden Wood. I thought much of Tess and the maid in those days, and grew morose and withdrawn, not the best of travelling companions. My mood didn't lift until we were well across the Vales of Fortune.

We avoided the cots of the herdsmen and the small towns in the Vales, quickening our pace as Hickathrift's health and stamina improved. As the Oak Moon, the first moon of winter, began to wane, we reached the Hills of the Dead that border the Great Waste. We camped that night where the hills rise from the downs that riddle the Vales of Fortune. In the twilight, the hills rolled eastward, granite-topped and gorse-backed—a gloomy sight that stayed with me long after the night hid their shapes from my eyes.

After a dinner of galsa root (which I'd grown quite fond of) and fresh cheese that I'd begged from a shepherd while Hickathrift hid out of sight of the flock, I asked him about those hills and how they'd gained their grim name. Hicka-thrift told me of the great wars that had raged in elder times, long before the struggles of the Hill Lords against Yarac's army.

By all accounts, those were terrible times to live, Cerin. All the world was in turmoil. The Southern Kingdoms writhed in the grip of endless warrings—not the petty squabbles that continue to this day, but whole armies meeting on the field of battle, fighting to the last man. In the Trembling Lands, the Hill Lords defended their halls against an influx of raiders riding north from the Widelands. Algarland and the mys-hudol of Auldwen were at odds. In Kohr and Drarkun Wood, the yarg wars raged for long years.

At that time these lands were called the Hills of Bre. They were ruled by King Wellstarre, along with the Vales of For-tune and most of Eldwolde. The legions of the Dark swept over the King's high seat in Estelleaad, leaving the Golden City in ruins, and Wellstarre met them in one last great battle in these hills.

The Dark legions were slain to the last creature, for Tua-than came to Wellstarre's aid. Secret-laden Jaalmar was there, with Truil the Father of Stone and the Sky Lord Grey-min. But Wellstarre took a wound in that last battle and died . . . as did many, many of his men.

He spoke as if he saw those armies clashing before his eyes, and I leaned forward, transfixed by his tale.

Many were the heroes that fell. Achel and Lankin were among their number, as were Locween of the Axe, bold Galan, and his sire Halmoc. Jalenna, who fought with a spear bladed at either end, and her brother Yuln, the Shapechang-er, died there. It's said their ghosts still haunt these hills—

theirs and the shades of the Dark who were slaughtered in that battle. They are shunned by the Kindreds now, these hills, and named the Hills of the Dead, for nothing lives here save hill-gaunts.

My eyebrows lifted in a question.

Carrion-eaters. I doubt we'll meet them, for they range nearer the Great Waste where they can harry the caravans.

Later that evening when I brought out my harp, something of the grim nature of the hills edged into my playing. I thought of all that Hickathrift had told me and found myself composing a lay that told of the fall of Wellstarre and his knights. The tune came readily to my fingers, the words striding through it with a sure skill that didn't quite seem to be my own. Hickathrift complimented me when I was finished singing it for him, a warm smile twinkling in his eyes.

I wondered then, as I had before, that one so used to the golden tongues of the Harpers of Wistlore should find my own verses favourable in comparison. Though I was secretly pleased at his praise, there were times when I felt that he was more kind than truthful.

Hickathrift was already asleep when I finally put my harp away and lay down to stare into the star-laden sky above. Winter's chill was strong in the air, though thus far we'd been spared snow. Just the same, cold winds muttered through the hills, and I sought the warmth of my mantle, wrapping it tightly about me and wishing that nature had given me a coat as warm as my companion's.

That night I had a strange dream. I found myself in a grove of hazel, alder, and thorn, in the company of strangers—men and women with haunting eyes. They were a tall folk, the women standing shoulder to shoulder with the men, clad in trousers and gowns of sheep's wool and well-worn leather trim. Their cheekbones were high, their eyes dusky like Meana's, with gold flecks in the pupils. Their brows were broad and smooth, and each one's hair ran from auburn to a bright rust-gold.

It seemed that they spoke to me in a language that was old when the land was young, a tongue I didn't know; but in the dream I understood and conversed with them. What we spoke of, I forgot by the time I awoke; but later, when I played the roseharp, echoes of their speech hovered in my memory, and strange turns that I recognized as their touch came into familiar tunes.

Our crossing of the Hills of the Dead took two more days, although we spent three nights all told camped in the bleak range. Each night the strangers visited my dreams, and we walked and spoke in that grove of old trees. I came to realize that they didn't so much speak to me as through me. I felt as if I stood in their midst, unseen to them. At times, I'd occupy the same space as one of their number, and then it seemed that I answered some query put to me or put forth a question of my own—though in truth I spoke not at all.

The last night I sensed the presence of the Grey Rose among them—though I caught no glimpse of her—and that dream stayed longer in my memory, so that when I woke I didn't feel so much that I'd dreamed as that I had been in some fey elsewhere. These were the Tuathan, I realized, Meana's kin. But when I spoke of them to Hickathrift, he shook his heavy muzzle in disagreement.

I'd say not. The lore books give the Tuathan another seeming, and those records were written by folk who trod the same earth as they in those elder days. Tyrr Stormbringer was as dark-haired as a raven, while Avenal was as fair as the harvest corn. Not all of them even wore the shape of men. Jaalmar had a head like a brecaln or another of the great cats and Greymin a hawk's, while some were like the kemys-folk— half beast and half man. The Sea Lord Jarl had a fish's tail from the waist down. . . .

I was unconvinced but had to bow to his superior wisdom. Tess had told me of the Tuathan but never given shapes to their names, so I had nothing to judge my dream-folk by except the intuition that had given me their name. Even Hickathrift, while he could tell me who they weren't, still couldn't place them. He worried at the riddle all that day, for his knowledge of the old lore was great, and it troubled him that he could not identify my dream-folk.

Late in the afternoon the wind grew so chill and the sky so laden with clouds that I was afraid that the first of the winter's storms was upon us. A howling wind buffeted us as it shook the sparse vegetation and drove refuse from the Great Waste before it. Grit stung our eyes, and we dodged clumps of brush that rode the wind like balls. From where we were, I could see a faint shimmering that marked the beginning of the Waste. At this distance it looked more like water than a sea of sand.

It remembers. Hickathrift's gaze followed my own. *The Waste remembers when it was an ocean in ages past, and it plays with illusions of water as we do with our memories. If you were to walk those sands, you'd find shells and preserved fish that are like stone, while here we are—leagues and leagues from the nearest sea.*

We turned north to enter the grasslands that border the Waste. The yellow grass rode as high as my waist, and it filled our sight like a sea as well, rolling toward the horizon until it finally washed up against the mountains on one side and the desert on the other. Clumps of blackthorns were scattered about like small islets in the ocean, and the grass whipped against us as the storm followed us north. Hickathrift's thick pelt kept him warm so the cold didn't trouble him, but I had only the thin clothing of the southlands and my mantle with its tattered hem. I thrust my hands deep into my tunic and huddled against the growing cold, my harp heavy on my shoulder.

After a half week in the grasslands, we came at last to a land broken with winter-dead willows and dried reeds and rushes. The marshy ground underfoot was half-frozen and passable, and at length we stood looking over the Qualan River at the point where it splits in two before it runs into Kamera Bay, the southernmost reaching of the Inner Sea. I was for building a raft to cross over. Hickathrift insisted on bearing me across upon his broad back.

Our crossing was unmarred by misfortune, but by the time we reached the other side, I was shivering with the cold and sure that I'd come down with a fever. My right arm—with which I'd held my harp above the water, for all that its otter-skin case should've kept it dry—felt like lead. I could hardly move it.

I built a fire on the riverbank, in a hollow away from the wind, and huddled in front of it, refusing to press on until I was thoroughly dry. The cold cut me to the marrow, and my teeth chattered. I knew that if I didn't find some warmer clothing soon, I'd die from exposure. Again I envied Hickathrift his warm coat.

We spent that night by the fire and fared on the next day. A light snow fell throughout the afternoon and evening, continuing until just before midnight. We walked all that night. Any wood we could find was too damp for a fire, and I was afraid to lie down, knowing that my exhaustion and growing weakness might never let me rise. Hickathrift, although warm, was in little better shape, for he was still recovering from his wounds.

We were a sorry pair by the time we reached the banks of the Winding Clay. We were cloaked in white, for it had started to snow once more. I collapsed on the shore to stare listlessly across the cold water. As dawn neared I thought I saw a light on the opposite bank and pointed it out to Hickathrift.

Calman's hut, he rumbled. *We'll find shelter there.*

Once more I took hold of the fur on his back while he waded out into the icy water. Sometime during that crossing I must have blacked out, for my next recollection was of waking on a hard bed that was too short for my long frame. I opened my eyes to find a broad bearded face peering into my own.

CALMAN WAS A DWARF.

He stood just over four feet. What he lacked in height he more than made up for in breadth. I'd never seen shoulders so wide, a chest so deep. He wore his hair and beard long, and both were black, streaked with sudden greys—almost as grizzled as Hickathrift's fur. His trousers and shirt were made of rough homespun cloth, mottled brown in colour, while his boots and jerkin were a bright scarlet leather. Finan would've like them. A broad brow and nose highlighted his face; his eyes were dark, almost black, and he was wrinkled with the passage of many years.

My first wakening to him—in a strange chamber, with him standing over me, his head too close to the floor because of his height—came as a rude surprise. I started back, knocking my head against the headboard. As I sat up, the room spun. Steadying myself, I wondered if my fever had made me see what looked like a big man shrunk down like a closed concertina; but no, he still looked the same.

He stepped back, and I saw Hickathrift lying in front of a hearth, soaking up the heat of a large fire. He nodded solemnly to me.

So you've returned to the living, Cerin.

Rubbing the back of my head, I attempted a smile. The dwarf left my bedside to busy himself by a low table across the room. The cabin was log-walled and chinked with dried mud. The floor was made of rough wood and the rafters of roughly hewn timber. The only stone was in the hearth, and it was fieldstone. Besides the bed on which I lay—it had to be Calman's from the size of it—I saw a table with woodworking tools and a half-carved statue of a stag on it, a low chair in front of it, a cabinet across the room that stood under a shuttered window, and the table where the dwarf was busy.

He returned with a bowl of steaming soup in his hand.

"How long . . ?" I began, returning my gaze to Hickathrift.

"It be two days," the dwarf answered.

Shakily, I took the bowl he offered and murmured my thanks. Outside the building, the wind howled like a thousand furies, but with the smell of the soup rising to my nostrils, I had more interest in food than in the weather.

I looked about some more as I ate and saw a chest at the foot of the bed, another stuffed under the worktable. A thick rug of goat's pile lay beside the bed, and a rough blanket covered me. On the mantel stood three completed statues— one of a bear, one of two frolicking wolves, and a third of a slender man playing a set of bagpipes.

When I saw that instrument my throat went tight, and I almost choked on the soup.

Telynros. The roseharp—

Then I saw it lying under my pack at the foot of the bed, tucked between the chest and the wall. My hand still trembled as I lifted another spoonful of soup to my lips, but now it shook with relief. I must have clung to the harp for all that I'd blacked out when we crossed the river.

Later, after two more bowls of soup, I felt strong enough to sit by the fire. I leaned against Hickathrift's side and remarked on the soup's almost woody flavour.

"Aye," the dwarf said. "Wood be much of its making, indeed."

I glanced at Hickathrift and he laughed, deep and rumbling.

A great delicacy in my homeland, he said, *is the inner bark of a white pine. It's best taken when the tree is young—in the spring, from the south side of the tree.*

"But that's bear—or at least mys-hudol—food," I protested.

And you never eat nuts or fruit?

"That's different."

"No different," Calman said.

I gave up. How was I to argue with a bear and a dwarf? I said as much, and they both grinned.

"How did you come to live here?" I asked Calman.

The humour fled the dwarf's face. He looked at me strangely, as if he were appraising both my question and myself before answering.

"Questions be awkward betimes," he said, glancing at Hickathrift, "and there be many folk not wanting to answer them. But I find no real harm in the telling.

"It were years ago, by any reckoning, and I dwelt in the halls of my kind in Maelholme—there where the mountains fall into the Westron Sea. My clan be the Clan Stonestream, and fair were the times I had there—till a pair came from the north, knocking at our great stone doors with a child in tow.

"Ye'd have to have seen them—all rags and tatters they

were, but I knew one of them to be gwandryas. When they begged sanctuary, for all it were the middle of winter, I'd not let them step one foot into my hall.''

He paused, frowning, and I turned to look at Hickathrift.

The enmity between dwarfland and the gwandryas is old beyond reckoning. The reason itself is almost forgotten, but—

''Not forgotten!'' Calman cried, striking his knees with a fist. ''Were they that stole the Truil-stone from Deepdelve and for that they be ever cursed!''

It was the gwandryas of the Waste who stole it, Hickathrift said.

Calman shook his head. ''Of the Waste . . . or the Grassfields . . . it be all the same.''

Hickathrift shrugged, unwilling to argue the matter. Looking at the dwarf's furious features, I worried what he'd do if he ever learned who my father had been. I didn't want to be sent out into the storm, but, given a chance, I'd have braved the elements rather than face Calman's fierce anger. His face was red above the edges of his beard, and his dark eyes were black with anger.

''They were proud, those two,'' he continued after a moment, ''proud as erlkin for all their rags, but I were proud too. Nowhere was there the one could work stone or metal better than I. And I'd never have it said that I guested gwandryas—even such a tattered pair, with their squalling child.

''I sent them away with a curse on my lips, and the one of them returned that curse. 'No more skill be yours!' I was told as they turned back into the storm. I laughed, with that doom ringing 'bout my ears, but then . . . ah, then! The metal in my forge ran 'tween my tongs like water, ran like a stream into a crack in the stone of my smithy, and the tongs shattered in my hands. Harper's Curse it were—took my skill from me.'' He looked bitterly at my harp. ''Damned Harper's Curse!''

I knew a chill at his words. I was twice damned now—son of a Harper and a gwandryas. If he should learn. . . .

''Here I came then,'' he said, ''winter on me, chill winds blowing, snow piled high as a mountain in its drifting. This cabin I built—for wood heeds my call—and plants I grow. But there's not a stone answers my skill, not a metal I can forge. I! I who were the best can do nothing. I can use an axe—crafted by another. My hearth—were built by another. . . . A dwarf I be, not a damned wooder!''

He grimaced in his beard, slowly clenching and unclenching his fists.

''The . . . Harper . . . What was his name?''

''He? Were no man—were a woman! Eithne Gwynn her name!''

I'd felt it coming before he spoke my mother's name. My mind reeled as his tale took hold, and the cold of the storm outside settled in my bones. I knew anger at the dwarf for sending my parents out into that other storm fifteen years ago. If it hadn't been for him . . . But then, I pitied him as well. A dwarf unable to work in stone or metal—what worse curse could there be?

Calman regarded me steadily, and I grew afraid. If he should guess . . . and yet . . . that it should be my own parents—it seemed too evil a coincidence.

It was your mother, Hickathrift confirmed.

His voice cut through the tumble of my thoughts.

''You knew?'' I asked him. Then I turned to Calman and met his unwavering gaze. ''And . . . and you? You knew it was my mother who cursed you and still took me in?''

Calman ran a hand through his long beard, and it seemed that the anger in his eyes softened.

''Fifteen years be a long time,'' he said. ''Time enough to consider and remember and regret. The son need not pay for the parents' ill deeds.''

His fingers twisted and pulled at his beard as he spoke, and I watched their movement, then looked up to meet his gaze when he paused.

''We have no quarrel, ye and I,'' he said. ''I ken now the lesson that your mother meant for me to learn. Let the past be. But kenning her lesson. . . .'' His fingers stopped their nervous twisting, and he held his hands before me. ''It be still hard.''

"I'm sorry," I said.

And I was. It would've been kinder to kill him. I knew how I'd feel if someone took my harping from me.

"Be ye truly sorry?" Calman asked.

He leaned forward again, peering as if he tried to read my heart. I nodded helplessly. Calman beamed with delight.

"Then ye'll help me?"

"Help you? How can *I* help?"

Calman rose at once and went to the foot of the bed. Reverently, he lifted the harp's case and brought it to me.

"Lift ye the curse," he said simply as he placed the case in my hands.

I stared at him aghast. Lift it? I had no such knowledge. But if I refused—would he turn me out, as he had my parents? I looked beseechingly at Hickathrift.

Help me! I cried, shaping the words with my mind.

I can give you no aid in this, he replied. *Only remember what we spoke of before—gifts such as the roseharp can be used as a focus to wake your own hidden talents.*

I was too ensnared in panic to realize that I'd mindspoken. That in itself was a great wonder. Instead I clutched the case and tried to still the thundering of my pulse. I had no talents. But I remembered Meana telling me I had magics, and I was heir to my father's fey strengths. . . .

"Ye be of their blood," Calman said. "Blood to blood . . . only ye can lift the curse from me now."

I swallowed with difficulty..

"I . . . I don't know how."

Hickathrift stirred behind my back.

You must try, he said. *Your mother is dead—only she could have lifted the curse. She . . . or one of her blood.*

I felt trapped. My hands trembled as I undid the bindings that held the case closed. The otterskin fell away, and once more I looked on Telynros—my gift from the Grey Rose. Its finish glistened in the firelight, and the rose in its head shimmered and glowed with a pale inner light.

My hands still shook as I tuned two strings that sounded false. Calman watched me like a hawk, his hands twisting at his beard until it was a matted tangle, his gaze beating down at me until I had to turn away. I stared at the roseharp's strings, looking for inspiration in their silver lengths.

Begin with something you know, Hickathrift said softly, *and the rest will follow if you remain attuned to it.*

I nodded, thinking: attuned to what?

Hesitantly, I plucked at a string, then another. Their sweet tones rang out in the confined space of the cot, rebounding from the walls so that their echoes multiplied. It seemed as if a hundred strings were sounding. I tried a chord, my hand moving slowly as if a weight was tied to it, then ran through a series of triplets.

The sound filled the room. As the notes rang out, I smelled a sweet scent like that of roses, and, closing my eyes, I called up the features of the maid of the Grey Rose. When I saw her, with her gentle fragrance all around me, the weight left my fingers. I played with a sudden confidence. I heard voices singing harmony—an unseen choir that sang with the voices of the red-haired beings from my dreams in the Hills of the Dead—and I marvelled.

Opening my eyes, I looked at the dwarf and saw a webwork pattern of spider-thin threads, red and gossamer, wrapped about him like a cocoon and knew it to be a visualization of my mother's spell. My harping moved into strange ground, echoing music I'd heard in dreams but never played, and I saw a way to lift the curse. It was but a matter of unwinding those gossamer red threads. . . .

Words spilled from my throat—sounds that had meaning but were in a tongue I'd never spoken. I watched the first thread unravel and fall from the dwarf. It drifted to the floor and dissolved. Half my mind marvelled that I could do—was doing—what I did, but the other half was listening to the thrumming of my blood as it moved through my veins.

("Blood to blood . . .")

The gift of my parents' blood moved in me and something hidden was stirring into life.

("You lack no magics . . .")

Another thread drifted, feather-slow, to the floor. I realized that it was more than a different view of the world that had set me apart from the villagers in Wran Cheaping, and more than love that drew me to my fostermother. I understood little of what I was doing, but I knew enough to understand that what rose in me now had always been there, a fey hidden secret that had required only the catalyst of Meana's gift—and a need—to stir it awake.

A third and fourth thread fell from the dwarf, and now I could see a visible change in him. His spine stiffened. A far-off look came into his eyes. He rose from where he sat to take a small hammer and chisel from the chest under the worktable. Like a man in a dream, he worked a small stone free from the side of the hearth where his pots and pans hung and sat down again in front of me.

Against the fey ringing of the roseharp, the clacking sound of a chisel cutting into stone filled the air. He kept time with me, for all that the music I played was not a rhythmic music. It passed through so many varying time signatures, from bar to bar, that I'd have been hard put to follow it myself had someone else been playing it.

My head was beginning to ache when the last of the threads fell free. The music I drew from the roseharp faltered.

"Look!" Calman cried. "O blessed Truil, look!"

In his hand he held a small harp carved from stone.

No sooner had he spoken than the spell I'd worked took its toll. Sharp pains lanced my temples, and my hands fell away from the harp. The instrument would've fallen from my lap if Calman hadn't caught it. I remember thinking his speed wondrous for one of his bulk. That, and Hickathrift's words, were all that I retained as a black wave came sweeping over me.

You did well, Cerin, he rumbled, *and more than well. Sleep now. Garner strength. . . .*

And so I did.

THE FIRST MORNING AFTER THE LIFTING OF THE CURSE, I had a long talk with Hickathrift. My head was filled with riddles and worries and, try as he might, there was little he could do to set my mind at ease.

"It was a cruel lesson," I said of my mother's curse.

Hickathrift nodded his grizzled head in agreement.

And yet I don't doubt that she meant to lift it herself once it was learned. She couldn't know that she would not live to see that day, so we shouldn't be harsh in our judgment of her.

"And yet . . ." I nodded.

Calman was wrong to turn them away—gwandryas or not. But the stubborn pride of the dwarfkin is known the length and breadth of the land, Cerin. The Truil-stone that he spoke of, that the gwandryas of the Waste stole from Deepdelve . . . your maid of the Grey Rose was still young when that deed was done. Wistlore didn't exist, and the Cradle of the Kings was the centre of learning. Don't you think a grudge held that long is one held too long?

"What was the Truil-stone?"

Truil is the Tuathan Lord of Stone. The Stone was his gift to the dwarfkin, for they were his children. The High Lord of the dwarves wore it in his crown until it was stolen.

"Why did they steal it?"

Hickathrift shrugged. *The gwandryas say it was in payment for the raids that the dwarves had made against their own camps. Too many years have gone by for the truth to be known, and the bitter enmity between the two clouds any understanding that could be reached. The Stone is gone—lost in the Great Waste—and Deepdelve itself fell in the dwarves' war against the Wormlands. It lay north of the Vales of Fortune, under the Perilous Mountains, and there its ruins still lie for all anyone knows. I doubt not that the mountains themselves fell in on those hidden halls, and nothing remains of them. Only dwarves and Loremasters remember it now.*

Our talk turned then to the events of the night before—how I'd lifted the curse and used mindspeech. I tried to describe what it was that I'd felt awaken in me, but words proved inadequate. It was like the echo of a quiet song, playing softly in the deepest reaches of my mind. A sound, a stirring so faint that I could almost forget it was there at all. But when I thought of it, or reached for it, the song grew stronger, the stirring quickened, until I drew back from it.

But this is a rare thing, Hickathrift said, *no matter your bloodlines. Mindspeech. The Wyslings have it, as do the erlkin, the kemys-folk, and my own kin. But for a man to have it . . .* He shook his head as his voice trailed off, then added: *And the fey strength itself . . . I hoped you could lift the curse, for the blood of your mother runs in you. But what you've described to me . . . that is the essence of magic itself. What the Wyslings call* taw, *their inner strength. That is what stirs in you.*

It seemed more a burden to me—as if I was no longer alone in my own mind, for all that the stirring was a part of me.

"I'm not so sure I'm pleased to have it."

Such powers are not a matter of desire. One has them or does not.

"Perhaps . . ." I sighed and glanced at my harp. "I wanted to find magics, but not like this—not inside myself. The only spell I ever wanted was the one that music could weave. I wanted only—"

To be the Songweaver, Hickathrift said with a gentle smile as he used the name the maid'd given me before she left.

"That's all."

Hickathrift was quiet a moment.

I know a Harper in Wistlore who was a friend of your mother's. His name is Eoin Fairling, and when we reach the Harperhall, I'll introduce you to him. For her sake, and your own skill, he might well take you on as his prentice, although the Masterharper Caradoc is likely to lodge a protest. Eoin was your mother's friend, but Caradoc was foremost among those who raised their voices against her and so had a hand in her exile from both the Harperhall and Wistlore itself. Caradoc can be eloquent—where's the Harper that isn't?— and I don't doubt that he'll try to sway Eoin from accepting your pledge.

I wondered if I could be happy in the Harperhall, knowing that its present master had been instrumental in my mother's exile. Then I smiled. From what Hickathrift said it seemed unlikely that I'd ever get the chance to find out, even if this Eoin Fairling was willing to take me on as a prentice. I said as much to Hickathrift, but he shook his head.

Wistlore isn't ruled by despots. If Eoin is willing to take you on, Caradoc can do nothing.

"And they don't need to know who I really am. I could use Tess's surname, or the one Meana gave me. Who would be the wiser then?"

You mustn't hide you lineage, Cerin. The relationship between prentice and master is based on trust, and beginning it with a lie would be a poor showing of that trust. It would go worse for you if the truth was discovered later.

I suppose my features wore a resigned look, for Hickathrift laughed.

How will it be so hard? he asked. *You've already slain a Waster and lifted a curse—deeds fit for the hero of a ballad. Now it's time for you to discover what happens to a hero after the ballad is done.*

"I don't look forward to meeting this Caradoc."

A teasing look came into Hickathrift's eyes.

You could always look to your dream-folk for help.

I laughed with him, and then Calman returned with a sled laden with stone. The conversation turned to the storm and other matters while I helped him unload the sled and we set about preparing dinner.

But later that night, I lay in my cloak by the hearth and thought of my red-haired dream-folk, and I wondered. Who were they? If not the Tuathan, Meana's kin, then who *were* her kin? For I knew for certain that she'd been among those strangers on the last night that I dreamed of them.

That riddle, coupled with the strange stirring inside me, made it hard for me to sleep. I tried to fashion some plan for the coming days, but knowing nothing of Wistlore except what I'd heard secondhand, I had little to base my planning on. Did I even want to be prenticed in the Harperhall? Once I had—but then I'd met the Grey Rose, and my life had changed.

I'd come a long way as a musician on my own. But I knew as well that, for all that I had Meana's gift—and Telynros was a princely gift, beyond compare—I could only teach myself so much. If I wanted to earn the blue cloak of a Harper, I had to study under a Harpmaster. There was no other manner in which to earn the title.

And what of the maid herself? I looked to meet her again— only where . . . and when?

I thought I'd never sleep, but soon I began to nod off. The only thing that disturbed my rest that night was the howling of the wind outside the cot.

WE STAYED WITH CALMAN FOR ONE WEEK, ALL TOLD, AND the storm kept us inside most of the time. Winds feathered with wild snow roared about the cot, sending small drifts scurrying under the door and shaking the shutters. Calman and I worked hard to keep a path clear from the front door to the privy, but each morning we'd find the drifts piled against the cottage as high as my waist. If the door hadn't opened inward, we could easily have been trapped inside until a thaw.

Hickathrift and I rested mostly, conserving and gathering our strengths, while Calman sat with his chisel and hammer, cutting wondrous shapes out of the stone he'd gathered. He hummed strange tunes under his breath as he worked, breaking into song every so often. When he sang, the words seemed to come forth with a gruff rumble, like the earth shifting deep underground in the hollowed holdings where only the dwarf-kin made their homes.

I accompanied him on the roseharp from time to time. He'd grin at me through his beard, and the tap-tapping of his hammer would follow the rhythm of my harping and the meter of the old dwarf-songs he sang. Our friendship was forged during that time, tempered with the sharing of our music that needed neither speech nor explanations.

One morning we woke and the wind was only a quiet whisper outside the cabin. I rose from my place by the hearth to pry the door open and look outside. For the first time in days

I could see the surrounding countryside, and my mouth gaped open in amazement at what I saw.

I was used to snow, for it fell in the West Downs, but what I saw now was like the legends of the frozen northlands where the spring never came. Drifts were piled higher than my head, covering the hills. The Winding Clay was frozen over, capped with snow. The trees were half buried under their own blinding white mantles. I shook my head at the wonder and wildness of the sight.

"Aye," Calman said from behind me. "The first storm of winter be ever a wild one."

He pushed by me, shovel in hand, to clear a new path to the privy. I stepped back inside, shivering with a sudden chill, for now that the storm had ended, a deep cold had settled over the land. Adding a few logs to last night's coals, I had a merry blaze going by the time Calman returned. I stirred the porridge I was making one last time and poured it into three bowls. We ate in silence.

Hickathrift and I left later that morning. I was clothed more warmly—in ill-fitting clothes, true, but I didn't mind. Better to be ungainly and warm, I thought, than fashion-conscious like some courtly jack-a-dandy and cold. Calman and I had fashioned some of his extra gear into a sturdy travelling cloak, and I had a pair of his boots as well, with two pairs of thick socks so that they'd fit. He also gave me a pair of snowshoes, for which I was especially grateful. With the snow so deep, they were all that would keep me from sinking to my waist in the heavy drifts.

Calman appeared to be genuinely sorry to see us go, and for my own part, I knew I'd miss him as well. I'd come to love the dwarf's company and the snugness of his little cot.

"Ye return this winter," he said, "and I'll still be here. As for Drarkun—the wood be quiet, for now. Stirrings and mutterings, tree groan and tree spite there—no more. But north, a shadow stirs. Though ground be frozen, it speaks of the Dark awakening."

Hickathrift nodded solemnly. *This is the message we bear to the Wyslings—that Damal has risen.*

Calman spat in the snow. "That, for the Dark Queen." He scowled, then regarded us both steadily. "I be here while the snow lies. But come the springtime it's mountain-deep I be faring, westward and westward, to the halls of my kin. And there ye'll be welcome too, Loremaster Trummel and Cerin Songweaver."

I shook hands with him. He muttered a gruff farewell as we stepped away.

Across the white fields we fared. Hickathrift's broad paws kept him from sinking too deep, while my snowshoes kept me above the drifts. As we left the cabin and the Winding Clay behind, the sparse woodlands began to thicken, heralding the borders of Drarkun Wood.

We made good time, huddling together under the trees in a cold camp that night. By midafternoon of the second day, we were well within the wood. I carried my snowshoes now, for the snow was not so thick in the old forest. The winter silence was broken only by a lean wind that rustled through the pine and cedars. Among the trees, clumps of snow disturbed by our passage fell from the smooth branches of elms, oaks, and maples. The only life we saw was a covey of wood pigeons that we startled into sudden movement and an odd white-furred hare.

The deeper we moved through the forest, the more a feeling of disquiet stole over me. The spark of feyness inside me touched another power—something harboured in the trees themselves, like an old malevolence that watched us, hating our presence. I thought of Damal then. I'd not truly considered her before. I knew little enough about her—only that she was a daughter of the Daketh, of Yurlogh Tyrrbane himself—but I seemed to sense her presence in the watchful sentience of the trees.

I'd slain her comrade Yarac, I thought, realizing the implications of that deed for the first time. And didn't Hickathrift and I fare northward to set the Wyslings on her scent? I wanted nothing to do with her, but she could well be setting a trap for us in this hateful forest.

I don't think so, Hickathrift replied when I voiced my fears.

Drarkun Wood harbours its own evil, a reminder of the yarg wars when it was a Daketh holding. The forest doesn't forget. We are the intruders.

"Is the whole forest like this?"

It was the feeling of evil that made me so uneasy. There were no twisted trees or malignant growths I could point to, only the impression that something awful waited for its chance to strike. Hickathrift shook his head.

There are other beings hidden in its depths that avoid intruders as well, but mean them no harm. Remnants of the kemys-folk, mostly—the halflings. Horsemen with the torsos of men, fauns, and even the manbull are said to dwell in its secret places—places that no living man, Wysling, or Loremaster has trod in uncounted years.

The last of the raewin is said to live in this forest, and she I would dearly love to meet. She's an antlered maid, with a doe's body and the upper torso of a woman. Shy as a unicorn and fierce as a mandrake—and just as much a legend as either of them, I fear. Though once it wasn't so. . . .

That night we slept huddled together for warmth again—though it was I that needed Hickathrift's cozy fur to curl up against, rather than he needing me. My harp stayed in its case—too cold to play now. I dreamed that night of hidden dells peopled by beings who were half beast, half man. Kemys-folk, Hickathrift called them. Halflings. I had no longing to meet any of them. My longings to see magical beings had brought me enough grief as it was.

The Grey Rose walked my dreams as well—more a suggestion of her presence than an actual vision. She was always close to my thoughts by day, so I thought it little wonder that I'd dream of her at night. The red-haired folk that I took to be her kin remained absent, although sometimes, when I hummed to myself as we walked along, I could still hear a trace of their voices in my ear. They were like distant echoes—like the shepherd pipes I'd heard from time to time, drifting over the West Downs when I had walked the hills at night.

We spoke little on that journey, eating sparingly from the stores that Calman had replenished our journeypack with, and it seemed we made little progress, for the woods seemed the same whichever way I looked. Hickathrift guided us, following the prompting of some inner compass, I guessed, for there was nothing else to mark the way.

Underfoot, only a light crust of snow covered the thick carpet of pine needles, twigs sticky with resin, and the mulch of the hardwoods' leaves. It was warmer as well, for overhead the boughs of the pine made a canopy that held back the snow and kept out the worst of the wind.

Though the evil presence I sensed intensified the longer we were in the forest, we passed through it without mishap. On the eighth day after we had left Calman's cabin, we stepped past the last trees. Fields white with winter lay in front of us. Tall, bare-limbed trees, dark against the snow, were scattered sparingly amongst them. Beyond the fields lay the frozen waters of the Lake of Lanesse.

I fastened my snowshoes to my boots once more, and we set off across the snowy expanse. A wind crept up and met us, while, from behind, I thought I heard a long sigh echo through the forest, as if our passage had been a minor troubling, and even the trees were thankful that we were gone. I looked back. For all that we'd passed through safely enough, I had no wish to dare its depths again. Out in the fields, with the open sky above me, I felt safe once more.

We've come too far east, Hickathrift said. *We'll have to turn west, but another day will see us in Wistlore—no more than two.*

We made camp in a stand of willows by the lake's shore—a cold camp, as they'd all been since we left Calman's cabin. The first night in the forest I'd begun to lay a fire, gathering fallen limbs and branches, and Hickathrift had looked aghast.

Are you mad? he'd rumbled. *Light a fire in this place, and the trees themselves will wake to kill us.*

As his mindspeech came to me, I'd heard a muttering in the trees, though I could see gnarled limbs reaching for me out of the corners of my eyes, and hastily scattered the wood that I'd gathered.

Even now, outside its boundaries, we were too close to risk the forest's wrath. We ate a cold meal, then crowded together against the cold breath of the wind.

WISTLORE

All the knowledge
that a Loremaster hoards
like a magpie its trinkets,
and all the histories
wrapped sweet-tongued
in a Harper's blue cloak,
are still no match
for the eye that sees
the secret truths,
the ear that hears
the hidden wisdoms.

—from the SONGWEAVER'S JOURNEYBOOK

THE NEXT MORNING DAWNED GOLDEN. THE SNOW BLINDED
us with its glare, the sun was splendid in a blazing blue sky,
and my heart lifted as if the fairness of the day was a portent
of how things would turn out. Before the day was done I'd
look on Wistlore at last. The Wyslings and Loremasters there
would answer my riddles for me, and, with my heart at peace,
perhaps I'd take up the harp under Eoin Fairling's tutelage as
Hickathrift had suggested.

And yet . . . Wistlore had exiled my parents. What welcome could I honestly expect from those who lived within
her walls? I shook the foreboding from me, not wanting to
spoil the day.

The afternoon was drifting in to evening when we finally
saw Wistlore. It was a wondrous sight, rising tall and proud
from the snowy fields. High stone walls encircled higher
round towers, and the main keep rose tallest of all in the

center. As we drew near, I saw that each merlon of the battlements had a statue carved into it. They were astonishingly lifelike, and all the Kindreds were represented—dwarves, erls, mys-hudol, mankind, and beings for which I had no name.

Some I recognized from legend and lore. Unicorns and centaurs reared in the air; fauns played about the feet of nymphs and wood spirits that were more beautiful than any maid I'd ever seen, except for the Grey Rose. Along the machicolation above the gatehouse was the most astounding carving of all.

A statue of a woman sat on a stone tree-stump, her face hidden behind the spill of her hair. To one side knelt a man with stag's antlers lifting from his brow and the head of a harp poking from the folds of his cloak. On the other side was a being, partly goat and partly man, who played a set of reed-pipes. About their feet cavorted all manner of strange beings and wildlife. There were twisty folk that were more like roots with hints of human features. Others were like flowers with maidens' faces. Hare sat with fox, squirrel with raven, while starlings perched on the piper's shoulders. The sheer beauty of it took my breath away.

It's said that long ago, before the Kindreds walked the world or even the Tuathan came, these were the gods of the earth.

I glanced at Hickathrift, surprised at what he said.

"Doesn't Wistlore revere the Tuathan?" I asked.

The Kindreds do. Dwarves raised these stone walls, but the carvings on the gate were crafted by muryan. Those are the gods of the weren still . . . and the gwandryas.

I shook my head, still not understanding.

"But I thought the gwandryas were the enemies of Wistlore," I said. "Why are their gods depicted on its walls?"

It's written in the record scrolls that once the work was completed, there was no one who had the heart or will to command a change. Gods of the weren they might be, but there is still such a peace about them . . . and a quiet beauty. . . .

I nodded. My neck was sore from craning upward to view these wonders. As I regarded the three weren gods the fey-ness that was stirring in me prickled—my father's blood recognized them, I supposed.

Finally I looked down, for we'd reached the great brass-bound oaken doors that served as gates. A voice hailed us as we stepped up to them.

"Who approaches? State your name and business."

I looked about for the source of the voice, then noticed Hickathrift frowning. He glanced at me and shrugged.

I am Hickathrift Trummel, Loremaster, and my companion is Cerin Kelledy from the West Downs.

We'd decided that I should use Tess's surname until I had a chance to talk with the masters and explain my lineage.

There was a short silence, as if our unseen questioner was considering Hickathrift's reply; then the gates swung slowly open. Hickathrift padded forward, but I stood where I was, suddenly apprehensive. From outside its walls, Wistlore appeared truly wondrous, but there was also something forbod-ing about it. Merely my own nervousness, I realized as I hesitated. I was unsure of my welcome once my lineage was made known, and the brusque tone of the man who'd hailed us had done nothing to ease my worry.

I moved forward at last, following Hickathrift, to meet the owner of that voice. He was tall, clad all in shining mail. A long halberd was in one hand, and a narrow sword sheathed in a finely worked scabbard was at his belt. Under his helm, his hair was golden, his features pinched and thin. I'd no need to look to see that his ears tapered into fine points to know him for an erl.

The eyes told me all—almond-shaped and strangely gold, with an otherworldly light flickering in their depths. I drew in a quick breath as I realized what he was. At last I'd met with one of the erlkin, but I was disappointed. The old tales recounted a gay folk, quick to anger perhaps, but neverthe-less merry—not grim-eyed warriors like the one standing in front of me.

"Greetings, Loremaster," he was saying. He bowed from

the waist to Hickathrift and added a short nod to me. "Your quarters will be prepared immediately. If you'd fare to the main hall, I'll have word sent when all is ready."

Hickathrift acknowledged him with a nod and moved on. I followed, still looking about with wide eyes, but my wonder at Wistlore was tempered by a curious feeling. I misliked the feel of the place.

It could be nothing more than the fact that the folk here had exiled my mother from their halls, I knew, but Wistlore was still nothing like I'd expected. The courtyard was strewn with straw, bedraggled from the slush of the wet snow and trampled by many feet. Underneath, the ground was hard mud. We made for the keep that stood directly opposite the gatehouse. To the left and right rose the towers I'd seen earlier, three on each side. Below them were many smaller buildings against the walls—to serve as stables and barracks, I guessed.

But Wistlore seemed more like an armed camp than a place of learning to me. Men-at-arms—mostly erlkin—lounged in the courtyard, but few other folk. There was an oppressive atmosphere that reminded me of the last few verses of "Luthan's Fall," particularly the last verse.

> The brooding walls of Yoland's keep
>   that secret hoards like gold;
> too many are the shades that weep
>   in dungeons, dank and cold.
> Were all the sons of Caeldon come,
>   their strength could not prevail;
> Death herself, flees swift, undone,
>   and cannot pierce the veil.

Perhaps I'd come expecting too much; my head filled with endless daydreams of the place, I'd looked for a magical glamour to shine from the very walls. Yet Hickathrift was strangely quiet—puzzled where he should've been cheered. It was hard to read his feelings, since his ursine features were so unlike a man's, but his eyes were hooded and brooding, and I thought that he shared my misgivings to some extent.

We entered the keep through tall, broad doors. After the brightness of the snow, the hall seemed as dark as a cavern, so I stood in the doorway for a moment and let my eyes adjust to the dimness. There were tapers along the walls to light the hall; at the far end was a dais, while all along the wood-panelled walls ran long benches and tables. There were nooks and entrances, that might have led to shut-beds or corridors, between some of the tables. Huge rafters criss-crossed, while the ceiling above them rose to the height of a full-grown oak tree.

We made our way to one of the many hearths that were scattered along the length of the hall. They were round field stone affairs, constructed so that they could be approached from any side, with metal flues that rose straight as saplings to draw the smoke. The flues joined pipes that carried the smoke out through the chimneys I'd seen on the roof outside.

I saw that the wood-panelled walls were carved with scenes from old legends. I recognized Bearwulf fighting the worm on Drummas Peak from a tale Hickathrift had told me on our journey. There were wall hangings depicting similar scenes as well, cunningly woven and brightly coloured. I sat down on a bench, unclasping my cloak and folding it beside me. My harp and journeypack I placed at my feet, along with my snowshoes. Leaning forward, I warmed my hands at the fire.

Hickathrift settled down by me. Though he sat, his head was still level with mine. The hall was almost empty, though here and there were a few erls in mail, a number of clerical-looking folk in plain brown robes, and two mys-hudol—a stag and a large fox. They looked curiously at us. I felt that the mys-hudol were speaking to Hickathrift, but though I strained my mind to hear, I caught none of their speech.

I examined my feelings as I sat there. Wistlore was both more and less than I'd pictured it to be. I'd never seen a building of the Kindreds on such an immense scale except for the ruins of Banlore. At the same time, it was plainer, more mundane than I'd imagined. The erls I'd seen so far were no different from the mailed warriors I'd seen passing through Wran Cheaping. What the place lacked the most, I suppose, was the sense of magic I'd expected.

While I was occupied with my thoughts, a slender maid approached me with a stoneware mug of steaming tea. Her hair was light brown and her features strong rather than pretty. Her eyes were downcast as she proffered the mug. I thanked her as I took it, and she started, slipping away quickly as if she was afraid of me. I frowned and turned to ask Hickathrift of this, when a young man wearing a brown robe similar to the maid's came up to us.

"Master Hickathrift," he said. "Your rooms are readied."

Hickathrift rose at the words. I gathered my belongings and slung them over my shoulder. With my tea in hand, I followed Hickathrift and the man through the hall to one of the openings which led into a corridor. We walked along the stone-walled passageway—again lit with tapers—until we came to an ante-chamber. I realized, from the distance we'd walked, that some of the corridors must lead to the towers I'd seen from outside. The others probably connected the upper floors of the keep with the main hall below them.

We climbed three flights of narrow stairs until we came to another corridor with a number of doors leading from it. Our guide took us the length of the passage and opened two doors.

"These are your rooms, sires," he said, standing aside so that we might enter.

Like the maid's, his features were strong. I wondered if all men appeared coarse next to the delicate features of the erlkin.

Hickathrift glanced into his own room before he followed me into the other, a stark room with only a washstand, a small bed, a chest, and a table and chair for furnishings. A tightly shuttered window was set into one wall. Opposite it was a small hearth where a fire burned cheerily, warming the room. Our guide lit the room's taper from his own. Bowing, he backed out through the door.

Our thanks! Hickathrift called after his retreating form. He received no reply.

I placed my belongings at the foot of the bed and sat on

it, sipping my tea. Hickathrift prowled about the room. He seemed immense in the small quarters. His heavy muzzle shook slowly from side to side, his nose wrinkling.

"So this is Wistlore," I said.

I kept my voice light. If it wasn't all I'd expected, I'd also seen very little of it so far.

Hickathrift glanced at me with a strange look in his eyes.

I don't doubt that it bears the same name, he said, *but if I'd never seen the shape of its buildings before with my own eyes, I wouldn't know it. I've yet to see a smile or a look of cheer on the face of any we've met. And Leof—the stag who was in the main hall—when I entered, he mindspoke a warning to me. "Tread softly," he said. That and no more, for all that I questioned him. It makes no sense. What could have happened?*

I shook my head slowly. "Maybe there's a war brewing. At least so it seems from the guards and the weaponry." A sudden thought struck me, and I added: "Perhaps Damal has already made herself known. That would account for the change, wouldn't it?"

Perhaps. But these are halls of learning, not war. The change runs deeper, I fear.

I shook my head again, for I'd nothing else to suggest. Taking another sip of tea, I set the mug aside and reached for my harp. For all the hard journeying it had undergone, it looked no worse for wear.

"Why don't we look for Eoin Fairling?" I asked. "I'd dearly love to meet him, and maybe he can tell us what's happened."

Hickathrift shook his head. *My head's spinning. First let me settle my thoughts.*

"Fair enough."

I finished tuning the roseharp and began a quiet tune that I hoped would settle our jangled nerves. It was a gentle air, not complex, filled with what I could remember of my summer days in the company of the Grey Rose. In some ways I yearned for a return to those simpler times. My fingers were a little stiff—I'll never recommend cold weather to keep one's fingers limber—but they warmed up soon enough.

I half expected to hear my dream-folk weaving their harmonies into the music, but the only sound that filled the room was that of my harping. Hickathrift nodded his head in time to the tune, and we both relaxed, enjoying the music, the warm room, and each other's company.

A sharp rapping at the door soon spoiled the peace of the moment. I broke off playing in the middle of a bar and looked up. The door opened, and a man entered. I took an instant dislike to him. This didn't happen to me often. In Wran Cheaping my feelings toward the villagers ran more to indifference, and the last time I'd felt this way was at the Beltane fair a year and a half ago.

I'd heard that there was to be a minstrel come up from the Southern Kingdoms, and, after hurrying through my chores, I'd gathered up my harp and made for the fair in a cheerful mood, hoping to learn a new song or three from him. One glance, however, and I'd turned away, not even staying to hear a verse. Something about the man repelled me, though I couldn't have said what at the time.

Later I learned that he'd lain with Jorna, the innkeeper's daughter, against her will. He fled before anyone could raise a hand against him, taking with him a purse of gold that he'd stolen from Ralen Tagh and a brooch worth at least two gold coins that Jorna's uncle had given her.

With the same feeling in me now, I regarded the newcomer with some apprehension. He was not overly tall and wore a well-fitted light brown robe, belted at the waist, with a short sword hanging from the belt. His dark hair was cut short. He was clean-shaven and heavy-jowled. There was an odd look in his grey eyes when he turned to me that reminded me of a bad-tempered cat: subtle and sly, waiting to work mischief.

"Greetings, Master Hickathrift," he said. His voice had an oily texture to it.

Greetings, Feador, Hickathrift replied, his own voice edged with a wary tiredness.

"I have been sent to warn you that it is unlawful for an unlicensed Harper to play within these walls."

I stiffened with anger. Unlawful? Dangerous lights gleamed in Hickathrift's eyes when he answered.

There have been many changes since last I was here, Holdmaster. I wasn't aware of this latest ruling. Are there any more that we should be aware of?

Scorn licked at each of his words, and it wasn't lost on the man.

"Such is the law," Feador said with a shrug. "I was only told to tell you. Also, you are summoned to the Judgment Room. The Lord will speak with you now."

The Lord? Since when has there been a Lord in Wistlore? Who is he?

"You've been gone a long while indeed, Master Hickathrift. William Marrow is our Lord, by ruling of the Inner Council. Will you keep him waiting?"

No, Hickathrift replied. *Your Lord may wish to speak to us, but I've a word or two for him as well. Lead on.*

I replaced my harp in its case and shouldered it as Hickathrift rose. Without another word, we followed Holdmaster Feador down the hall.

THE JUDGMENT ROOM WAS THE MOST MAGNIFICENT CHAMBER I'd yet seen in Wistlore. Rich tapestries hung from floor to ceiling and heavy drapes covered the doorways, but where the walls showed through they glittered like sunlight on mica. A profusion of tapers lit every crook and cranny. Lines of statues stood on both sides of the main entrance, so realistically sculpted and painted that at first I thought they were alive.

At the far end of the chamber was a dais where a number of beings sat, watching us. These were the Inner Council, I guessed.

In the center was a tall man, white-haired and bearded, in a golden robe that was slit down the front to reveal a loose cotton shirt and leather trousers. His face was wrinkled with the weight of many years, the lips thin and thoughtfully pursed, the piercing blue eyes appraising us. He was a formidable-looking figure, though a closer scrutiny revealed a faint trembling in his hands where they gripped the arms of his high-backed chair, carved from a single piece of oak.

Beside him sat a woman wearing a shimmering white robe that revealed more of her well-endowed form than it hid. Her hair was as black as a raven's wing, her skin pale as snow. She smiled warmly at us when we entered, but there was a distant coldness in her eyes that set my inner senses to prickling and made the hairs at the back of my neck hackle.

To her left was a red-haired man with small, feral eyes set in a round face. He wore a cloak of Harper's blue, and, from the delicately carved instrument that lay beside his chair, I wagered he was the Masterharper Caradoc. I had heard that his harp was worth a king's ransom.

Beside him was an enormous brecaln who regarded us with unblinking amber eyes. The hill cat's fur was striped orange and white, and the tip of its tail flicked with annoyance.

To the right of the central figure—he'd be William Marrow, the Wysling Lord, I realized—sat an erl who looked much like the one who had met us at the gates, save that his clothing was richer. Completing the council was an erl woman. Her hair was red-gold, her face suntanned and openly honest. She wore a modest green gown, embroidered with red and yellow threads, and was the only one who seemed at all sympathetic toward us.

I wondered, as I looked on the might of the Wistlore's council, what they wanted with us. I had the feeling that we were about to be judged for some heinous crime, yet we hadn't done anything. Feador led us to the open space before the dais and withdrew. For a long moment the council studied us, then the central figure spoke.

"What mad folly possessed you to venture into our halls masquerading as a Harper?"

I was distracted by a rustling sound that came from behind us and glanced back to see a number of erls entering the chamber. Some held spears, and others were notching arrows in their bows. As the silence following the Wysling Lord's question lengthened, I suddenly realized that it had been addressed to me. I looked up to find him frowning at me.

"Masquerading as a Harper?" I repeated. "You wrong me. I've done no such thing. I came here as Hickathrift's companion, hoping to find the true tale of my parents in your lore books."

"Is that instrument not a harp?" he asked, indicating Telynros's otterskin case.

"Yes, but—"

"This is a grave offense," the Wysling pronounced, "and one that we cannot let go unpunish—"

"Hold one moment!" I said, breaking in. Anger stirred in me. "Who are you to judge me? You're no Lord of mine. I'm not your vassal."

"Who am I?" he roared. "I am William Marrow, appointed Lord of this council and all of Wistlore. When one enters our halls, bearing an unregistered harp, and has the gall to play it within our halls, it is my right to question this affront."

Hickathrift stirred uneasily beside me, but before he could speak I was already answering.

"Were you among them?" I asked softly. "Did you have a hand in exiling my mother from these damned halls? And do you mean to deal with me now in the same way?" My anger grew, unchecked.

"Damned halls?" the Wysling cried.

The dark-haired woman beside him put a hand on his arm, trying to bridle his anger, but he shook it off.

"Who was your mother, then, that we treated her so poorly?"

"Her name was Eithne Gwynn."

The red-haired man whom I'd taken to be the Masterharper laughed loudly.

"So her whelp has returned to her defense," he said. "What do you want of us, with your rags and poverty, boy? And where did you get that harp? Stolen, I'll wager."

"Caradoc!" the erl woman in the green gown cried, her tone reproachful.

"Stolen?" I shouted at the Masterharper. "As was your own? For surely you never earned that instrument."

Caradoc lunged from his seat, his eyes blazing.

Hold! Hold! Hickathrift cried, his voice cutting like ice through my mind. *Does madness reign here? What is this talk of unregistered harps and of licenses needed to play one? Have the Daketh stolen your reason? I've been gone for less than a year to find Wistlore, the great halls of learning, like some armed camp with restrictions placed on the simplest of pleasures. Dark Yurlogh must take great joy in seeing this.*

"You are a fine one to speak of the Daketh," William Marrow said. "The tales of your own doings in the south have preceded your arrival, Master Hickathrift. They paint a sorry picture of a Loremaster. True, you aided in the destruction of a Waster, but in doing so you allowed the greater foe to escape."

What do you mean?

"Surely," the dark-haired woman beside William Marrow replied, "you've not forgotten your own lore—the learnings that foretell the coming of Damal, the Dark Queen? That is why we are an armed camp, Loremaster. The days of doom have arrived, brought in part by your own deeds."

I looked at the faces of the council members, trying to understand what the woman meant.

Whatever else the maid of the Grey Rose might be, Hickathrift said, *she is not Damal.*

Horror welled up in my soul as I comprehended. They thought—

"No!" I cried. "There's no evil in her!"

"Listen to her consort," Caradoc remarked. "Grey Rose, indeed. She's a Dark Rose, boy, with a soul as black as Yurlogh's heart."

I strode toward him, my fists clenched in rage, but I got no further than the foot of the dais before three guards stopped me with lowered spears. A low growl rumbled from Hickathrift's throat. From the corner of my eye I saw him rise to his full height, towering over the erl guards. A half dozen of them rushed forward, threatening him with leveled spears.

The bowmen lifted their weapons and drew their shafts back to their ears. Dark fires raged in Hickathrift's eyes, but he backed away from them. Then William Marrow's voice cut through the air.

"This ill becomes you, Master Hickathrift. Understand— we are not plunging blindly into this darkness. Auguries have been taken, and the wise have gathered from many lands. We seek to put an end to her threat for all time."

We were warned that the evil was trying to enter Wistlore. How could we have guessed that it had such a strong hold— so soon?

He seemed to shrink into himself with defeat.

"What do you mean?" the Wysling demanded. "Who warned you?"

Hickathrift looked into the eyes of the old Lord and smiled bitterly.

Why, the maid of the Grey Rose. The very one you mean to destroy sent us north with the warning. Amusing, isn't it, that she'd want to warn such wise and brave folk against herself? There is madness in these halls, William Marrow.

"Master Hickathrift," the Wysling said sorrowfully. "I fear that the only madness in these halls lies within you and your companion. By your own words you have damned yourselves. It's obvious that you are both in league with the followers of the Daketh, if your souls don't already wallow in their dark worship.

"Were we the evil beings that your young companion thinks us, we'd have slain you out of hand. But we are not. You will be imprisoned until we can decide how to deal with you. When the threat has passed and we have the leisure, you will appear before us again and judgment will be passed. Are all in favour? Kentigern?"

The brecaln regarded Hickathrift thoughtfully as the Wysling called his name. Slowly, he nodded acknowledgement.

"Caradoc?"

The Masterharper inclined his head and grinned.

"Tamara?"

"Regretfully, yes," the dark-haired woman said.

"Selwyn?"

"As you will it, my Lord," the erl on his right replied.

"And Merla?"

"I fear," the lady in the green gown said, "that an injustice is being done."

"The vote goes against you," William Marrow replied.

Merla sighed. "As you will it, then."

"So," the Wysling continued, turning his gaze from his peers to where Hickathrift and I stood, ringed by erl guards. "We are all in agreement. I will tell you that a large party has already been sent in pursuit of this creature you call the Grey Rose. She has been seen in the Southern Kingdoms where, Tamara has told us, she seeks the last of the caryaln. With the shadow-death, she could loose a doom on this land that we could never contain. But do not let your hopes for her rise. She will be taken long before she has a chance to wield the caryaln."

I was still stunned from all that had happened and could hardly believe that they saw the maid in such a light. I wanted to tear the smug lies from their faces, but with the guards surrounding us, I knew my first movement would be my last.

I thought of Meana's fey powers and told myself that the Lord's words were just empty boasting. Her means of travel were beyond mortal understanding—how could they track her? But these were folk used to magic and power, I realized, and I feared for her. And for us. I didn't know what they had planned, but I knew they meant us ill. My stomach churned, and I felt as if there was a hard rock in it. My mind was numbed at how things'd turned out. I hadn't expected to be greeted by great crowds of cheering folk, but this. . . . This was the stuff of nightmares.

"Take them away," William Marrow ordered.

His voice broke into my thoughts. The guards made ready to carry out his orders.

"One moment," Caradoc said as I bent to pick up my harp. "I want the boy's instrument."

My heart caught in my throat, and I clutched it to me.

"No!"

But the guards forced it from me. One of them carried it to the dais and placed it in Caradoc's hands.

I strained against the arms that held me fast as he undid the bindings and Telynros was revealed to the council. A sigh whispered through the chamber as the light of the tapers caught its splendid workmanship. Caradoc plucked at the strings. In horror, I watched them snap at his touch. A discordant ringing filled the room. Despite the bright lighting, a shadowed pall hovered over us until the sound faded. As the strings broke, something inside me seemed to break as well.

"No matter," Caradoc said, staring bemusedly at the broken strings. "They can be repaired. And if not, it'll still look fine hanging in the Harperhall." He glanced at me, malice and victory in his eyes. "It seems that I, at least, was correct. This is too fine a harp for the likes of you. It was stolen. No doubt of that. Should its rightful owner come to claim it, it will be given up freely."

Tears streamed down my cheeks as I was led from the Judgment Room. That last was too much. I didn't care who saw them fall. In the hallway outside, they took Hickathrift in one direction, me in another.

I despair, his sorrowful voice murmured in my mind. *Forgive me, Cerin, for leading you into this.*

It wasn't your fault, I replied. *We might still prevail.*

They were brave words, but nothing more than words. Hope died in me, and all I knew was a terrible sorrow. I don't know where they took Hickathrift. They returned me to the tower room from which we'd first been summoned to the council. As I stepped inside, the door slammed shut. I heard a heavy bar thud into place outside, locking me in.

THE HOURS DRAGGED BY IN MY PRISON, INTERMINABLE AND dreary. As soon as the door had closed behind me, I'd rushed for the window and flung the shutter open. Through iron bars, the rough winter wind blasted my cheek, and I knew there was no escape through the window. Even if I broke through the bars, there was still a drop of a hundred feet or better to the courtyard below.

Unrelenting despair gnawed at me. I paced the chamber, throwing myself onto the bed at times. Sleep was far from me, however, and no sooner was I lying down that I'd rise to pace the floor once more. At one point the door opened and three erl guards entered with lowered spears. A brown-tuniced server placed a bowl of barley-meal on the table—I flung it against the wall—and they departed, leaving me to the silence of the four bare walls. At length I knelt by the fire and tried to lose myself in the swirl of its flames.

They flickered and danced merrily and made me long for my harp so that I could play a tune for them. And with the harp, I thought, perhaps I could magic up a tune to cast down the walls of this foul keep, like Minstrel Ravendear had done when Koldeer locked him in the dungeons of Corby Crag. But this was no song of old, no tale where the brave hero was expected to prevail. I'd neither harp nor music—and if my father's blood left me heir to any magic, it did no more than stir vaguely inside me. I had only myself, locked in this tower, and the endless dance of the flames in the hearth.

Their movement hypnotized me and seemed to spell out the tale of my failure, but with wistful understanding rather than mockery. I imagined Tess's face amongst the flames, and it seemed that her voice issued from the heart of the fire.

Look for friends along the way, she said, *and look for them in strange guises.* . . .

I smiled bitterly. There'd been one or two—Hickathrift and the dwarf Calman—but that was all. The folk of Wistlore meant me only ill.

Tess's face slipped away into the flames, and others' took its place. I saw a childhood memory of my mother, a handsome woman with strong features and gold-green eyes that warmed a little as they looked on me. Over her shoulder I could make out my father's visage, battle-scarred and proud.

Caryaln, my mother whispered, *caryaln. The shadow-death for Wistlore. Caryaln.* . . .

I shook my head, bewildered by what she said and troubled

at seeing faces I knew only from Tess's descriptions. She smiled sadly and faded. My father's features remained a moment longer. Before he vanished, I heard his voice crying: *Shield and horn, sword and spear . . . caryaln. . . .*

The fire paraded a hundred faces before my eyes, both those of folk I knew and those of strangers. I saw Finan and the Trader Haberlin, the villagers of Wran Cheaping, strange grim visages of men who were war-worn and weary, beings that were more beast than man. The folk of my dreams were amongst those images—the Tuathan, for all that Hickathrift denied it.

Once, the flames showed a hazel grove in some hidden wood and two of the red-haired folk standing in it. There was a woman, blindingly beautiful, who seemed to be arguing with an older, handsome man. Sometimes he turned, as if to look directly at me. Then he'd shake his head slowly, and the woman would begin to speak to him again.

They faded until all that remained was the grove. Then the trees became trees of fire that swirled and flickered. From the dance of flame-boughs and leaves, the Grey Rose smiled at me, her rust hair mingling with the fire.

They've stolen the roseharp, I told her, my voice bitter. *And they mean to destroy you. They've named you Damal, the Dark Queen of the Daketh, and they mean to kill you.*

I know, she said. *The darkness festers like a sore inside their hearts. Beware, Songweaver, lest they rob you of your light. Oh, beware. . . .*

Her face drew back until the image showed the whole of her sweet form. My heart caught in my throat, for she was standing at the brink of a bottomless abyss, with huge misshaped shadow creatures threatening her from all sides. As I leaned closer to the image, the flames flared. A strange, haunted fire burnt there now, and from the corners of my room the shadows seemed to draw away from the walls and approach me. I cowered by the hearth, unable to move.

Then a sound at the door broke the spell that held me in thrall. The fire burned as normal, and the shadows were dormant by the walls; I turned as the door opened. Merla—she of the green gown—slipped inside, closing the door softly behind her.

"What do you mean?" I asked, but not unkindly. Of all the folk in the Judgment Room, she alone had seemed willing to help us.

"I want to help you," she said with pity in her eyes. She glanced curiously at me, hunched over the fire, and added: "What are you doing?"

What the fire'd shown me, I meant to keep to myself. I understood little of it, but I knew instinctively that the images had been for me alone.

"Nothing," I said. "I was only warming myself. How can you help me—and why should you?"

A strange look flitted across her eyes that was swiftly hidden.

"Do you want your freedom?" she asked.

"Yes."

"Then that is what I offer."

"But why? What will you gain from helping me?"

"I'll tell you," she said and came to sit by the hearth with me.

She was silent for a long moment, and I wondered if she was going to explain or not. She finally spoke.

"In the Judgment Room, your words and Hickathrift's rang too true. I've felt a darkness blossoming inside these walls, and I fear that I can pinpoint its source as well—but to what avail? Tamara, the dark-haired witch, and Masterharper Caradoc are behind it. They've put a spell on William Marrow and most of Wistlore, so who is there to turn to? Even my brother Selwyn was ensnared by their lies."

"Is there no one you can trust?"

"If Robin, the younger Marrow, were here, he'd make his father see the light before it was too late. But what use is there in wishing? He studies with Ler Yrill in Magdal, in the Southern Kingdoms. No, I have only you."

"But what can I do?"

"This maid of yours," she said. "The Grey Rose. She seeks the caryaln in the Southern Kingdoms. You must help her find it. With its power you can defeat Tamara and Caradoc, and then the folk of Wistlore will listen to reason. It was Tamara's sorceries that first discovered the Grey Rose, and now she's set the hounds of the Daketh upon the maid's trail.''

I remembered the vision in the flames and the shadow creatures threatening the maid, and I shivered.

''The Wysling Lord knows nothing of this,'' Merla added. ''He thinks—for this is what Tamara has told him—that she's conjured up the help of the Tuathan to hunt down the Grey Rose. If she succeeds . . .''

''Why would Tamara do this?'' I asked.

''I fear that *she* is Damal. Somehow, she's stolen the true Tamara's shape and now wears it for her own. Nothing can defeat her but the caryaln—the shadow death. It was a weapon from the elder years, and the last of its kind. Legend says that only the sting of the caryaln can send the Dark Queen back to the realms of the Daketh.''

What she said explained much. Now I knew why Wistlore was so changed from how Hickathrift had known it.

''And Caradoc is her ready ally,'' Merla said. ''It was he who worked the hardest to have your mother exiled from Wistlore. He lusted after her, but she spurned him and gave her heart to a gwandryas. In revenge he set the Harperhall against her. He's a bitter, small-minded man, quick to do hurt where he can. Now that your mother is gone and you've come, he turns the hardness of his heart on you.

''In you he sees Eithne in her youth. She was ever the more skilled Harper and, by rights, should have become the Masterharper when Curran Wemyse died. Through guile and trickery Caradoc stole the position and had her cast forth.

''Would you have revenge on him? Then, I tell you, this is the way. Seek the Grey Rose and the caryaln. Bring the shadow-death to Wistlore to defeat those who'd hold our beloved halls in thrall. And you must succeed, for there is more at stake than simply Wistlore. Unchecked, Tamara's power would eventually enslave all of the Kindreds. Then the Daketh would rule, and despair is the only gift they have to give us."

I was moved by her speech, and it answered many riddles; but it brought forth others.

"Why don't *you* seek the caryaln?" I asked.

"It is the Grey Rose's to find," Merla replied. "I'd offer her my help, but how could she trust anyone from Wistlore now? She wouldn't accept my aid."

"Then why should I?"

"Because this is your only hope of winning free from here and helping her. Gods! If you don't trust me, at least take your freedom. Once beyond the walls, you can follow your own path. Who can hinder you, if you travel secret and swift?"

I could think of many—Tamara in particular, if her power was so great. But I agreed with Merla on one count: I should at least attempt to take my freedom. With that decided, I rose to my feet.

"I'll take your help. It was fairly offered, and I was rude to be so distrusting."

"I blame you not."

Tess's words rang in my mind. (*"Look for friends along the way—and in strange guises . . ."*)

Here was unforeseen help, but not in such a strange disguise. The erl woman was fair and worthy of a ballad for her courage in striving against our unnatural foes, as well as for her beauty.

"What about Hickathrift?" I asked. "Can you free him as well?"

She shook her head. "His is a greater power than yours, and Tamara has imprisoned him with her own magics. They are too strong for me to attempt a counter-spell. That is why I came for you; the council didn't think you enough of a threat to set more than two guards outside your room. A simple sleeping spell has rendered them helpless. Pray with me that Tamara doesn't sense my hand in it, or I will be undone."

She took my hand to lead me forth.

"Come. Let us go."

I held back for a moment.

"What about my harp?"

"That, too, is beyond me. It lies in Caradoc's chambers, bespelled by his magics. To fetch it would set the whole keep alert. I have this, though."

She proffered a small dagger in a worn leather sheath. I took it gingerly, for my inner senses warned me it was evil, and drew the blade forth. It was smithed from a strange, mottled metal and had thin runes scratched along the length of the blade. Shuddering suddenly, I resheathed it. I realized then that I'd sensed the dagger's evil long before Merla had given it to me—it was that, as much as my justifiable suspicions, that had led me to distrust her.

"This is Tamara's," she said. "Natural steel can't harm her. This was made by an erl smith from the ore of a fallen star. Don't use it unless you are physically confronted by her, for it can only be used once."

"Why not creep to her chambers and strike her down now?" I asked.

It seemed to be the obvious thing, and my suspicions reared once more.

"To strike her with it now would wound her sorely," Merla explained, "but not to the death. Only the caryaln can kill her. I've given you the dagger to protect you along your way, in case she should follow you. Now come. We must hurry before we're discovered."

I fetched my journeypack and cloak. Finan's tinkerblade and the snowshoes were still tied to the pack. Laden with my gear, I took the erl's hand once more, and she led me forth.

I was unhappy at leaving Hickathrift and the roseharp behind, but it didn't appear that I had much choice in the matter. For good or ill, I had to leave them behind and seek out the Grey Rose. Together we'd search out the caryaln and return with it to put an end to Damal. I only hoped that Hickathrift would understand. But there was this at least: I had hope again. Somehow, we'd prevail.

* * *

WE CREPT THROUGH THE DESERTED HALLS OF WISTLORE with a silence born of fear. I'm sure I had never moved so quietly before—although, to my nervous ears, my pulse was drumming loud enough to wake the whole keep. We traced the path that the guide had led Hickathrift and me along until we reached the main hall. All was silent. The hearthfires were low and the folk in their shutbeds and chambers.

"What of the guards outside?" I whispered.

"I'll put a glamour on you so that no one will see you," she replied. "But you must be cautious. It won't last long or stand a close scrutiny in bright light, so keep to the shadows. Here." She opened the tall doors of the hall just wide enough for me to squeeze through. "Be on your way."

I slipped through, pausing to glance back once I was outside.

"Thank you," I said, "and please forgive my suspicions. I'm unsure of so much these days that I don't know where to turn."

"You are freely forgiven," Merla said softly. "Luck go with you, Cerin Gwynn, Eithe's son."

The doors closed on her final words. Taking her advice, I crept to the walls where the shadows were thick and hid myself in their shrouds. I looked to the gatehouse; there was no way out there. The gates were locked shut, and guards patrolled in front of them. I took to the stairs that led to the walkways on the walls. Looking over the merlons, my heart quaked at the drop below me.

Still, what choice did I have? At least there was snow below, tall drifts glistening in the moonlight. Taking a deep breath, I climbed atop the battlements. Lowering myself as far as my arms would reach, I took another deep breath, offered a quick prayer to the tinker Lord Ballan, and let go.

I tried to roll with the fall, but my belongings got in the way. I landed with a jarring thump that knocked the breath out of me. The snow was deep, and I sank out of sight. Clambering up, I stood unhurt in the moonlight and brushed the snow from my mantle.

Which way should I go? The Wysling Lord had said that

Meana was in the Southern Kingdoms. I knew roughly where
they lay, but what other road was there? My only hope lay in
making my way south and trying to find her.

Looking back at the high walls, I thought of Hickathrift
still trapped inside. For a moment I balked at leaving him
behind; then I realized that Merla knew what she'd been
speaking of. If Tamara had him so well guarded, any attempt
to rescue him was doomed to failure. With one of us free at
least we had a chance.

I took out my snowshoes and silently thanked Calman as
I tied them to my boots. Calman, I thought. I'd forgotten
him. The dwarf might help me where no other would. He'd
said he would be at his cabin until the spring. Well, winter
still held the land fast in its cold grip, so I'd go to him and
lay my troubles before him. Maybe he would help, for Hickathrift was his friend as well. If nothing else, he could give
me some advice.

Greatly heartened, I set off eastward, skirting the walls of
Wistlore as best I could. The snow-covered Lake of Lanesse
shimmered on my left in the bright light of the Wolf Moon.
Far to my right lay the dark tracks of Drarkan Wood.

I walked all that night. Dawn found me at the spot where
Hickathrift and I had quit the forest. I looked at the dark wall
of trees. Even in the morning light, the forest stood grim and
forboding. I remembered Hickathrift's tales of the place, and,
although we'd seen nothing strange during our passage
through it, I remembered as well the evil presence I'd sensed.

Drarkun Wood seemed to watch me. The bare limbs of the
winter-gaunt oaks and elms were like skeletal courtiers before the court of the deep green pines. The wind stirred the
trees, sending shadows scurrying under the laden boughs of
the pines. Each motion quickened a new fear in me, until the
forest held all the terrors of my imagination in its depths, just
waiting for me to set foot within it.

My mood wasn't surprising. I still feared pursuit from
Wistlore, for all that my escape had gone smoothly, and my
surroundings were desolate. All I could see were the death-

like hardwoods, the grim green pines and cedars, and the endless white pall of winter that lay over all. And I was alone.

Then I caught a splash of colour out of the corner of my eye. I moved closer until I could make out the scarlet berries and jagged leaves of a holly brush. Its unexpected finery cheered me, and, shaking my premonitions from me, I strode boldly into the forest.

A hare exploded from the snow almost at my feet, nearly sending me flying in the opposite direction until I stilled the quick drum of my heart. I took a last glance back at the open fields; then the evergreens closed in overhead. Although the sun was bright outside, the wood was all in shadow, for the trees made a perfect roof above me. I undid my snowshoes, strapped them to my pack, and tramped on over the soggy carpet of pine needles and cedar branchlets.

It'd taken Hickathrift and me almost seven days to pass through the wood before, with another day added on for the distance that lay between the forest and Calman's cabin. I doubted that I could make much better time. I was still weary from the journey to reach Wistlore, and I was not nearly so well provisioned this time. Nor did I have Hickathrift to warm me by night.

But behind me, the hunt would be on now. I couldn't imagine what sort of pursuit Tamara would set on my trail. At the moment, in the middle of this eerie forest and all alone, my imagination was all too vivid.

GWENYA

Like a windsong
quicksilvering through the trees,
or a dream remembered
in the morning's twilight,
the old mysteries still dwell
in their hidden places.
I've heard their voices,
secret and shy,
join with my harping,
and sometimes
catch them dancing
in the corner of my eye.

—from the SONGWEAVER'S JOURNEYBOOK

I WALKED ALL THAT DAY UNTIL I GREW SO TIRED THAT I could hardly put one foot in front of the other. I made a rough camp, and, remembering Hickathrift's warning, I didn't light a fire—much as I wanted its companionable warmth. A mug of tea would've been welcome as well. Instead I made do with one of the three bannocks that were still in my pack and a handful of nuts from the bottom of an almost empty sack. Measuring my provisions against the number of days it would take me to reach Calman's cabin, I realized that I'd simply have to tighten my belt.

When I was finished with my meager meal, I rolled up in my cloak and tried to sleep. I missed Hickathrift and worried for him. I yearned for Meana, wishing, not for the first time, that we were both simple villagers and could live out our lives in Wran Cheaping or some such place rather than being forced to skulk across the countryside as outlaws. Whatever romantic notions the old ballads had given me about the life of a brigand had long since fled me.

My worries wouldn't let me sleep. I lay awake for a long while, listening to the creak and moan of the forest around me. Unpleasant visions crept into my mind so that I kept starting awake whenever I did begin to nod off. The last time it happened, I realized that it was more than my imagination that had set my nerves on edge. Something touched my mind, and I shuddered, remembering the horrible experience in Banlore when the Waster's thoughts had reached out to touch my own.

I lay there helpless as an evil presence washed over me, thought tendrils hesitating when they touched my mind. I tried to hide from their scrutiny. Scarcely aware of what I was doing, I imagined the wood empty of my presence, the trees where I lay standing alone and undisturbed, while a cloak hid me from the spying presence. Vaguely, I sensed a confusion in the questing thoughts. They looked this way and that, trying to discover where I was hidden, but the cloak held fast. I waited with inheld breath until at last they slipped away, deeper into the forest, still searching.

When they were gone, I let out my breath and breathed a prayer of thanks. I had no doubt that it'd been Tamara's mind I sensed; only she would look for me in such a fashion. The power of her mind was stronger than Yarac's had been, and now I was sure that she was Damal, the Dark Queen. I knew, as well, that if I hadn't managed to hide myself from her, my flight would've ended there. I could never have withstood a concentrated assault from a mind as strong as hers.

Now that she was gone—for the time being, at any rate—I had the leisure to wonder what it was that my father's blood had left me heir to. To be able to use my mind in such a way—hiding from Damal, mindspeaking, lifting Calman's curse. . . . I tried to think of all I knew of the gwandryas and found I knew very little. Neither Tess nor Finan had told me much about them. Hickathrift had said that they followed the ways of the old gods, like the weren. Weren blood ran through their veins. . . .

I lay back, pillowing my head on my pack, frightened at what stirred inside me yet eager to know more of it. At length I fell into a dreamless sleep, my weariness overriding my need to understand it all at once. As I slept, I tried to keep my protection against the questing thoughts. The cloak seemed to hold, for when I woke in the morning I was still undiscovered. I ate sparingly from my diminishing stores, broke camp, and fared onward.

Throughout that day, the thought tendrils came looking for me, slipping from the surrounding forest without warning to hover near me. The forest—the spirit of Drarkun Wood itself—was disturbed by my passage; it was this disturbance that drew the search to me, time and again. But as I hid successfully from each new probe, my confidence grew.

At mid-day, while I was taking s short rest, they came on me with such a force that it took all of my newfound guile to hide. They swept back and forth across the wood like a storm while I lay shaking, not daring to let down my shield for a moment. When at last they left, I sat up and leaned against the bole of an old pine. I was filled with relief, silently thanking my father for this gift of his blood, when a new sound came to me.

I sat still to listen, then realized it was mindspeech that I heard. The words were in an alien tongue and were not directed at me personally, yet I sensed in them such pain, fear, and loss of hope that I stood hastily. The mindspeech seemed to come from the west, so I went in that direction, treading warily. The sound grew louder the farther I went.

The forest was all pine here; the trunks were so thick that my hands wouldn't have met if I had stretched my arms about them. The lower branches of these giants were dead. Many of them had fallen, and, with the canopy of boughs high above like a roof, I felt as if I was striding through a gigantic hall. There was no snow on the ground here, only a thick covering of needles, pine cones and long-dead branches.

The mindspeech grew stridently shrill as I came to a dip

in the ground and saw its author. In the hollow, trapped under the limb of a large pine, was a woman—or so I thought at first glance. I caught glimpses of tanned skin among the brown and green boughs of the tree—a slim arm and a woman's face framed by long tresses of auburn hair.

As I hastened forward, the tumult in my mind ceased, and the woman's gaze locked onto my own. Her eyes were green, deep and penetrating. I saw then that she was without clothes and—

I stopped dead in my tracks, my mind reeling. Under her bared breasts, below her waist, were not a woman's buttocks and legs, but the torso and haunches of a deer. I saw, too— at first they'd been hidden in the criss-crossing of the branches—that two small horns sprouted from her brow. The part that was a deer was mahogany in colour, the sides heaving for breath. The part that was a woman seemed entirely out of place. Except, I realized as I took in the impossibility of what I saw, there was nothing unusual about her—for the being that she was.

She was a raewin.

I think this meeting, more than any other marvel, truly brought home the truth of magic and the old myths to me. I'd confronted a Waster, been befriended by a talking bear and a dwarf, discovered the stirring of power inside myself, walked the halls of Wistlore with its Wyslings and erlkin, known the magics of the Grey Rose. . . . Yet marvellous as such things were, none of them touched me as deeply as this mingling of woman and beast that lay before me now. The sheer wonder that such a being could be staggered me. Something expanded inside me—my worldview, my understanding of the mysteries of the world, perhaps. I was not sure what. I only knew that I was changed.

I stood there, staring foolishly, when her mind touched mine again, gently this time. I shrugged to show that I didn't understand the words. But their meaning was evident—she needed help. I was willing, but, eyeing the bough that trapped her, I doubted my ability. The bough was as thick around as

my waist and three times as long as I was high. To lift it I'd
need a lever of some sort, so I fell to searching for one.

I stepped from the hollow as my search took me farther
away. No sooner was I out of her sight than the tumult rose
in my mind again. Suddenly, I was frightened. Not by what
she could do to me—she was helpless, after all—but that her
cries would be heard by Damal as she mindsought me.

I scrambled back to where the raewin could see me, trying
to project an image of the lever I was looking for and what I
would do with it once I found it. Her mindspeech gentled
once more. An image formed in my mind of her standing
free and kissing me lightly on the brow. I read this as thanks
for what I was attempting and returned to my search. This
time, she remained quiet.

When I found a length of wood that would serve my purpose, I returned to the hollow. The raewin's gaze met mine
as I stepped into view, and a weak smile touched her lips. I
tried to project comfort to her but couldn't find an image that
she'd understand. What could a cozy hearthfire mean to her?
I settled on repeating what I intended to do with the lever
and fell to.

I thrust my pole into the ground near where the bough
trapped her hindquarters and pushed up. At first the wood
sank into the soft needles. When it finally found purchase, I
put my back into it. The bough lifted a fraction of an inch.
The raewin began to squirm, trying to free herself. I sent her
a quick image of her lying still—showing the bough falling
if she didn't abide by my warning. She lay quietly, and I
managed to lift the bough another fraction.

The pole slipped in my sweaty grasp, and the strain told
on my back. I realized then that I should've found a log to
thrust under the pole so that I would be pushing downward—
utilizing my weight—rather than up. But it was too late for
bright thoughts now. If I let the bough down again, it might
come down wrong, shifting and crushing her. It was a mir-
acle that it hadn't done so already.

With another effort, I lifted the bough a touch higher. I
could hardly bear the strain now. If I could only rest for a

moment. . . . But there was no time. I squared my shoulders, losing the last distance I'd gained, and put all my strength into one surge. As I did so, I sent her an image of herself scurrying free.

She was quick to obey. When the last part of her torso had worked free, I dropped the bough. I couldn't have held it for a moment longer, whether I wanted to or not. It came down with a crashing thud. Branches trapped the raewin again, but they had neither the weight nor the size of the bough that had trapped her.

I dropped the pole and hastened to her side, pulling her free of the remaining branches. This close to her, I marvelled at the smallness of her stature. The top of her head would come no higher than my chin, if she was standing.

When at last I had her free of the imprisoning branches, she lay panting on the ground. I knelt by her, feeling for broken bones. She shivered at my touch, drawing away until I spoke soothingly, showing that I meant no harm. Then she lay still, only trembling slightly as I completed my examination. She was so afraid that I wondered if she'd ever seen a man before; then, thinking how cruel my own kind could be, I realized that she most likely *had* seen men before— hence her fear.

I projected an image of her moving her hind legs. She did so, grimacing a little at the pain. Nothing was broken, I decided, and I smiled to think of how my years of tending Tess's goats now stood me in good stead. I knew enough of how the musculature and bones should look and feel in a body like this. All she'd suffered were bruises. She was lucky; she could just as easily have been crippled from the accident.

I tried to question her about where her home lay so that I could walk her there, but I couldn't explain myself properly. She shook her head to show that she didn't understand.

Gwenya, she mindspoke after a short pause.

She indicated herself, then pointed at me, arching her eyebrows. It was her name, I realized.

"I am Cerin," I said slowly.

Ser-in, she repeated, making a song of my name so that it

chimed and echoed in my mind. *A-meir, Ser-in. Col-neh . . .
ah!*

I must have frowned, trying to understand, for a look of
apprehension flitted over her face. I reassured her quickly,
and the look passed to be replaced by a smile. She took my
hand and drew my face to hers. Our lips met once—with her
half raised from the ground and myself leaning forward—then
she lay back again.

I arose, suddenly flustered, and went to where my journeypack lay. The taste of her kiss was pleasant on my lips,
but I felt strange—as if I'd forsaken my maid of the Grey
Rose. Then I recalled the image Gwenya'd shown me of her
standing freed and kissing my brow. She was thanking me,
that was all. But the kiss still troubled me. My father's gift,
the weren blood, had stirred in reply.

Retrieving my pack, I returned to her side. I drew out my
two bannocks and the water sack. Slowly, I let her eat and
drink, sharing the last of my supplies with her. When she
was finished, I made a pillow of my journeypack and placed
it under her head. Then I covered her with my cloak.

Col-neh, kwessen, she murmured in my mind. *Ar moorlig. . . .*

She was asleep before the last word finished echoing in my
mind. I settled down beside her, watching her sleep while I
tried to decide what to do with her. The forest was quiet, and
when the night came, the shadows grew long until I could no
longer separate the trees from the spaces between them. I
shivered and, weary from my efforts, nodded beside Gwenya
until I fell asleep where I sat.

I AWAKENED WITH A START, THINKING ONLY AN HOUR OR SO
had passed, to find that I'd slept through the night; the forest
was dim with the morning's light. I looked for my new ward,
but she was gone. I rubbed my eyes. Had I dreamed the
whole thing? Then I saw the bough that had trapped her and
my pole leaning against it. No, it had been real enough.

My cloak was folded by my journeypack. Upon it lay a par-
cel wrapped in large green leaves. I opened it—wondering,

as I did, where leaves could be found at this time of year—to find a fresh supply of bannocks. There were a dozen or so loaves, smaller in size than those I'd brought from Calman's cabin. Gwenya must have left them for me to replenish my provisions.

Suddenly ravenous, I bit into one, relishing the hearty flavour, and soon finished it. I immediately regretted eating the whole thing at once for, small though it'd been, I felt as if I'd just polished off a brace of pheasants on my own. There was some magic about them, no doubt about that. In the future I'd eat no more than a third of one at a single sitting.

I noticed small deer hoofprints in the damp pine needles as I was packing my journeypack. There were three sets. One came east, the other two went west. She'd left, returned with these provisions for me, then retraced her way homeward. Wherever that home might be, I wished her safety in reaching it. My own path led the opposite way.

I thought of Hickathrift as I walked. He would've liked to have met the raewin. Instead, he was still trapped in Wistlore. I wished, as well, that I could've communicated more clearly with her. I had questions about Drarkun Wood that only a denizen of it could answer. Also, I wondered what other beings might dwell hidden in its depths.

THE REMAINDER OF MY JOURNEY THROUGH THE FOREST passed without incident. I still felt the animosity of the trees for my trespass, and, once or twice each day, Damal's questing thoughts swept over me, but I weathered each new probe with growing strength and confidence. As for the trees, I could only make my trespass as short as possible and hope that they could perceive that I meant them no harm.

As I had fallen asleep the night before my last day in the forest, I'd heard a strange troubling music that disturbed my dreams and kept me tossing restlessly as I tried to sleep. I'd heard it once before, two nights earlier, and as it had sounded, vague and distant, the subtle hint of evil that hung about the trees grew almost palpable, as if the music was feeding it . . . enraging it.

When I awakened on what proved to be my final day in
the forest, I was surprised to see the edge of the wood in the
distance. The night had been well upon me before I'd camped
the night before, so I hadn't seen the tell-tale lightening between the trees that beckoned to me now. I got to my feet
and hastened ahead, glad to be safely through those cursed
woods for a second time.

But as I made for the fields, that weird music began to
sound once more. I heard it dimly, in the recesses of my
mind, and quickened my step. It set my teeth on edge, and
I was afraid of what it might herald. The music grew in equal
proportion to the tempo of my flight, fiery notes cascading
in discordant progressions. The forest trembled around me,
stirring into life as the hateful sound swelled in volume. Then,
as a sudden crescendo built layer upon layer of the music, I
heard a baying that was like the howling of wolves—but human in timbre.

Ahead, the end of the forest was some two hundred yards
away. I glanced back over my shoulder and saw three shapes
flitting through the trees toward me. Fear lent speed to my
flight, but they were gaining quickly upon me. Looking back,
when I should have been watching where I placed my feet, I
ran headlong into a low, dead branch. The branch snapped,
and I fell to the ground.

Raising my head, I saw that my pursuers were too close
for me to escape now. I could see what they were as well,
and my fear grew. I had no name to put to them.

They were hybrid creatures, like the raewin, with the bodies of wolves and small dwarfish torsos where the wolves'
heads should be. White fur covered them shoulder to toe.
Although they had human faces, there was a canine set to
their features—long jowls, frothed muzzles, wide-set eyes.
Bright fangs gleamed sharp and deadly in their slavering jaws.
Whether the forest had sent them against me, or they were
creatures of Damal's, or they were even born from the hellish
music that still resounded and scraped at my mind, didn't
really matter. They meant me harm, and I had to defend
myself.

I forgot both Finan's tinkerblade and the dagger that Merla had given me. Rising to my feet, I brought up the branch that I'd broken as I'd fallen, but I was too late. The first of the creatures bowled me over before I could steady my balance. I struck it with my fist, then lunged to my feet. Taking a hold of my makeshift club, I swung it at the next of my attackers. I caught my victim square in the chest with the blow and heard the crunch of its ribs cracking.

The third threw itself against me, knocking me to the ground once more. I despaired as its stubby hands clawed at my face, but then . . . a horror! The beasts backed away from me with rolling eyes as the branch in my hand came to life and shaped snake-like coils that wound themselves about my arm. I tore the coils loose and flung the branch from me.

My attackers were still backing away from me, and I soon saw why. The trees themselves had become possessed with unnatural life. Their branches reached down for us, impossible wooden fingers opening and closing as they looked for holds. I knew now that whatever these wolf-beasts were, they didn't belong to the forest. The first one I'd struck with my club was caught fast in a wooden grip, and its life was being crushed from it.

We fled, the remaining beasts and I fled for the open fields just within sight.

Branches grabbed and roots twisted up to trip me, but my terror was so wild that I was strong beyond my normal power and won free each time, panic gibbering in my mind. When I reached the fields, I ran as far as I could until the press of the snow drifts brought me to a halt. I collapsed to lie panting. The wolf-beasts hadn't been so lucky. Of one there was no sign, but the other hung from a tree at the very edge of the forest, a branch looped tight about its neck.

I lay shivering in the snow, unable to move. The trees at the edge of the wood bent toward me, their branches reaching for me. Shaking with repulsion, I watched them for long moments until at last I fought my way to my feet and stumbled away, sinking thigh-deep in the drifts.

The music was gone now, although uncomfortable echoes

still hissed and whispered just beyond my consciousness. I'd
lost both my pack and snowshoes in my mad scramble for
freedom, so I had to fare as best I could through the snow-
choked fields.

The going was slow. Darkness lapped at the edges of my
mind threatening to overcome me. I felt numb—weak from
my struggle and flight and from my fear. I could still see the
gnarled branches reaching for me, all my terrors of the forest
come to life. I had no idea why it had waited so long to
attack. At that point it was simply too hard to think. All I
wanted to do was to lie down in the snow and sleep. But I
knew that meant only death—a sleep from which I'd never
wake.

Onward I fared, blind and unthinking, trying to leave the
horror behind; but it stayed with me. I'm sure I caught a
fever of some sort, for I was babbling deliriously by the time
night fell. Out in the fields, the winds swept down and cut
me to the bone with their soul-numbing cold. When I finally
saw the lights of Calman's cabin in the darkness ahead of me
I hardly knew what they meant, let alone if I'd ever reach the
haven they promised.

I dragged myself through the last few drifts, hope welling
up to drown my despair in a sudden moment of lucidity.
When I reached the cabin, I tried to hammer on the door but
I could only manage a feeble scratching. Calman took so long
to answer that I was sure he heard nothing. Visions of freezing to death on his very doorstep were flashing through my
mind when the door opened suddenly, and I sprawled forward into the cot to look up into Calman's bearded face. I
tried to speak, but the words lodged in my throat.

"By the Truil-stone!" he muttered. "Look what the winter's dumped on my step."

The darkness I'd held off for so long swept over me at last.

ONCE AGAIN I AWAKENED TO CALMAN'S FACE PEERING INTO
my own, but this time it was a welcome and familiar sight.

"Be but a day ye've laid abed this time," he informed me
when he saw I was awake.

I managed a wan smile.

"Can ye sit up?" he asked. "I've the soup on, and other company besides. Would hear your tale, be ye able. And where be Hickathrift?"

When he said there was company, I sat up, head spinning, to look about the cabin. A dark-haired, clean shaven man sat by the hearth. He met my gaze with clear blue eyes, and a warm smile hovered on his lips. He was stocky, although a head taller than Calman, with a well-weathered look about him: scuffed leather boots, patched trousers and shirt, and strong hands and jaw that'd known the sun and wind. By the door lay a heavy cloak and a journeypack that were obviously his.

"Good morn," he said, "or rather good afternoon, for the day's wearing to its end. My name's Galin Cathainsson."

I nodded a greeting to him. In the same way that I'd taken an instant dislike to Holdmaster Feador in Wistlore, I found myself intuitively liking this man. But, because of Wistlore, I was now wary of any and all strangers.

"Calman was telling me about you and your Grey Rose last night. I'd hoped to hear your harping, but I see you didn't bring the instrument with you."

"It's lost, I fear."

All my troubles rose up in a swell—the attack of the forest, Hickathrift and the roseharp lost in Wistlore, the council's accusations of the Grey Rose, and the ill luck that plagued us both. I tried to put the worries from me as Calman approached with the promised soup.

"Be forest soup again," he said with a grin.

I thanked him and took a spoonful, sure that I'd lost my appetite. But my body craved the nourishment, whatever my mood, and I soon finished that bowl and a second. When I was done, I joined them at the hearth. I peered into the flames for a while, half expecting to see faces in the fire, but there was only the wood burning and the red-hot glow of the coals, the lick and dance of the flames. At length I sighed and began my tale.

"A raewin?" Calman exclaimed when I told them of Gwenya. "Be a sight to see, that!"

I nodded, remembering how the sight of the woman joined to a deer had affected me. I felt the strangeness again as if the earth moved under my feet. Then I thought of the wolf-dwarves and returned to my tale. When I was done, we sat quietly for a long while, and only the sound of the fire crackling touched the room. The raw edge of the terror I'd known as the trees came to life and attacked me was not so sharp now. Still I doubted that I could look on any tree for some time to come without shivering.

"They be a cruel lot in Wistlore," Calman said at last.

"So it seems," Galin agreed. "I always knew them as a stuffy sort of folk. But now, with what you've told us. . . ." He hesitated a moment, then added: "Pardon this question, Cerin, but I feel it must be asked. How well do you know this maid of the Grey Rose?"

I could feel myself bristling to her defense.

"What do you mean?"

Galin glanced at Calman.

"Could there be any truth in the council's accusations?" he asked.

A vein began to throb in my temple, and I saw red for a moment. Was I the only one in all the world who trusted her? But then I saw, through the wave of sudden anger, that he meant well by the question. I drew a deep breath to steady my nerves and answered.

"I'd trust her with my very life."

Galin nodded. "I thought as much from all that you and Calman've told me, but I thought the question needed asking."

I looked at him, my curiosity plain. Before I could ask him why he thought it important, he answered my unspoken question.

"I want to help you," he said, "as I'm sure Calman does too."

"Aye," Calman said forcefully. "The folk of Wistlore be unkind folk and deserving of any sorrow we bring to them for what they've done. Hickathrift be my friend. Locked in stone be not for him. The woods and the wilds be his domain.''

The dwarf was stroking his beard thoughtfully as he spoke. I looked from him to Galin, startled at their offer. I'd thought that they might be able to advise me as to what I should do next, or where I should begin, never dreaming that they'd join me. I was not so surprised, perhaps, that Calman should want to help, for Hickathrift was his friend as well and he knew me, but Galin was a stranger.

''It could be a long journey,'' I said.

''Then better the three of us fare it, than the one alone,'' Galin said.

''But you—you know nothing of me.''

''I know injustice,'' Galin said.

Before I could say anything else, Calman spoke up.

''Where be the dagger the erl gave ye?'' he asked.

I brought it from under my tunic and handed it over. Calman wrinkled his nose with distaste as he took it from me. Galin leaned forward, interest plain in his manner.

''Be darkness wrought in its making, sure enough,'' Calman pronounced when he'd drawn the blade from its sheath. It glinted wickedly, bringing a chill to the room. ''Be not of this world, this blade.''

''Its metal came from a fallen star,'' I said. ''Or at least that's what Merla told me.''

''Aye, but the workmanship . . . that be from another realm, one that those shiny stars in our own skies have never seen.''

I looked at him, puzzled, but he didn't elaborate.

''Be an unseemly thing,'' was all he said, ''not fit for decent folk.'' He slipped it back to its sheath and returned it. ''Best ye hold onto it, though. Be a time coming—like your Merla said—when it be of use, maybe.''

We sat quietly again, each with his own thoughts.

''Your plan's the best,'' Galin said at length. ''To go into the Southern Kingdoms and look for both your maid and the caryaln,'' he added when I looked up. ''I've travelled through them once or twice—lived in Liammoir for a year and a half once. I've friends down there who might help us, but it won't be easy.''

The flames spluttered, for the fire was low.

"I be fetching wood," Calman said, rising.

"I'll give you a hand," Galin said.

I began to rise as well, but Calman waved me back.

"Two be enough," he said. "Best ye rest all ye can, while ye can."

They threw on their cloaks and went out. I could hear them scrabbling in the woodpile alongside the cabin. Leaning against the hearthstones, I savoured the warmth still trapped in them and eyed Calman's latest stonework with admiration. One piece portrayed a Harper and a bear—Hickathrift and myself, I realized. I looked at the stone bear's cunningly chipped features and sighed, missing my friend.

A sudden shout from outside roused me from my reverie. Startled, I rose and hurried to the door, throwing it open just as Calman and Galin came up, their arms loaded with wood. It was dark outside—a starless night—and I could see little.

"What. . . . ?" I began.

Silently, they pushed by me, faces set with grim purposefulness. Galin dropped his load in the middle of the floor and reached for a longbow that leaned against the wall. I hadn't noticed it earlier. With practised ease, he had it strung and an arrow notched in a moment. Springing to the door, he let loose a shaft, then kicked the door shut as soon as the arrow left his bow.

"Got one!" he cried.

I looked about, bewildered, as he notched another shaft. Calman took a two-headed broad-axe from the wall beside the hearth and took a stance beside the door.

"What is it?" I demanded.

"Be dwarwolves," Calman said.

"The beasts from your tale," Galin added at my uncomprehending look. "More than two score of them. They have us ringed in, Cerin."

My skin prickled as I thought of the hybrid creatures. And,

remembering their attack in the forest, I cocked my head to listen. There . . . faintly . . . I could hear the strains of that hateful music once more. I shivered, thinking of Damal. For all that we'd just been speaking of her, I'd almost forgotten that she'd still be searching for me.

"Where do they come from?" I asked. "From the forest?"

"They be left from the elder wars," Calman offered. "Could dwell in Drarkun."

"They were bred from dwarves," Galin said, "like our good friend here. The Daketh took them and twisted them to their own needs. They're not as strong as yargs—but strong enough. We don't have much hope of standing them off here. The walls of the cabin are solid enough, but the shutters and the door won't stand up to a determined assault."

"Would ye had your harp," Calman said. "Ye could play them a death tune, like the Harpers of old. When Rhynn Rhymemaster slew the troll in that old tale Hickathrift told us—were a song that slew the beast, remember? Not axe. Not sword."

I remembered. And if I had the roseharp . . . but it was in Wistlore. And while I might've conjured up a cure for Calman's curse, I doubted that the vague feyness stirring in me was a match for two score dwarwolves. Still, the music that had drawn them here droned faintly in my mind. If music had brought them, music might send them away again.

The feyness in me—that Hickathrift'd called my taw— quickened. It was a power, he'd said. Weren blood—my father's heritage. And them my mother's blood seemed to speak to me, telling me what tune I'd play to work this magic. My fingers curled at my sides as I imagined what strings I'd pluck to make that tune sound. But what use was it to dream of a harp or what I'd do with it? I didn't have one, and I said as much.

Silence greeted my words until Galin set his bow against the wall and turned to us.

"You haven't got your roseharp," he said, "but we could still make one for you."

I looked at him as if he was mad.

"Aye, that we could," Calman agreed. "There be power in my hands since ye gave me back my skills, Cerin. Be not so hard to fashion strings and tuning pegs for a harp."

"It'd take too long," I protested.

"I've some small skill in woodworking," Galin said. "If you can give me the measurements, Cerin. . . ."

We looked at one another. It was the height of folly, and I think we all knew it, but hope rose in our breasts.

"I made a harp once," I said. "Long ago, in the West Downs. I could do it again, easily enough, but it takes time. . . ."

Without further discussion, we fell to. Outside the cabin the strange yelps and cries of the dwarwolves chorused unabated while we began to dismantle one of Calman's chests for the wood we'd need.

THE DWARWOLVES ATTACKED THE CABIN THAT NIGHT. THEY came in a clamouring, howling wave, throwing themselves against the walls, then claws ripping at the wood. The door shook under their onslaught. It was sturdily built and held fast—but for how long? The music that I heard as a constant drone built into a crescendo just before their attack. When it was at its loudest, the creatures were at their strongest, yammering and growling in a frenzy as if their numbers had doubled. And all the while, we worked on the harp.

Galin was more than a little skilled at woodworking. Between the two of us, we had the roughs laid out well before midnight. We used the planks from the chest we'd dismantled and the thick legs of one of the tables for the two supports.

"Well, it won't be a beauty," Galin remarked as we looked on our handiwork, "but as long as it plays, it's work well done."

As we whittled the various lengths of wood into usable shape and carved the pegs that would hold the joints in place, Calman built up a roaring fire and sat scowling into its heat. It wasn't enough for what he needed. Not until he'd added a good store of his precious coal to the wood was the heat to his satisfaction. Galin and I stripped off our shirts as the temperature rose steadily in the cabin, but Calman, undisturbed by it, began his work.

He fashioned long wires from two melted-down bronze pots, winding other strands about them for strength. I'd argued against the making of the strings, but Calman insisted that those made of gut were useless for harp magic.

"Be once living," he said. "Play them, and your tune will hold their ill will. Be not as strong as metal, nor as pleasing."

I couldn't dissuade him. Like a fairy smith in an old tale, his fingers fairly flew over their work. By the time Galin and I had the roughs fitted, he had five strings completed. He set me to carving molds for the tuning pegs then, while Galin fitted the soundbox together.   ·

An hour after the dwarwolves commenced their attack, the music in my mind faded until it was a drone once more. The creatures retreated. We knew they'd be back, though, and didn't let up on our labours. I asked the others about the music that I heard in my head, and they regarded me blankly. They'd heard nothing. I worried at that riddle as I carved the molds.

The music faded, and the dwarwolves withdrew; when it grew strong again, they attacked. Somewhere, someone was devising that music. To my mind, there was only one person who had the skill and the animosity to do it, and that was Caradoc, the Masterharper of Wistlore. To him—when our work was done and the harp ready in my hands—I'd direct my magic.

At dawn, Galin fell back from his labour with a sigh.

"I can't go on without a rest," he mumbled.

Rolling out his cloak, he curled up by the door, as far from the heat of Calman's fire as he could lie without being outside.

Calman scorned rest. Twenty-six of the strings were completed now, and only five remained. As he worked on the last of them, I put aside the completed molds and began to bore holes into the supports where the tuning pegs would be set. I completed the last hole as Galin awoke. He smiled at my work, and we both went to help Calman in casting the pegs.

As they were cooling, the droning in my head swelled into that hellish music once more.

"They're attacking again," I said.

No sooner had I spoken than the dwarwolves essayed another assault. This time, one of the shutters gave way. A dwarwolf fell into the room, carried by the momentum of its lunge. Calman's axe was in his hand and flying through the air before Galin or I had time to realize what'd happened. The axe caught the creature full in the chest. Before another could come in, Calman leapt for the window—again surprising me with the speed at which his bulky shape moved—and set his shoulder against the broken shutters, holding them closed. Thuds and a steady clawing at the wood outside lent speed to our efforts.

While Galin and I held the shutters against the beasts, Calman grabbed leftover boards from what had been his chest and hammered them across the window. We fell back from it with a sigh of relief when the makeshift barrier held.

When a lull in the attack came—heralded by a lessening of the discordant measures that sounded in my mind—we opened the door just wide enough to heave the carcass of the dead dwarwolf outside. I'd had a good look at the creature while it lay on the floor. Even in death it was a fearful thing to look upon.

The fur was more yellow than white, I saw now that I had a clearer and less hectic view of it, though this beast's pelt was stained from the gaping axe-wound in its chest. It was indeed a cross between a dwarf and wolf—though who would breed such a thing, and to what purpose?

Left over from the elder wars, Calman had said. The Daketh had created them for their own foul uses. Then I thought of the raewin—was Gwenya the Dark Gods' product as well? She hadn't seemed evil to me. And what of the other kemysfolk, the halflings? Were they all creations of the Daketh? Then I remembered that Hickathrift had told me that the Tua-

than themselves were hybrid forms. I shook my head. Such
riddles were beyond me.

While the dwarwolves held back, we returned to the harp.
Galin and I set the pegs in place, then busied ourselves string-
ing it. Calman hunched by the doorway, axe close at hand,
chiseling away at a piece of stone. He had his back to us, so
we couldn't see what he was making. When we were finally
done, having just fitted the last string into place, he approached us. In his hand he held a small rose carved from
stone—grey rock shaped to make a grey rose.

"This be to mind ye of the other," he said gruffly.

Cunningly, he set it into the wood where the forepillar
joined the neck. When he stepped back, I touched the carving
with a trembling finger. My throat was thick with emotion,
and when I turned to him, I saw him through a mist.

"Thank you," I said softly.

He grinned, tugging at his beard.

We stood back then to admire our handiwork. It was a
primitive instrument and would never win any prizes for its
beauty, but so long as it was serviceable, it was work well
done. I closed my eyes and tried to reach down to that fey
stirring inside me as I approached the harp. The harpspell I'd
thought I could feel rise up in me echoed in my mind as I
took the instrument onto my lap and began to tune it.

The pegs turned smoothly in their holes and held firm when
the strings were tightened. The instrument's tone was dull,
especially when compared to Telynros's, but music could be
made on it.

"Spell their deaths," Calman said as I tuned the last string.

I nodded grimly and began to play.

My father's blood quickened magically inside me, and my
mother's gave me the positions that my fingers must assume.
My left hand struck a chord while I plucked a melody with
the fingers of my right. The notes fled the harp more crisply
than I'd imagined they would, bounding from the walls and
filling the cabin with their sound. Calman grinned in his
beard, and Galin smiled. Then—in the middle of my tune,
with the magic stirring—another music awoke in my mind.

The drone that had lain dormant swelled now, growing from a half-forgotten echo into a thunder of sound. And again the dwarwolves attacked.

The noise of their clawing and scrabbling cut through the music my harp made. Frantically, I played the tune through to its end, then began again, playing with more force this time. Dull thudding came from the door. The hellish music that drove the dwarwolves to their attack became a howling cacophony in my mind.

The pounding at the door accelerated, drumming in time to the hateful mind-music. The dwarwolves had found something to use as a battering ram and, from the sound of it, they'd break in soon. I tried to concentrate on the magic I was trying to spell and saw instead an image of the roseharp. It hung in an ornate room—its brave strings broken, its magic fled. Then I saw Caradoc, the Masterharper of Wistlore, crouched below it, playing his own harp, and I knew for certain who'd set the dwarwolves on my trail. I lost the scene and opened my eyes to Calman's cabin once more.

My hands fell from the harp. I could see—I *knew*—what music to play to make the magic work, but I couldn't transfer that intuitive knowledge from my mind to my hands.

"What's wrong?" Galin asked.

He gathered up his longbow, fitting a shaft to its string.

"The power was in the roseharp, not in me," I said, dejected with my failure.

Caradoc's music boomed louder in my mind, and the thudding at the door increased.

"Be three powers of a Harper," Calman said. "Sleep, laughter, and tears. Those enchantments be in the music itself, in the man, not in the harp. Play ye one of them, Cerin."

"I don't know them."

All our labours, our hope, had been for nothing. Despairingly, I realized that there was only one place where those skills—a Harper's skills—could be learned. That was in Wistlore, the very source of our troubles. What a cruel jest.

The music in my mind swelled to an impossible volume. I staggered under its onslaught; then the door burst open with a great rending of wood. Shards flew about us, reminding me of the Waster's appearance in the Grey Rose's cabin. The dwarwolves were upon us.

Galin's bow spoke twice. His shafts feathered as many of the beasts. Then they were too close for bow-work. Calman's axe hummed above his head. He swept it in a wide arc in front of the door, killing the next beast that rushed in. Galin swung his heavy bow. We were too late to hold the door against them, though. Four of the creatures were in the cabin, while more filled the doorway. I lunged for my pack and Finan's tinkerblade, but too late. A dwarwolf bowled me over. I turned to grapple with it, my fingers locking around its neck.

The creature pummelled my head with blows. I felt my grip loosening on its throat and despaired for all our lives. It would've been better if I'd died in Drarkun Wood and not brought this death to those who'd befriended me. A forlorn thought of the Grey Rose swept through me. I lost my grip, and the creature's teeth were nearing my throat when a fierce cry rang through the small interior of the cot like exultant thunder. It drowned the roar of Caradoc's hellish music in my mind, and suddenly the air was filled with the stench of burning fur and flesh.

Yaln ser brena! I heard above the din of our struggle. *Ren Carn ha Corn! Yal!*

The dwarwolf that was on me screamed and fell away, its pelt in flames. I scrambled away from its thrashing form and rose to see the last of the creatures bolting for the door, where a wondrous being stood. It was Gwenya.

The last beast tried to scurry by her. She turned as it squeezed past and pointed a rod that she was holding in her hand at the fleeing creature. A shaft of flame erupted from the end of the rod, and the dwarwolf crumpled to the ground, its pelt hissing where the fire touched the snow.

Bren ser meir, Ser-in?

I lifted my gaze form the charred corpse of the dwarwolf to meet her deep green eyes. The concern was plain in her eyes, and I smiled to show that I was unhurt. Behind me,

Calman and Galin were beating the smoldering corpses of the slain with a blanket so that the fire wouldn't spread. I stepped toward Gwenya, entranced by her strangeness where I was repulsed by the dwarwolves.

"My thanks," I said aloud and sent an accompanying image of myself kissing her brow.

She smiled warmly, moving forward until I was looking down into her face. Caradoc's music had stilled at her first cry, while in my mind the sweet tones of her voice were still ringing. I bent to kiss her brow, but she lifted her head so that our lips met.

Het ser meir, she said.

She stepped back, smiling at the blush that was starting up from my collar.

Quen, she added, motioning for me to follow.

Outside, the snow was littered with dead dwarwolves. Gwenya motioned again. I looked where she'd directed me, and my eyes went wide. A male counterpart to her stood in the snow, regal and proud. He was taller than her by a foot, with two sweeping antlers where she had only the small horns.

If Gwenya seemed strangely wondrous to me, her mate filled me with awe. His eyes were a dark amber, stern and piercing. He held his head erect, the twelve-pointed antlers gleaming.

Kalseth, Gwenya said.

I supposed that she was introducing me. I swallowed drily.

"My . . . my thanks to you as well, Kalseth," I said.

A-meir, Ser-in, he replied.

His voice was deep and clear in my mind, and his antlers dipped as he inclined his head toward me. I saw that he, too, carried a small rod in his hand. Looking closer at the one Gwenya held, I saw that it appeared to be no more than a hollowed tube, carved from a wand of white ash. Thinking of the havoc they were capable of wreaking, I wondered why Gwenya hadn't simply used hers to free herself from the pine bough in Drarkun Wood.

I managed to put my question across to her, and an image formed in my mind of the inside of a stone room—perhaps a cave. Gwenya was in the chamber, and I saw her leaving, and forgetting the rod where it lay on a small shelf. The next image showed her trapped by the bough, helpless. Then she showed Kalseth, with the impression of a great distance separating him from where she was trapped.

The rest I knew. As she was answering me, Calman and Galin approached. The raewin grew nervous at their presence, standing their ground but fidgeting with their rods and lifting their hooves and setting them down in the snow.

"Be thanks we owe ye," Calman said. "Your coming was timely."

His eyes were wide with wonder, and Galin's no less so. Kalseth nodded a greeting to them as well. An awkward silence developed, and the raewin were growing more nervous, when Galin said:

"Ho! Who comes there?"

I turned to see a figure in a brown cloak coming from the direction of the Winding Clay. He'd obviously caught sight of us and was waving his arms to attract our attention. It was impossible to make out any details at this distance. The raewin chose that moment to spring into motion.

"Gwenya!" I cried after their retreating forms.

Dursona, Ser-in, her voice echoed in my mind. *Dursona. . . .*

The word hovered, breathy, in my inner ear—a farewell of sorts, I thought. I shaped it with my lips and knew with a sudden insight that the raewin's language was the same as that of the Tuathan, the folk from my dreams.

"Dursona," I murmured, though they were now out of sight. "Dursona, and many thanks. . . ."

I was sorry to see them go, but the stranger was now within hailing distance. Calman had his axe in hand, and Galin was notching another shaft when the man called out:

"Put up your weapons. I'm unarmed and mean no harm."

Regardless of his assurance, we waited for him to approach without lessening our guard. The hood of his cloak lay back on his shoulders, revealing erl-like features and a shock of golden hair, with a thin beard of the same hue sprouting raggedly from a narrow chin. He was slim, and wore loose brown trousers, a rust-coloured shirt and jacket, and boots of dark brown leather. He slowed his pace as he neared us, his attentive gaze going from the dead dwarwolves to our faces, then to the forest where the raewin had disappeared from view.

"What's happened?" he asked. "Were those deer-folk the fabled raewin? And what caused the dwarwolves to attack? It's passing strange that so many should gather to attack one small holding. Do you have some great treasure hid away in there?"

He fired his questions at us, one after the other, without giving us time to answer any of them. His green-brown eyes twinkled with curiosity.

"What would ye of us?" Calman demanded brusquely.

The stranger's eyes narrowed at Calman's tone.

"My name's Robin," he said. "I heard a great clamour rise up while I was crossing the Clay, and, thinking there was someone in need of help, I came to offer what I could." He looked at the dwarwolves again. "I can see the struggle was fierce, and ask again: what caused their attack?"

"They want me dead," I said.

"You? Why? What've you done—slain their chieftain?"

"Not yet. He hides in Wistlore, beyond our grasp for the time being."

Calman shot at me a look as I spoke, as if to say that I told too much.

"What would ye of us?" the dwarf repeated.

"Wistlore?" Robin repeated, ignoring Calman's question. A grave look shrouded his eyes. "Now you speak a strange riddle. Who in that place of learning would do such a thing? I'd hear the whole tale of this, if you'd tell me."

"Ye be asking too many questions without answering our own," Calman said, fingering his axe.

"Heed me, dwarf!" Robin said, suddenly standing straighter so that he seemed to loom over us. "I've told you my name, and why I came—to give aid if it was needed. Nothing more. I hadn't thought to claim questing here and," dangerous lights now kindled in his eyes, "if you do not put down that axe, I'll take it that you mean to attack me and will defend myself accordingly."

The moment was suddenly charged with tension. I could sense Calman tightening his grip on his axe. In another second he was liable to strike the stranger.

"Wait a minute," I said, placing my hand on Calman's arm to restrain him. "We've been through a lot these past few hours, stranger, and we aren't prepared to welcome whoever happens by. Our enemies are many, and you—you could be easily one of them."

I wished I knew whether or not we could trust him. This constant distrust wore heavily on me, for all that it was necessary. A thought came to me then.

"Do you know Wistlore at all?" I asked.

"Very well," he replied, "though I've been gone these past five years or so, studying in the south."

"Do you know a Loremaster named Hickathrift?"

"Hickathrift Trummel?" Robin asked. "Bether 'n' shin! I know him well. He taught me all that I know of woodslore when he first came to Wistlore from the Aulden Woods. Wait a minute." He looked at Calman. "I know you now. You're Calman Stonestream—Hickathrift's often spoken to me of you. We share a friend, Master Stonestream. Now won't you put down your axe?"

Calman continued to glower at him, saying nothing. I understood his suspicions, but thought that he was carrying them perhaps a bit too far. Galin suddenly broke the silence.

"I say we trust him."

"So do I," I added, hoping I wasn't making a mistake.

"Be it so," Calman said finally, lowering his axe. "I'll offer ye guest-rights, stranger. If ye have weapons, leave them at the door."

Robin opened his cloak to show that he carried no weapon, and I wondered at his earlier statement of defending himself against Calman's axe. How could he have accomplished that without even a dagger to his name? There was more to him than appeared at first glance, it seemed, and I hoped again that we weren't making a mistake.

When we were back inside, Calman nailed a blanket across the door while I built up the fire once more. As I readied a kettle of water, Robin asked me of Wistlore again. I remained silent for a moment, weighing his claim of friendship with Hickathrift against my suspicions. In the end, the tie with Hickathrift won out. If he proved false, we were still three to his one.

"I'll tell you," I said as I poured 'round the tea.

So I told my tale through again, making shorter work of it this time. I left out much about Meana and why I was now looking for her, but this time added the fact that it was Caradoc who'd set the dwarwolves upon us.

Robin remained silent throughout, fixing me with an unblinking gaze. A look of wistfulness came into his eyes when I spoke of Gwenya, and he straightened in his seat when I told of the council of Wistlore, leaning forward and remaining tense through the rest of the tale. When I told of Hickathrift's imprisonment, anger flickered in his eyes.

I could sense something about him as I spoke, a familiarity that I found hard to understand. When I was done, he was quiet for a long moment.

"A raewin," he murmured at last. "Hickathrift and I once spent six months in Drarkun, searching for her, but to no avail. And now he's imprisoned, and madness reigns. . . ." He shook his head, as if coming out of a reverie. "I forget myself. These are grave tidings you have of Wistlore. Tamara and Caradoc? Caradoc was always mean-spirited, and I can see him playing a part in all of this, but Tamara? Hoof and Horn! She raised me as her own child when my own mother passed away. . . ."

I stared at him, aghast. Calman's hand was on his axe once more, and Galin edged toward where his bow leaned.

"Who are you?" I asked, my voice almost a whisper. Had we let one of our foes into our midst?

"I thought I'd said as much," he replied. "My name's Robin—Robin Marrow, and now it appears that I'm a Lord's son.'' He looked at us, smiling bitterly. ''Oh, put up your weapons! I mean you no harm. I told you that I've been gone these past five years. I was in Magdal, studying under Ler Yrill.''

That rang a bell for me. Merla had said the same of him, and she had spoken well of him, too.

''When I left Wistlore,'' Robin was saying, ''it was a bright, sunny place of learning, not the warcamp you describe. Bether 'n' shin, but these are fell times. There was talk in the Kingdoms of trouble brewing in the north. That's why I was returning home sooner that I'd been expecting to.''

''So you knew nothing of this?'' Galin asked.

Calman kept a firm grip on his axe and scowled, while I— I didn't know what to think.

''Not a whit,'' Robin replied. ''I find it . . . difficult to accept, to be honest with you. My father's always been stern and stubborn at the best of times, but never evil. And never, never have there been prisoners kept in Wistlore's halls, nor erls patrolling the keep. Ah, poor Hickathrift. He never cared to be inside stone walls for long.''

''You say you're recently come from Magdal?'' Galin continued. ''If I remember rightly, that lies just north of Lord Audager's lands. Is there news there of a maid like Cerin's Grey Rose?''

''This is the first I've heard of her . . . Alken's daughter, you say. . . . ?'' Robin's voice trailed off, and he was lost in thought. ''The muryan have a song of her. She was unnamed in it, as well . . . the elder folk are careful with their names.''

''What song is that?'' I asked.

He cleared his throat and sang a verse of it softly:

> Twilight, hooded, forth did go
> from hollowed hill, from hallowed hold;
> Alken's daughter, 'neath his banner,
> shook the moors with bitter laughter;
> Alken dead and barrowed was,
> Alken's daughter forsook love;
> Twilight, star-clad, freed of vow,
> fled the Dark from then to now. . . .

Hearing a song of my maid of the Grey Rose from another's lips were strange. The worry I felt for her like a constant ache welled up in me, and I was sad, thinking of her on her own in the south, fleeing the Dark Queen's shadows.

"I don't have the whole thing," Robin said, "but it seems to tell of the same maid." He shook his head as if to clear it of unbidden thoughts and looked at me. "She named herself Meana to you? That means 'twilight' in the old Sennayeth tongue. If you're going south, you might do well to fare to Magdal and ask Ler Yrill of her, for there's little doing in the Kingdoms that he's not aware of."

We sat quietly for a while, then Robin turned to me again.

"What way do you plan to take?" he asked.

"We be going our own way." Calman answered before I could speak. "And ye?"

Robin laughed at Calman's continued suspicion, but I saw that the humour didn't reach his eyes. I saw only sadness there.

"From all you've told me," he said, "perhaps you do well to mistrust me. But I was only going to tell you that something stirs in the Great Waste, and the Hills of the Undead are uneasy, as if the old ghosts were waking. I was followed the whole of my journey north until I crossed the Qualan. I thought you should be warned."

"Now we be warned," Calman said shortly.

"As for me," Robin continued, ignoring the dwarf's comment, "I'll have to skirt Drakun now, adding a month to my journey at a time when it can ill be afforded. With the madness in Wistlore, dwarwolves hunting, Wasters awake . . . the whole land appears to be marshalling for a war. I fear its coming greatly."

He regarded us each in turn, and we all saw the apprehension in his eyes.

"And Damal," he added softly, "the Dark Queen, is come. . . ."

The conversation languished after that. No one offered to revive it, so we took what comfort we could amidst the shambles that the dwarwolves'd made of Calman's cabin. Galin and Robin rolled themselves up in their cloaks by the hearth. I fashioned a carrying bag for my new harp before I took my own rest. Though there was no magic in the instrument, it'd still ease the long journey south. I'd missed having an instrument to play.

When I was done and laying out my own mantle, I glanced at the doorway to see that Calman was still sitting in front of it, his axe in hand, his gaze fixed on Robin's sleeping form. The blanket that blocked the doorway did little to keep out the cold. I shivered from the chill and huddled closer to the fire, wishing that Calman would rest. At the same time, for all that I thought Robin could be trusted, I was thankful that Calman stood guard.

Deepdelve

Under mountain   deep they were
who remembers   Truilkin
Hammers silent   dark the halls
who remembers   Truilkin
Gold no longer   glitters bright
who remembers   Truilkin
Long ago and   long it was
who remembers   Truilkin

—"Deepdelve"
from the SONGWEAVER'S JOURNEYBOOK

THE DAWN CAME GREY AND DREARY, WITH A CHILL WIND heralding the possibility of heavy snows before nightfall. We crouched in front of the hearth, sipping scalding tea and thinking of the road that lay before us.

"Be fearful weather for travelling," Calman remarked.

"But travel we must," Galin said. "I fear dwarwolves more than the weather, if the truth be known. Out on the road, without the raewin's aid. . . ."

"You do well to fear the dwarwolves," Robin said. "But once you've crossed the Clay, I doubt they'll pursue you." He turned to me then, adding: "I'd like to go with you, Cerin, to help as I can in your quest for this Grey Rose, but I must away to Wistlore. From all you've told me, I'm long overdue."

"No matter. Three travel swifter than four," Calman said, making little sense, except to emphasize that he wanted Robin excluded from our company.

"By that reasoning," Robin said with a smile, "I'll travel swifter than you all."

He rose from the hearth, set his mug aside, and gathered his cloak about him.

"I envy you your friends, Cerin," he said. "They're true to you, and that's a gift not lightly given. But I must away. Travel safely, trust few and, with any luck, we'll meet again in Wistlore. And this time I can assure you that your guesting will be more to your liking." He nodded to Calman and Galin. "Farewell to you both. And perhaps, Calman, when your quest is ended, you may come to think more kindly of me."

He pulled aside the blanket at the door and stepped outside.

"Luck to you all!" he called back and was gone.

I walked to the door and watched him disappear across the fields, his figure dwindling into the distance. He moved quickly indeed, I thought. Behind me, Calman sighed and set aside his axe. When he began to gather provisions for our journey, I turned from the door to give him a hand, musing as I worked on all that had befallen me since the Grey Rose first came into my life.

My mind was more on her than on the task at hand. I stuffed dried apples and bannocks into a sack but pictured Meana in my mind. She wore the white shift that I'd first seen her wearing in the Golden Wood. Her rusty hair gleamed softly in the sunlight; her dusky eyes were warm. I worried for her constantly.

Since the dwarwolves had fled, I hadn't felt either the touch of Caradoc's fell music in my mind or the thought tendrils that'd sought me as I travelled through Drarkun Wood. While I was thankful that they were gone, I feared that Caradoc and Damal only ignored me so that they could concentrate all their attention on the Grey Rose.

"Be ye sleeping?"

"What?"

I looked up to find Calman grinning at me.

"Ye've not made a move for a good ten minutes," he said.

"I was just thinking what you'd look like without your beard," I said, matching his grin with one of my own.

Galin roared with delight.

"Be not a pretty sight," Calman said, trying to look grim.

His unsuccessful attempt had us all laughing in the end, loosening the tension that'd lain on us since the dwarwolves' attack. I felt the immediacy of my worries draw back somewhat. Hickathrift's imprisonment and Meana's plight were still constant aches, deep inside me, but I realized then that if I lived them every moment of every day, I'd wear myself out long before I could be of any use to anyone.

WE LEFT THE CABIN AT NOON, CROSSING THE WINDING CLAY without mishap, and stepped out briskly once we reached the opposite bank. Calman seemed to have enough snowshoes to outfit an army, for we all had pairs on our feet as well as spares in our packs in case of breakage. The storm held off, and we made camp just before dusk in a small hollow among the low hills. Clouds hid the stars that night as the storm gathered, and I took to my blanket early, falling asleep to the murmur of Calman and Galin's voices as they discussed the road ahead.

All too soon it was morning, and Calman was shaking me awake.

"Be wild snow and winds soon," he said, "and a long road afore us. Need be to cross the Qualan ere the storm strikes."

I roused myself, blinking sleep from my eyes. Only the second day of our journey, and already I felt as if we'd been on the road for months. I had yet to manage a decent time to rest and recuperate from all that'd befallen me these past few weeks. It seemed as if I was constantly on the road from here to there, with never a chance to catch my breath in either place.

There was hot porridge waiting for me by the fire, simmering in a small black pot. Galin nodded to me as I filled a bowl. He looked as sleepy as I felt. I was scraping the bottom of my bowl clean when Calman swung his pack to his back.

"Do ye be coming?"

"You're a hard taskmaster," I muttered, exchanging weary looks with Galin.

He shrugged his shoulders as if to say that travelling with dwarves had its hazards as well as its benefits. I cleaned my bowl and shouldered my pack and harp. They seemed twice as heavy today as they had the day before. I glanced at Calman, whose pack was so loaded down that I marvelled that he could even lift it.

"I'll cook and carry more than my own share," he replied when I mentioned it, "but bedamned if I'll wait for ye. Come. The wind's rising, and the snow be on us soon."

We trudged all that day under oppressive skies and crossed the Qualan River at midafternoon. Like the Clay, it was frozen over, so the crossing was simpler than when Hickathrift and I had come this way a month or so earlier. Westward we could see the storm hovering on the backs of the Perilous Mountains. Calman led us another three leagues before we camped for the night. While Galin and I gathered fuel for the fire, Calman readied the camp. We were in a small stand of winter-bare elms, and he tied a blanket between two boles to stave off the bite of the wind.

Much later in the evening we sat talking quietly by the fire, warming cold hands around mugs of hot tea. A small sprinkle of snow was falling, spluttering on the fire.

"I'm from Algarland originally," Galin replied to the question I'd just put to him. "It lies far to the north, beyond the Wall of the World. Surely, you've at least heard of it?"

"I have kin there," Calman said.

Galin and I smiled. We'd already learned that dwarves had kin everywhere, if half of what Calman told us was true.

"My uncle travelled there once," I said.

"The town I was born and bred in," Galin continued, "is called Hab-on-the-Water—a fair little burg that sits on the shore where the Waine flows into the Norde Sea. My people live mostly by fishing, although there are also farms, and some live by the longbow and spear—hunters and trappers. There's only one pass through the mountains, and that lies some thirty leagues or more north of Wistlore. In the dales we call it the Door to the World.

"I might've been living there still, if it wasn't for a tinker who came to my father's steading one fine summer's night. He stayed over with us and offered to take me on the road with him when he left. Well, I thought about it—for perhaps half a minute—and agreed readily enough. I was the youngest of three brothers, you see, and had the choice of working for one of my brothers or homesteading on my own. I had always had my eye on the horizon rather than the task at hand, and I doubt my father was all that sorry that I made the choice I did.

"Well, I travelled with that tinker man for three years, and wound through the Grassfields of Kohr down to Lillowen, taking ship from there to the Widelands. From there we came back north, hugging the coast and skirting the Trembling Lands, to pass through the West Downs of Eldwolde and on into the Southern Kingdoms. His name was Tomaj'n Tufty, that tinker. We parted ways some years back. . . . in Thekeldale, I think it was."

"This was your first trip home, then, in all those years?" I asked, feeling somewhat guilty that it was because of me that he was postponing his trip.

I think he read that guilt in my features, for he smiled.

"Truth to tell, Cerin," he said, "I wasn't much looking forward to going back. I was just tired of wandering without a purpose. I've felt more alive these past few days than I have in years, and I'd rather be on this quest with you than listening to my brothers discuss what a waste I've made of my life."

"Did you never want to settle down?"

I thought of Tess, who had grown tired of the world and made her home in Wran Cheaping, and of Meana and how I'd wished more than once that we could have lived hidden away in her cottage in the Golden Wood, with no one to trouble us and only the odd friend like Hickathrift or Calman or Galin to come by for a visit, much like Finan used to visit Tess and me.

An odd look came into Galin's eyes and for a long time he said nothing but stared into the fire. I remembered something he'd said before—about knowing injustice—and wished that I hadn't reminded him of whatever it was that was now troubling him.

"I settled down once," he said softly. "It was a funny thing. When the time came I realized that there was more daleblood in me than I'd let on, even to myself."

He glanced at me, and I saw a misting in his eyes.

"I met a woman," he said. "Her name was Susan Wims. She was neither tinker nor any sort of travelling persons, but she came away with me from her father's farm in Vogan. We journeyed up through Denn and Lower Eyre and finally settled down to homestead in Brennocksdale. I never thought that there could be so much joy in ploughing a field and building a cabin, and for the first time I understood what it was that bound my father and my brothers to the soil. It wasn't for the earth itself—though there's joy in its richness, never doubt it—nor the owning of land. It was the sharing of that work with someone I loved, building a future together.

"We were homesteaders, and we claimed our farm from the wilderness. But a time came—during the second year we lived there—that Lord Brinan's men came riding in and demanded a tithe. They came with mocking grins on their faces, and I turned back their demands with hard words. I. . . ."

He clenched his fists as the memory rose fresh within him.

"I never thought what I was saying. We'd worked that land, grown our first crop and seeded our second, raised the cottage from logs we'd cut down ourselves . . . no one helped us. Where was Lord Brinan when we were building? And why should we pay a tithe to some Lord we never knew had claimed those acres, when he'd done nothing for us?

"There were three of them—of Brinan's men—and I drove them off with a well-placed shaft or two to show them I meant business. But if I'd known. . . ."

There was such a hurt and anger in him that I wanted to comfort him, but words were hollow and empty-sounding at a time like that. We sat quietly, Calman and I, and waited for him to finish.

"They came back—three-and-twenty of them this time— with the Lord himself at the front of them. They bound me to the old birch that stood in front of the cabin and burned the place down . . . burned it with Suara . . . still inside. They beat me with the hafts of their spears and left me for dead. And I would've died—only my hate sustained me. I hung in those ropes all that night and half the following day. I'd be hanging there still but a tinker came by—I had the mark on the tree, you know?"

I nodded. Tess had one cut into the door of our cottage as well—a circle with a cross in its center, a tinker-rune that said there was a welcome for the travelling folk in the place with that mark on it.

"The tinker's name was Twintale Callum—he was a Kelledy on his mother's side, so perhaps he was kin to your fosterfolk, Cerin. He knew my old travelling companion Tomaj'n as well, though that had been before I took the road with him.

"So Twintale cut me down and nursed me back to health. I was sorely hurt, but I healed. I was driven by my need for vengeance—on Brinan, on his people, on whatever he held dear or laid claim to. I meant to take everything from him, as he'd taken all that had meaning from me.

"It was six months before I was strong enough to travel again and another half a year before I was fit enough to take my war to Brinan and his people. I haunted the forest near his manor for a month and stalked him every time he left his hall, until I finally caught him alone. He was hunting boar in the forest, and his men were scattered from here to Dalker, chasing the hounds.

"I leapt from my tree and unhorsed him, had my knife at his throat before he could lift a hand to defend himself. I let him look at me, and I told him who I was, for I meant for him to know why he died. I'd had the chance to shoot him from a distance a hundred times or better, but I wanted to see the fear in his eyes before I drove the dagger home."

He paused and looked from Calman to me.

"I had him helpless and at my mercy, but, looking at him and the pitiful figure he cut, I knew all of a sudden that to kill him would mean nothing. It wouldn't bring Suara back. It wouldn't return to life what I'd lost. It all meant nothing now. The rage ran from me, and all that remained was my sorrow. I stood and looked down at him, then walked away. Suara's memory was too dear to me for me to soil it with his death. But I wonder, you know. . . ."

He sighed deeply, the pain etched deeply in his features.

"I wonder," he said, and his voice was so low that I had to lean forward to hear him. "Did I do the right thing? Suara's still dead, and he still lives. . . ."

His voice trailed off, and silence hung around the campfire. Calman was the first to break it.

"Ye did right," he said.

I knew he was thinking of my mother and the lesson she'd taught him of the worth of hate. But that hate had stemmed from the wars between the gwandryas and the dwarfkin that lay centuries in the past. What'd happened to Galin was a far more immediate thing, and I wasn't sure that if I'd been in his place and that it was Tess or Meana that lay dead . . . I wouldn't have cut Brinan's throat.

"When we be done this quest," Calman added, "maybe Cerin will write ye a Harper's satire about this Lord Brinan. Give it a month or two to run about the Kingdoms, and he'll be too shamed to lift his head let alone be thinking of hurting folk."

I was about to say that I was not a Harper, so I couldn't write a satire, but then I saw the hopeful look in Galin's eyes and swallowed my words.

"Would you?" he asked.

I nodded. A well-written satire—one that could catch the fancy of both the common folk and the highborn—could destroy the life of its subject through derision alone. It was a powerful magic, slow to start, but long-lasting. Children know its worth instinctively—mark the words to their rhymes if you will—but in the hands of a trained Harper such a small, spiteful rhyme can take on giant proportions. And while I wasn't a Harper by way of title, I knew enough of how to put words together to write a decent satire.

"I'll begin tomorrow," I said, and wished that Damal were so easy to deal with.

Galin regarded me gratefully, and although the pain was still in his eyes, he began to discuss in a businesslike voice plans for what we'd do once we reached the Kingdoms.

"Barring Brennocksdale," he said, "I've made some good friends while travelling through the Kingdoms. It's my thought that once we're as far south as Tulla, we take the time to look one or two of them up and see what help they might give us."

"Be a good rede," Calman said. "We'll stick to your friends, Galin, and circle wide around this Ler Yrill the Wysling brat spoke of."

"I'll follow your lead as well, Galin," I said.

I wasn't quite as ready as Calman to belittle Robin's advice, but as I knew next to nothing concerning the Southern Kingdoms, I thought it wise to have Galin as our guide. Galin was with us; Robin was not.

We talked for a while longer. When the other two readied themselves for sleep, I sat up, my weariness gone for the moment. I fed wood to the fire as it needed it and watched the light snowfall sparkle in the glow thrown by our small campfire. The full brunt of the storm was still no more than a threatening promise. I prayed that it would hold off as long as possible, for I'd no desire to be snowbound in these lands— not with those I cared for being either in, or soon to be in, the clutches of our foes.

I thought on Galin's grim tale as I stared into the flames and toyed with the opening lines of the satire I'd promised him, but my thoughts drifted to our present troubles and the worries I had for the days to come. I added more wood to the fire until the leap and twist of its flames reminded me of the hearthfire in Wistlore and the faces I'd seen, the voices I'd heard . . . how much of it had been real? Was that what Tess's far-seeing was like?

So much had happened since my escape from Wistlore that I'd had little time to think about it. I leaned forward now, studying the flames, opening my mind in hope that the visions might return and that this time I could make more sense of them. The fire danced red and orange, and my face became hot. I thought I saw something and tried to reach out with the feyness that stirred inside me. I saw—

Damal!

I reeled back from the fire, clutching at my head. The thought tendrils that had scoured Drarkun Wood were back. I thought I saw the Dark Queen's eyes gathering the night to themselves. They became forbidding, all-seeing. Sibilant voices hissed in my ear. She told me what she'd do to the Grey Rose, to Hickathrift in his cell in Wistlore, to Galin and Calman. Her words were foul, obscene. They made me gag as she described in minute detail what was in store for all of us when, finally, she had us in her grasp.

Desperately, I raised what strengths I could muster to weave a shield, to cloak us from her awful gaze. The weight of that gaze bore down on me. The thought tendrils tore and shredded my defenses. I fought her while the whole night seemed to spin past, the stars wheeling in their dance, the darkness deepening, then lightening toward dawn.

Her laughter was mocking as I finally cast her out of my head. I shuddered when her evil presence was gone and picked myself up from the snow where I'd fallen. The fire'd burned down, but it was far from dawn. The stars were hidden behind a blanket of cloud that still dropped its snow in oversized flurries. I huddled close to the fire, not daring to look directly into it, and wondered if I'd fallen asleep and dreamed the whole thing.

But when I let the shield I was maintaining drop a touch I could feel her still—searching, unsatisfied. It was a long time before I composed my trembling limbs for sleep, and I worried that she might come again while I slept. I wove my defenses more tightly and vowed she wouldn't come this close to finding us again. She'd been in my mind, but I'd cast her forth without her learning our whereabouts. Of that I was sure.

So all I must do was maintain those defenses. While my companions led us forward on our quest, I'd hold off Damal's thought tendrils. I only prayed that I had the strength.

WHEN I AWAKENED THE NEXT MORNING THE SNOW HAD stopped, but the whole of the sky seemed to hold its breath as if waiting for just the right moment to loose the wild winds and storm it had threatened us with these past few days. Calman shook his head solemnly and hurried us through the breaking of our camp. As I was rolling up my blanket, I became aware of a sharp burning pain in my side, and my mind filled with a jumble of dark thoughts.

Damal! I thought, but this time it wasn't the Dark Queen. I opened my tunic and drew out the dagger that Merla'd given to me. It was this that felt like ice against my skin and caused the pain in my side. When I held it in my hand its maleficence reared up at me, too reminiscent of the evils that Damal had in store for us.

I tried wrapping it in cloth, but to no avail. At last I put it away in my journeypack where I couldn't physically feel it. From there it could only trouble my mind, but I was quickly relearning the skills I'd practiced in Drarkun Wood. I could sense Damal's thoughts as well, lapping on the borders of my consciousness, but my defenses held. Then I sensed something else, a warmth that was so familiar that it made my heart ache. My pulse began to drum as I recognized it for the Grey Rose's presence.

Somehow she'd become aware that I was seeking her. Her thoughts warned me of danger and begged me to turn back. Much as I longed to, I neither welcomed her nor gave any sign that I recognized her presence, for fear of putting Damal on her trail. Nor would I turn back.

My companions regarded me strangely, but when the immediacy of this fusillade of thoughts finally faded I went about my tasks without explanation. The matter was too complicated to begin unravelling for them now, and it was more

important that we begin the day's trek. There was time enough
for talk later, and I was weary from my struggles with Damal.
I thought it better to conserve my strengths for the physical
trials that lay ahead—and for the maintenance of my defenses
against Damal's return.

We set out, making the best time we could, but by mid-
morning the storm broke, surpassing all our fears. The wind
howled down on us from the north as if it was Damal's breath,
almost knocking us from our feet. Hard upon the wind rode
heavy snows and shards of ice that stung our cheeks with
terrible force. We wrapped strips of cloth about our faces.

Our snowshoes clogged with the wet snow, and we slipped
and scudded on the now dangerous terrain. We stopped a
moment, huddled together, while Calman brought a rope from
his pack. He put a loop through his own belt, then through
Galin's and mine.

"Be caves ahead!" he shouted above the roar of the storm.
"Shelter there, can we find them."

I was half blind from the driving snow and marvelled that
he could see anything. Taking the lead, he fought his way
forward, with the two of us in tow. Again and again Galin
and I were swept from our feet, brought up short only by the
length of rope that linked us with the others. Calman alone
was sure-footed, apparently less affected by the storm as he
trudged solidly before us.

Our snowshoes slipped where the footing was icy; in other
places not even they could keep us from sinking up to our
thighs in the deep drifts. I doubted if we went more than a
quarter league that hour.

I was exhausted already from my ordeal last night and this
morning and from the constant vigilance I had to maintain.
The storm beat at my body. The fierce winds and blinding
snow wore down my strengths. In my mind, Damal's thoughts
pummelled me—seeking, grasping. The energy I required to
face the storm was being channelled instead to forestall the
Dark Queen's search.

Move one foot forward, then another, I told myself, muttering the words like a litany. The wind bit through our

cloaks, and I was half frozen with the cold. I remembered
the snows on the West Downs. There, when it snowed, the
air became warmer. Here the storm's chill cut to the bone.
My teeth rattled, and my limbs shook from exhaustion.

At last I could go no further. Damal's search pounded at
my mind, and the storm stole the last of my strength. I fell
face forward in the snow and lay as one dead. I could feel
the rope at my belt as Galin tugged, trying to get me to my
feet, but it was no use. I was utterly spent and couldn't rise.
Calman fought his way to my side.

"Get up, get up!" he shouted, pulling at my arms.

I shook my head, rubbing my face in the snow. It wasn't
as cold as I'd imagined. In fact, a cozy warmth spread through
me, as if I lay on a bed of soft eiderdown where I could rest
until the ending of my days. . . .

"Be not far now!" Calman roared over the howling wind.
"Truil's beard! Will ye rise, Cerin, or freeze where ye lie?"

I couldn't move.

Between the two of them, they dragged me to my feet. I
protested feebly, demanding to be left in my comfortable bed.
Calman shook me roughly. He shouldered my harp, handing
Galin my pack, and they set off, half carrying me between
them.

I can remember little of the rest of that trek through the
storm. All I knew was snow and ice and cold, winds that
howled like dwarwolves, until, with snow-caked eyes, I made
out the bulk off a cliff rising in front of us. It reared out of
the blasting winds like an outlaw's hold in an old romance.

We moved onto the rock face to where a small opening
appeared, dark and welcome. No sooner were we inside than
the tumult of the storm became like a far-off thing, and Damal's thoughts abruptly ceased. I must have passed out then,
for when I woke I found myself lying in a dimly lit rock
chamber, heavy with smoke and warm as an oven. Galin was
fanning the smoke of a fire toward the cave's opening with a
folded blanket. When I sat up, he put the blanket aside and
came to me. All my nerve ends, especially those in my hands

and feet, felt as if they were on fire. I grimaced with the pain.

"Just a small touch of frostbite," Galin said. "You're lucky you got off as lightly as you did. Try some of this broth."

It was scalding hot and I could taste little of it, but as it went down I felt my strength returning.

"Where are we?" I asked.

"In the caves that Calman told us about," Galin replied, returning to his task of fanning the smoke. "Seems a recent rockfall cleared the opening to this one—or at least Calman doesn't remember it. He's gone deeper, exploring."

Speak of the Daketh, I thought as Calman appeared from the back of the cave. His step was light, and his eyes sparkled.

"Be here, be here!" he cried delightedly.

"What?" I asked.

"Deepdelve."

His whole face was alight as he spoke the word. Galin looked puzzled, but I understood Calman's excitement. Both he and Hickathrift had told me about the lost dwarfin halls.

"Years be long gone," Calman told Galin, "but once it was a great realm of my kin. Corman Glimmerhair was its lord. Lost it was in the elder wars when the Wormlords and their dragons stole it from the dwarfkin. The tale be that Truil made the mountains shift and buried it—if it be not a dwarfin realm, then it was to be no realm at all.

"All those years it be hidden from the eyes of man and dwarf. But now—Truil's beard! Whether it be a new turning unseen to me before, or the mountain itself shifted by Truil's hand once more, I have found the hidden door."

He plucked at my sleeve and beckoned to Galin.

"Many and secret were the entrances to Deepdelve, and many of the Kindreds sought them to no avail. Until today! Come, come. See the door, stone-made years gone. Come."

We rose to follow him, but he stopped abruptly. From the mouth of the cave we heard the howl of the storm as a dull moaning.

"Be a plan shaped between my ears," Calman said,

hunching down once more. "Beyond the cave be storm to end all storms. How long will it rage? Aye, and how hard be the journey through its snows? This be my rede:

"Outer doors of dwarfin halls be like will-o'-the-wisps—harder than star-silver to find. But once within, there be no struggle to find a way out again. Be warm in dwarfin halls, no matter how old. Be safe journey—safer than without. I ken the ways of stone." He tapped his chest with a thick finger. "In the mountain's breast I ken the safe ways and lead us true. Be doors under the Hills of the Dead—blind-hid from without, but easy to find from within. I say we fare dwarf ways. I will lead us safely."

Galin and I looked at one another. A warm hope stole through me. I'd eagerly fare the underground way rather than brave the storm outside. And, although I hadn't thought much on it, since we had entered the cave Damal's thoughts had ceased to plague me. Whether she was otherwise occupied, or if some magic in the mountains themselves meant we'd be freed from her menace for a time, I couldn't say. But if travelling by the dwarf ways meant we'd be free from her menace for a time, I'd take it.

From the look in Galin's eyes I saw that he was willing to brave Deepdelve as well.

"Lead on, then, Calman," I said, "and we'll follow you."

We returned for our packs and lit a twist of dried wood at the fire. With that flaming brand held aloft to light our way, we fared deeper into the cave. There were many rockfalls to clamber over, and the flickering light of our torch send shadows scurrying away in front of us. Then we came to a tumble of rock that blocked the entire tunnel.

The ceiling here was a good twenty feet from the floor. Calman pointed out a small hole near the roof which appeared just large enough for us to squeeze through. Without waiting for comment, he took the lead and was soon through it, lost to our sight.

"Be ye coming?" His voice echoed strangely through the small hole.

Galin and I made haste to follow him. Once the Dalesman

was through, I passed the torch to him. My harp and pack followed. I stood there for a moment with the only light coming from the small opening in front of me. As I squeezed through, I wondered at Calman's ease in essaying it, what with his broad shoulders and bulk.

On the other side the floor was a jumble of boulders and broken rock. We gingerly picked our way through them, the way leading downward all the while. At length we came to a blank wall, and the tunnel ended. Holding the torch closer, I made out squat runes cut deep into the rock, spelling an inscription, I imagined.

"This be the Dwarfhall of Deepdelve," Calman read, "the High Seat of the Lord of the Perilous Mountains and all the lands beneath."

"Here's something," Galin murmured. He traced a seam with his fingers.

Calman nodded. "Be craftsfolk in those days, clever with stone or metal."

The seam was the outline of a huge door, at least three yards across and twice that in height, but I saw neither handle nor keyhole.

"How will we open it?" I asked.

Calman looked from Galin to me, grinning hugely. He stepped forward and traced a spiral design with his finger, mumbling under his breath as he did so. At first nothing happened. Calman cocked his head and tugged at his beard while he regarded the door quizzically. Then he struck it once with his fist, and a dull rumbling filled the air. Slowly, the ponderous slab swung open. The grinding of stone echoed about us until the door stood ajar, revealing a dimly lit chamber.

"What did you do?" I asked curiously.

"How do ye play a harp?" he replied. "Be dwarf-spell that the youngest of my kin ken. Ha!"

He stepped ahead of us, chuckling to himself.

THERE WAS NO NEED FOR OUR TORCH ONCE WE PASSED THE great stone door. As Calman closed it with another dwarf-spell, Galin and I gazed about. We were in a broad tunnel with high ceilings from which misty globes hung that filled the tunnel with a dim light. It was brighter here than in a forest at twilight, but not much more so. I tried to get a closer look at the globes to see what they were exactly.

"Dwarf-magic be slow building," Calman said, following my gaze, "aye, but it be slow fading as well. Once these halls were as brightly lit as a meadow at noon by yon dalin. Now. . . . Were a small magic in those days—forgotten now. But be bright enow to light our way."

"A magic you can relearn now," Galin said, "once you've studied these."

"Aye."

"With such powers at the dwarves' command," I asked as we set off down the tunnel, "how did Deepdelve come to be deserted?"

The dalin might've been a small magic to the dwarves of old, but I imagined having a light like that in Tess's cot. No need for candles and straining our eyes while we wove our baskets or she mixed her herb simples. And when I thought of their secret doors and the enchanted weaponry that dwarves were famous for, I wondered how any enemy could best them in a war. A thief, like the one who stole the Truil-stone, I could understand. That needed only a cunning trickster—as much a fool as a brave man. But while one sly thief might steal in, how was an army to duplicate that feat?

"Were foul treachery, say the old tales," Calman said. "When first came the Wormlords, they be welcomed without fear. Gifts they brought and acted the part of kindly folk, but hid deep in them be a yearning for the dwarf riches garnered from the deeps below. One night they rose from the guest hall and fell upon Corman's folk, bringing ruin and death to many. Be a fierce battle till they be cast forth.

"But though the battle be won, that day were the death-knell of Glimmerhair's kingdom. Defenses be broken. Spells long in the casting be sundered that night.

"Came the elder wars, and the Wormlords brought the armies of the Daketh in by the secret entrances. Fierce battle there be again. The yargs and other fell creatures of the Dak-eth army be defeated, but Glimmerhair be slain. Dwarfkin be scattered. Many fled to older homes, westward and north. Came men then, to steal what remained. Then Truil brought down the mountain, and the secret entrances be lost and Deepdelve gone from the world.

"We be the first to tread these halls in many lifetimes. Be fine song ye can fashion, Cerin, of our coming here. Aye, and when our journey be done and all be set right, return here I will with others of my kin and build Deepdelve anew. . . ."

His voice trailed off. I could almost see his thoughts as he imagined how it would be, what he would do, and I was glad for him. After all the years of sorrow caused by my mother's curse, his fortunes appeared to be changing for the better. From his talk it was clear that he'd dreamed of finding and rebuilding these halls for many years. I'd never heard him speak at such length before, and, except for the night when I'd played the Grey Rose's gift of Telynros to lift my mother's curse from him, I'd never seen him so filled with joy.

But while I was happy for him, my own worries in no way lessened. I was still on guard against Damal's thoughts, and neither Hickathrift nor Meana was ever far from my thoughts. I had other, more personal disappointments to deal with as well.

Wistlore—all my life it had been a magical name, conjuring up images of learning, beauty, and folk that were wise, gentle, and kind. But now my dream of studying to be a Harper there was shattered, and the name was like a curse on my lips. Beyond the immediacy of my quest, I had no idea now of what I'd do with my life. . . . should I even be so lucky to survive long enough to do anything with it.

We entered a wide chamber then. Calman called for a halt, and I put my musings from me.

"This be the true entrance to Deepdelve," he said. "Here we will rest ere we go on. On the morrow, we will walk the deep stone-ways in truth."

We dropped our packs, and I set my harp against a wall.

While Galin and I rested, Calman strode back and forth across the chamber, unable to contain his excitement. Sometimes he'd stand as still as the stone walls themselves, his eyes glazed and unseeing, unless he saw something within himself. Then he'd start up his pacing once more, murmuring to himself.

"Bran's son Golnman, aye, and Bran himself—unless he be too old. Too old? Truil's beard! He be ten year-turnings younger than Hamon, and Hamon would come. Cormor and Taln—that be two more. Feldor. . . ."

He counted the names on his fingers, and I knew he was tallying how many of his kin would join him in the rebuilding of Deepdelve. When he came to sit with us at last—that contented smile still broadening his face—we made a meal of cheese curds and bannocks. For a while we talked idly of things that wouldn't bring our quest to mind. When the conversation fell, I stepped to where my harp lay and took it from its bag.

In the dim light of the dalin, the rough edges smoothed by the play of shadows, it looked a finer instrument than I'd remembered. The stone rose reminded me of Meana, and I tuned the instrument gladly, my fingers itching to play once more. My companions smiled when I had it in tune, urging me to begin.

I began with a simple air, a little uncertainly as it had been a while since I'd played, and the harp itself was unfamiliar to me. Soon I braved a more complex piece and, relaxing, played on until I wearied. I laid the instrument aside with a contented sigh and sat back.

"It'll be many years since a harp was played in these halls," Galin remarked. "I'm happy to have heard you play at last, Cerin. You have the touch."

"Aye," Calman said. "Be a sweet sound." He grinned, adding: "Aided, no doubt, by our own labours on it. Now I mind not the trouble of its making for the comfort it be filling me with this eve."

* * *

THE NEXT MORNING—IF MORNING IT COULD BE CALLED IN A place where the sun never shone and perpetual twilight ruled—we arose early and were soon on our way. The tunnel widened as we travelled down its slope, opening at length into a huge chamber that the whole of Wistlore could've fit into with little difficulty. Although it had been plundered of its riches long ago, the walls were still covered with unbelievably lifelike carvings. Statues rose out of the half-light— startling us considerably the first time—and furnishings of stone, metal, and even wood abounded. The dry air of Deepdelve had kept the wood from rotting, and, from that day onward, we had cheery fires most nights.

Looking at the statues and wall-carvings, I marvelled at their craftsmanship. They were similar to the ones I'd seen adorning Wistlore but more lifelike, if that was possible. Sometimes I was hard put to convince myself that they wouldn't step forward and speak at any moment.

"And who do ye think crafted Wistlore?" Calman said when I made the comparison aloud. "Truil's beard! Were dwarves built those walls and set the living stone in order. The muryan carved the gate stonework, but all the rest were crafted by my kin."

Throughout the chamber, small streams ran under delicately carved bridges, and emptied into fountains and pools adorned with reliefs and small statues. Dwarf-crafting was indeed long lasting, for although those basins were centuries old, I couldn't find a crack or a leaking seam in any of them.

That evening we took our rest in a small antechamber. We washed down our meal with crystal-clear water from the underground streams. I made music again that night and sang the opening stanza of Galin's satire for him. The grim smile on his lips told me that it was shaping up well. Afterward, Calman sang dwarf lays in his deep resonating voice, and Galin drew on a great store of tale and song from his travels— all of which I accompanied on our harp. I say our harp for, although I played it, they'd aided in its crafting. The more I played the instrument, the closer it drew us together.

As the days passed in the underground kingdom, I was

untroubled by either dreams or sendings. I'd heard no more from the Grey Rose and hadn't needed to use the mind-shield I used to keep Damal at bay once since we'd entered Deep-delve. I hoped that it was the dwarfin kingdom that kept the Dark Queen's presence away. Sometimes I worried that she must have captured Meana—why else was she unconcerned with us?—but I put those thoughts from me as swiftly as they arose.

The dagger in my pack was still like ice to the touch. I checked it often, but there was never any change except that the evil clinging to it seemed to grow more pronounced each time I inspected it. At last I hid it away at the bottom of my pack and looked at it no more.

One day we came into an enormous chamber that, unlike others similar in size, was undecorated except for two bas-reliefs on one wall. Opposite them, tiers of seats rose, enough to have seated at least three hundred dwarves, I judged, while under the bas-reliefs, there was a great stone throne, un-carved, with three other stone chairs set before it. The bas-reliefs drew our gazes, however.

They were cut into the likenesses of two men clothed in robes, and painted—the colour was still as crisp and bright as the day it'd been daubed on. They were red-haired and thin-featured; one wore robes of yellow, the other, rust, green, and grey.

"Who were they?" Galin asked.

"In Maelholme, where by my birthing," Calman replied, "there be the same figures cut into the walls of our judgment chamber—for so be this, I wager. They be likenesses of the Tuathan. In yellow be Jaalmar, he of Quiet Walking. The other be Truil, Stone-father."

Calman's words registered with a shock, for I'd recognized the pair as well. They had the same look as the folk from my dreams in the Hills of the Dead and bore a striking resem-blance to the Grey Rose. My memory scurried back, how-ever, recalling Hickathrift's words.

(The lore books give the Tuathan another seeming, and

*those records were written by folk who trod the same earth
as they did in those elder days. . . .)*

"That can't be so," Galin said. "I've seen their images in
the temples of the Kingdoms and listened often enough to the
druids of my own Dales describe them. This isn't their seeming."

"Be indeed so," Calman argued.

I shook my head, trying to puzzle this out. In the West
Downs, the Tuathan were not described, though we lit the
May fires for Willoney each spring and left tied corn-figures
for Mother Arn at harvest time. Tess spoke only of Ballan
but never described him. And Hickathrift, a Loremaster,
spoke of them as Galin did now.

"Tyrr is ever depicted with hair dark as a stormy wave,"
Galin was saying. "Truil like a dwarf, Freya and Weaywd,
gold as the dawn and winged. The others. . . . No. This isn't
their seeming."

Calman shot him a withering look.

"Aye," he said. "And ye be so familiar with them that ye
can say so with an assurance that will not falter?"

"But the druids, the temples . . . the old tales. . . ." Galin
said.

"They be man-tales," Calman replied, "Dwarfkin and the
High Erls—we be the elder races, walking these lands before
the coming of man, before trees moved or beasts spoke. In
Wistlore they speak as ye do. But be only Wyslings there
now—Wyslings and the younger cousins of the High Erlkin.
My folk knew the Tuathan, carved their likenesses. *This* be
their seeming. Fare ye into the Amberwood, Galin, and ask
the High Erls there, can ye even find them. Ask them of the
Tuathan. The High Erls and dwarfkin—we ken!"

Galin made no reply, while I looked at the bas-reliefs once
more. Tuathan or not, these *were* the folk of my dreams. I
shivered to look on them. There was mystery in their painted
eyes, wildness coupled with an elder knowledge. They were
crafted from lifeless stone, but it seemed that they breathed.

Take care, youth, came a woman's voice to my mind, *for*

the shadow of the Daketh is upon thee, and the Red Hounds run.

I started and looked to my companions, but they stood silently regarding the bas-reliefs and gave no sign that they'd heard anything.

Ye must not warn him, a man's voice gently reprimanded. *It is hard. . . .*

The woman's voice faded in the middle of what she'd begun to say and I heard no more.

We stood for a long time in that old judgment hall, deep beneath the weight of the Perilous Mountains. I didn't know what my companions were thinking, but my own mind was bent to the riddle of the voices I'd heard. I strained both my inner and outer ears to hear more. The fey spark in me prickled, but silence was my only reward.

Whose voices had they been? Meana's kin, I was sure— the Tuathan. What Calman had said supported that. But why would they speak to me? What did these Old Ones want with me?

We left the hall at last and travelled in a silence that lasted for the whole of the two leagues we fared before we stopped for the day. That night, after we'd eaten, I left the harp in its bag and went early to my blankets. Neither Galin nor Calman intruded on my thoughts as I lay there pondering.

(The Red Hounds run . . . the Red Hounds run. . . .)

The phrase kept repeating in my mind. A tremor of fear coursed through me until my arms and legs began to tremble. The feyness in me stirred uncomfortably. Why should those simple words worry me so?

At last I sat up.

"What are the Red Hounds?" I asked my companions.

Galin shrugged, but Calman's eyes narrowed.

"Why do ye ask?" he said.

I told them of what I'd heard, or imagined I'd heard, in the judgment room.

"Except for that phrase," I finished, "I'd think it all fancy. But the words trouble me. Why should they? I've never heard tell of these Red Hounds before."

"I have," Calman said slowly. "Once, though it were a long time ago. There be a tale among my folk that I heard told one long winter's night. From a storyteller the tale came, of how the Red Hounds of the Daketh once hunted a daughter of the Tuathan hill and under hill be the way she fled, but they caught her at last and slew her under a horned moon.

"It be said that so was the beginning of the elder wars, though the Loremasters in Wistlore have it another way."

Calman shifted, suddenly uncomfortable, but I was only half aware of him. With what he'd told me, my fears took on an ugly substance. His old tale was too close to the truth of what happened now. Damal sought the Grey Rose. The warnings of the Red Hounds, then, meant that the Dark Queen had loosed them on Meana.

"Be long since I thought of them," Calman added. "Be many years since that tale haunted me with evil dreams."

There was little more said then. I lay back on my blanket, worry for the Grey Rose foremost in my mind, until much later I fell into a troubled sleep. I remember glancing at Calman, just before I rolled over, to see him sitting staring into the fire with an unreadable expression on his face. The next morning he was in the same position, although the fire had long since burned into ash.

During the next few days of our journey, both Calman and I were withdrawn into our own thoughts. I sorrowed that I'd burdened Calman with old fears and tried at times to lift us all from the gloom, but to no avail. My own worries were too fierce for good humour. I feared we were too late, despite all the time we'd saved travelling through Deepdelve.

Galin caught our mood, and it was a sombre company we made as we fared through the dimly lit halls. At night my harp was still. There was no music, and little conversation as well.

"Be one sleep here," Calman said as we camped one night, "then we be faring up again to the Hills of the Dead."

I marvelled at his sense of direction—all underground as we were. Had I been alone, I was sure I'd have been lost long ago. My heart lifted at his mention of the Hills of the

Dead, for it'd have been there that the Tuathan had first come into my dreams. I hoped they'd come again, for I had questions for them now.

At length I took out the harp. Calman and Galin regarded me curiously, for it had been at least four days since I'd played it. Tonight, with our journey's end close upon us, I felt the need to play. A dozen tunes milled about in my mind, and my fingers touched the strings idly until a tune of my own came to hand. It was *The Fane of the Grey Rose*—first begun in the Golden Wood, completed outside Banlore, it seemed to hold the whole of my life in its cadences.

I closed my eyes and sang. Then I let the tune drift into an air that I'd heard Calman sing before. He took up the thread of the music and wove a dwarfish tale into it, his eyes twinkling like they had before the mention of the Red Hounds put a shadow in them. Galin sang a cheery ballad after that, and the bond that held us together grew firm once more. For the moment our troubles were set aside.

Much later, when the singing was done, I walked off by myself. I longed for the clean light of day once more, even if it meant braving winter in the Hills of the Dead. This endless twilight was wearing on my nerves. I tried not to think of the long search that lay ahead of us. The Grey Rose could be anywhere in the Southern Kingdoms, and they made up a vast area of land.

Instead, I looked forward to standing under the open sky once more, with the stars above us—for we'd be issuing forth in the late evening, Calman had said—and, by my reckoning, the Storm Moon would be in its first quarter. We'd be free of the stone halls, but what of Hickathrift, still imprisoned in Wistlore? And Meana, hunted by the Hounds of the Daketh?

I walked along, frustrated and lost in thought, and stumbled over something. I cursed the poor lighting once more as I looked down. At first I thought a man had tripped me, and took a hasty step back. Then, peering closer, I saw that although it'd once been a man, it was now nothing more than a skeleton clothed in rotted garments. I'd tripped over a large sack that lay by the bones of its hand. More than likely, I thought, this was one of the thieves Calman had spoken so disparagingly of, and the sack—why, it'd be the dead thief's booty.

I knelt by the skeleton. When I touched the sack, the cloth fell apart in my hands. Gold and silver sparkled in the dalin's dim light. Small carvings lay amidst coins, bracelets, and two large torcs. From under the precious jumble, the end of what appeared to be a small hunting horn jutted, a silver chain wrapped three times about it.

I returned to my companions with my newfound treasure in my hands. Calman pored over the torcs.

"Be not Glimmerhair's," he pronounced bemusedly.

He held one of them up to the light, peering at the small runes that were carved along the torc's rim. Shrugging, he laid it aside to look at the other.

"This is curious," Galin remarked, hefting the hunting horn. "What sort of a beast do you suppose it came from?"

I shook my head, and Calman grunted noncommittally. Tossing it up and down in his hand, Galin considered for a moment, then placed it against his lips and blew softly into it. A sweet sound issued forth and echoed against the roof and down the halls.

"It has a pretty tone. . . ." Galin began.

A muted cracking noise overhead cut his words short. We looked up, aghast. Seams were appearing in the ceiling. A few small stones fell on us.

"Put it away," Calman whispered. "Yon 'pretty tone' be weakening our roof. We must away."

As Galin slipped the horn into his belt, Calman shovelled the treasure into his own pack. Gathering the rest of our belongings, we fled up the tunnel that was to lead us to our exit. We'd gone no farther than twenty yards when, with a crack like a great peal of thunder, the whole roof of the chamber we'd just quit collapsed. Dodging shards of flying rock and choking on the sudden dust, we flew up the tunnel, expecting the whole mountain to come down on our heads.

When the noise had subsided, we paused to look back. The way behind was blocked, as surely as if there'd never been a passageway there. We could only go on now. Without bothering to discuss it, we silently agreed to forgo our rest for the night and trudge onward.

"I didn't know. . . ." Galin began, apologetically.

"Be none of us did," Calman said. "We be safe now—that matters, though there be more work now, when I return. What's done be done . . . no more of it."

We paced on, keeping to our own thoughts. My heart grew steadily cheered as the tunnel sloped ever more steeply upward. But after three hours of hard walking, we turned a bend to come up against another rockfall. This was an old one, not caused by our doing, but it blocked the tunnel effectively from roof to floor. There was no way of telling how thick it might be, either.

"There be little choice," Calman said. "Tunnel be blocked at both ends, and we be trapped like caged moles." He pointed to the mass of rock in front of us. "There be our road, so there we be digging. Hey?"

He had the right of it, and we fell to, throwing ourselves into the labour, casting boulders so that they rolled down the tunnel with a great noise and clatter. An answering rumble from somewhere above soon put an end to that. Then we had to carry the boulders down cautiously, moving with as much silence as we could muster. The tunnel itself was apparently none too sound.

We worked for a day and a night on that blockage, Calman directing us so that the obstruction didn't fall upon us as we were moving it. We despaired toward the end that we'd never clear a way through. We were soiled and grimy, our hands blistered—except for Calman's—our back's aching, our muscles weary, when Galin pulled a stone free and cried out:

"I'm through!"

We scrambled up to where he stood, working away until we'd cleared an opening large enough for us to crawl through. A half hour later, we stood on the other side, looking back on the great jumble of stone with sighs of relief.

A few more hours of rough walking finally brought us to the end of Deepdelve. There was another rockfall to clear away after we passed through the stone door on this end, but it took us no more than an hour's work. We crawled out into a cave and walked to its entrance to look out at last on the starlit rills and gullies of the Hills of the Dead.

We stood there, drawing the crisp night air deeply into our lungs, success burning in our hearts. When we explored a short distance from the mouth of the cave, we discovered that the snowfall on this side of the mountains had been light. We decided to make our camp in the cave and fare on in the morning.

As we turned to go back inside, I suddenly staggered under a mind-assault that came as swiftly as an adder's strike, with the force of an axe-blow behind it. Damal! I'd forgotten her.

I writhed in her grip, trying to build a shield against her thought tendrils as they snaked into my mind. Hideous laughter resounded hollowly through my mind and images blasted my senses. I saw Hickathrift mutilated by her minions, the Grey Rose nailed to a tree while leprous creatures capered about her, bloodied spears in their misshapen paws. I could smell their reek, the stench of blood. . . .

Steadily, I shook the horrors from me, locking my shield into place until all that remained was the fading echo of the Dark Queen's laughter. I felt Calman and Galin supporting me, their hands firm on my arms, while my body shook and trembled from what I'd undergone. I should have been prepared, I cursed myself. How could I have forgotten her?

My companions led me back into the mouth of the cave. By the time we were inside, I'd recovered sufficiently to move on my own.

"She knows," I replied to the unspoken question in their eyes. "The Dark Queen knows we are here. Now the struggle begins in earnest."

"Be sleep we'll be needing," Calman said. "Your limbs be weary—as be we all. We must rest. Garner strength."

I nodded, but I wasn't sure if I could sleep—not with the memories of those horrific images still clear in my mind.

THE RED HOUNDS

This I dreamed:
the empty eyes
in death's cowl
were my eyes;
the hand of spite
that plucks the heart
was my hand;
the boughs of a yew,
re-berried and green,
were my limbs,
for I was the tomb
to every hope.

—from the SONGWEAVER'S JOURNEYBOOK

MY SLEEP BROUGHT DREAMS. ALTHOUGH I HAD MY SHIELD up to protect my mind from Damal's assaults, it did nothing to stop me from dreaming. No sooner were my eyes closed than I found myself standing in a ruined land, a charred, miserable landscape that made me want to weep with despair.

Wherever I looked, I saw only bare rock, melted sand, and slag heaps, shimmering hellishly in the light of a dead sun that hung, dim and pallid, high above. My horror grew at so much desolation. The empty wasteland ran to the horizons on every side. Then, from behind me, the clopping of horses' hooves upon the barren ground broke the deathly stillness.

I turned to see five riders top a rise. In the vague light of the dead sun I could make out only a little of their features. They were faceless in that light, mounted on huge things unlike any horse I'd ever seen. Their legs were too long, their heads flat with jaws like hill cats'. Both riders and mounts were dark crimson. Long, curling horns sprouted from all their brows, and the eyes of the riders were pits of blackness set high in their shadowed faces.

The foremost rider lifted his horned head and howled at the sky. He pointed his lance at me, and the five of them thundered down the hill. I thought my heart would stop. With terror speeding my flight, I took to my heels and ran.

I seemed to run forever. They paced me, never gaining, but never falling back. My boots were soon worn through on the rough terrain. My feet tore and bled on the sharp stones. My breath came in raspy heaves, and sharp pains stitched my sides. And still they pursued me, herded me forward until an utter darkness reared before me.

I hesitated at its border. The thunder of the horned mounts boomed hollowly in my ears. Looking back, I saw the crimson riders approaching and put a name to them. These were the Red Hounds of the Daketh. When they were almost upon me, I plunged forward.

The dark embraced me, smothering me so that I could hardly breathe. I edged forward, afraid to take a step in that blind darkness, but more afraid of Damal's Hounds behind me. I could hear them move ever closer. The sound of their mounts' breathing neared; the hollow click of their hooves on the stone grew loud. Madness danced and capered on the borders of my mind. I didn't know where to turn, for the sounds came from every side.

Abruptly, blood-red flames erupted around me. I saw that I stood on the brink of an abyss that I doubted had a bottom. I swayed at the edge, unable to tear my gaze from the emptiness that fell away below.

I could feel myself leaning too close, and the abyss reached up to pull me down. Then something teased my consciousness, forcing me back from the brink. I lifted my gaze only to see the Grey Rose on the far side of the abyss, trapped in a similar circle of flames. She stood bravely in their midst, holding aloft a spear that appeared to be more shadow than any substance I could name. Two of the Red Hounds were circling her, lances lowered as they tried to thrust through the flames. She parried their blows with her spear, but I could tell she was wearying. How long had she been trapped there?

Again the sound of hooves arose from behind me, echoing on the dead ground. I turned to face my own pursuers. The horned heads lifted like skeletal tree boughs in the weird light, and the mounts' breath smoked from their nostrils. I tottered on the brink of the abyss as they lowered their lances.

"Away!" I cried, shaking my fists at them.

The lead rider laughed—he had Damal's laugh—and led the charge. The lance grew huge in my sight. I tried to dodge, arms pinwheeling for balance, then the weapon plunged into my breast. The pain tore a scream from me that seemed to echo infinitely. The rider lifted his lance, and I rose into the air with it, impaled like a boar on a spear. My chest was on fire, my eyes glazing—

Suddenly I lay awake, shivering in my blankets, my scream still ringing in my ears.

"What?" Galin cried, rising from his own blankets beside me.

His gaze went to me, then beyond, his eyes widening. With a speed that defied possibility, his bow was in his hand, then he had it strung, and an arrow sped from it to hum over my head. I twisted in my blankets to see shadowy shapes gathered in the mouth of the cave, stealthily entering. One dropped as Galin's shaft took it square in the chest. The others, seeing that they were discovered, gave vent to hideous cries and gibbering and charged forward.

I had scarcely time to gather my wits about me before I was grappling for my life with one of the creatures. I could hear Calman's battle-roar and the whistling of Galin's shafts above the cacophony of sound as I bent all my own efforts to besting the thing I fought. Its dank breath was foul on my face as I tried to force it back. Its iron thews held me like a vise, and I despaired of breaking its hold until opportunity gave me a small opening and I managed to throw the creature back.

I leapt to my feet before it could rise and lunged at it,

landing with a jarring shock on its chest. Under my boots I felt its ribs give way. Bile rose in my throat at the sickening sound, and I turned from the creature to find the battle done.

Across the snow fields in front of the cave the last of the creatures were retreating. Calman leaned on his axe, breathing deeply, still half asleep despite the battle. Galin brushed a lock of hair away from his brow.

"It was lucky you gave the warning when you did, Cerin," Galin said, "and luckier still that there were so few of the things."

I had opened my mouth to reply when a blast of raw power drove me to my knees. Damal's thoughts snaked into my mind, intertwining with my own. My eyes were open, but I couldn't see either the cave or my comrades . . . only a dark cowled figure that spoke to me, the words rumbling like thunder in my ears, although the voice the being used was no more than a whisper. I could see nothing of the shadowed features inside the cowl, but I knew Damal's voice.

Now I have you, witling, she hissed.

I held my hands over my ears, stunned at the volume of her mindspeaking.

Would you like to see your precious Rose?

Within the cowl a scene unfolded. I saw the Grey Rose fleeing across a hellish landscape that was all too familiar. She stumbled and wove to and fro from weariness, her features drawn and strained, a black spear held in a knuckle-whitening grip in one hand. A gasp of dismay escaped me when I saw the two crimson riders pursuing her.

The web draws to its close, Damal said.

I stared, yearning to be at Meana's side, numbed that even the cave could no longer protect me from Damal's assaults, railing at my helplessness.

My Hounds almost have her.

I watched Meana's flight across the slagged rock, the dead sun lending an unhealthy pallor to her skin. The Hounds followed at an easy pace, their horns gleaming in the eerie light, the nostrils of their mounts spewing thin streams of smoke that dissolved in the still air.

All that is lacking now, Damal said, *is the presence of her precious Songweaver. . . .*

For a moment, I thought that Meana turned and looked directly at me. I reached a hand to her, but Damal's harsh laughter pealed through my mind. The scene faded, and all I could see was the cowled figure and her shadowed face, the features hidden. Then that image, too, faded, and I was looking into the concerned features of my comrades.

"Cerin!" Galin was crying. "Cerin! What's the matter with you?"

I shook his hand from me and stumbled to my feet. I walked slowly to the mouth of the cave, stepping over the bodies of the dead creatures we'd fought moments before. Dispassionately, I looked closer at one of them.

It had the appearance of a human spider; that is to say, that while it had only four limbs, those limbs were thin, wiry, and jointed like an insect's, issuing from bloated spider-like bodies. Head and torso joined without a neck, and the eyes, now gaping wide in death, were huge—bulbous like a wasp's or a fly's.

I looked away. Reaching the entrance of the cave, I studied the land outside. An emptiness had settled within me. Somewhere the Grey Rose was being pursued by Damal's Hounds in truth, as we'd both been in my dream. The feyness that was my heritage from my father's blood lay silent inside me. Of what use was that magical potential if it was never at my call when it was needed? And Meana . . . how could I hope to find her in time?

Dawn was breaking, grey and dim as worn granite. I searched the landscape, and then I saw them. On a far hill they sat their weird mounts, dark red specks against the dull hills—the Red Hounds of Damal, of the Daketh. They remained where they were, still as the land itself, not approaching, only waiting . . . waiting. . . .

Suppressing a shudder, I returned to my companions and told them of my dream. I spoke of Damal's mind-search and assaults, of the Grey Rose's plight, and of how we'd been found by the Red Hounds. Calman started when I mentioned them and an unreadable look flitted across his features.

"What do you know of them?" I asked. "What are you hiding from us?"

I could no longer respect his silence. We had to know what it was we faced, and if Calman knew anything at all that could help us, he must tell.

"It be not that," Calman said.

I regarded him steadily, waiting for him to continue.

"There be a truth-sayer—a far-seer in Maelholme—who augured my future. Be little for her to find in my life, for all be overshadowed by yon Red Hounds. There be death when I meet them, she said, and would say no more."

He was visibly uncomfortable at having said so much, and I knew a sudden urge of pity. Ballan knew how many fears I had myself, and here was Calman ashamed of having the one. Too late I realized that I should have left well enough alone. If Calman had had information on the Red Hounds, he'd have told. I should've known better.

Our gazes met, and the dwarf smiled suddenly, as if he knew all my thoughts. He understood what drove me. I was grasping at straws; I'd take anything that would help the Grey Rose.

"Be not sad, Cerin," he said. "Though today be the day I face the Red Hounds, the wondering at least be done. Truil's beard! I've half longed for this day, just so it be done."

"These creatures," Galin said, changing the subject, "are they the Dark Queen's sendings as well?" He touched one of the dead beasts with the toe of his boot.

"No," Calman replied. "They be but hill-gaunts—carrion creatures that slaver for a taste of fresh meat. Be no one rules them. They run like dogs. Thoughts be of food—naught else."

I remember Hickathrift telling me of them.

"So I thought," I said. "Can either of you recall a land like the one in my dream? For if these Hounds are real, then so is that land, and it's there we'll find the Grey Rose."

"Only the Great Waste comes to mind," Galin said, "but even it's not so desolate."

"Be naught but a land of madness from what ye say," Calman said with a shrug.

His fear seemed to have washed from him, and he was the gruff dwarf of old once more. Only now I wore his fear, for if he fell to the Red Hounds, it'd be by my doing. I was the one who'd drawn him into this quarrel.

"Be not fit for life," Calman continued. "I ken naught like it."

"Maybe it's the realm of the Daketh themselves," Galin added.

"Perhaps," I said.

A grim purpose stirred in me then. I was done with hiding and skulking, with fear and the weakness fear brought. When next Damal touched my mind with her thought tendrils, I'd take the battle to her. And if her Red Hounds wanted us—I touched Finan's tinkerblade at my belt—let them be prepared for a bloody struggle.

Shouldering our gear, we set out from the cave. We fared across the Hills of the Dead, bearing southeast, keeping to a steady pace and pausing only once in midafternoon for a small bite to eat from our diminishing stores. To either side, the grim riders kept pace with us. I wondered why they didn't simply ride in and attack us immediately. Then I remembered Damal's words.

(The web draws to its close . . . all that is lacking now is the presence of her precious Songweaver. . . .)

I could visualize her in Wistlore, closeted with Caradoc, eagerly awaiting what she alone knew would befall next. By that reasoning, the Red Hounds were waiting for her word to attack us. But why was my presence required?

A small pack of hill-gaunts followed in our wake. They were waiting for something as well. The fall of night? If not that, perhaps they sensed the coming battle and were following to feed on the remains of the fallen.

"These riders," Galin said sometime after our midafternoon

stop, "are herding us. Whenever I fare more southward, those to our right edge in."

Since we were approaching the Southern Kingdoms, Galin had taken over the leadership of our company.

"I hesitate to lead us against them," he continued, "for their strength is more than ours. But if this keeps up, we'll be in the Great Waste before long."

I'd been watching the riders as well and agreed with him. We were being driven just as I'd been in my dream. Perhaps the Waste *was* the landscape of my dream. I'd not seen more than a glimpse of it, and, while that glimpse had shown me nothing like the desolation of my dreamscape, it was more likely that Meana was fleeing through the Waste than through the realm of the Daketh, wherever that might be.

"I think we should let them herd us," I said.

Galin nodded. "Perhaps they'll lead us to your Grey Rose. Then we'll have to trust in our wits and strengths to see us through."

As if they sensed our decision, the riders pulled away from the hills and rode toward us. Bow and axe came into my companions' hands. I reached for my tinkerblade, then remembered the dagger that Merla had given me so long ago in Wistlore. I was supposed to use it against Damal, but if these were Damal's sending, it might have some power against them.

I took it from the bottom of my pack and held it in my hand. Even through the sheath, I could feel its burning cold searing at my skin. I grimaced, but clutched it harder, dully recalling Merla's warning. It could only be used once and was meant for Damal's heart. No matter, I thought; my need was *now*. Against Damal's Hounds. The dagger's magics would do little good held fast in the hand of a corpse.

The riders thundered toward us, circling as they neared. They brandished their lances, and their horned mounts cut the ground with their hooves so that the sod flew. A strange keening arose in the air, growing louder and shriller as the riders spurred their mounts to greater speeds. Everything in my gaze shimmered and blurred. I went blind for a moment and heard Galin cry out in astonishment; then I fell dizzily to a rock surface.

Braying winds rushed about me; moanings pounded and wailed in my ears until an abrupt deadly silence fell. I opened my eyes fearfully—or was it that my sight returned?—and looked upon the desolate landscape of my dream.

An oath escaped Calman's lips, and he grasped his axe's hilt more firmly. I wondered what good it would do him here. The Red Hounds of the Daketh circled us still, at length coming to a halt and surrounding us like the points of a pentagram. One with a black skull burnished into his red armour stepped his mount forward, lowering his lance as he neared me.

The dream was vivid in my mind. I could see the lance plunge into my breast again, ending all hope, ending my life without having aided the Grey Rose. I lurched back, but not quickly enough. The tip of his lance brushed against me with the lightest of touches. A sheet of icy torment rushed through my body.

I staggered. Galin fired a shaft at the rider, but he turned his shield and the arrow bounced off the metal with a clang. The pain spun through me, tearing and rending, until it met the chill in my hand where I clutched the Dark Queen's dagger.

As the two pains met, a dark ice stole over my soul. Control of my body slipped away from me so that I was no longer myself. I became a vessel awaiting another's filling. That other was Damal. When she came, it was with a lapping of dark tendrils of thought that I already knew too well. They slithered into my mind and took firm hold of my body. Again I saw the cowled figure in my mind's eye, but this time I could see inside the cowl. I saw Tamara's face, and her gaze burned into mine. And hideously superimposed over her features was the hellish visage of Damal as she truly was.

Her skin was white, and stretched thin over the bone of her skull. The eyes were black, the brow high, the lips thin. Thick black hair fell to either side of her face, and blue veins throbbed at her temples.

Then she was inside me.

I fought her presence to no avail. Every strength I raised to push her from me she dismissed with power that burned with its potency. The feyness that was my father's gift to me stirred, but she hammered it down.

It is useless, witling, she said. *I'll grant you have a fey strength or two that surprised me at first, but how could you hope to stand up to me? I am of the Daketh, and their dark power is mine. As you fled from Wistlore I was always with you. I could have taken you at any time. My only setback was when that fool Caradoc set the dwarwolves upon you. But lo! Before I had to intervene and give away my hidden control, the raewin came to your aid. They are powerful creatures. . . . I will have to deal with them in time.*

Leave me! I cried.

But why? The stage is now set. Would you not see your Grey Rose one last time?

I didn't know what she had planned, but I fought her with renewed fury. My lips smiled with her smile.

I thought at first that you would lead me to her, Damal said, *but the Grey Rose has delivered herself into my realm. So now I have another use for you, precious Songweaver.*

Laughter pealed through the reaches of my mind as she set my body into motion. I turned to see the Grey Rose in front of me, exactly as she'd been in my dream except that we were both on the same side of the abyss. A circle of fire held her prisoner, and two of the Red Hounds threatened her with their lances. In her hand was a black spear that I recognized as a sister to the sword of the Hill Lord I'd once wielded. It was a caryaln weapon—the shadow-death.

A glad look came into Meana's eyes, for all that we were both trapped in Damal's domain. She spoke to me, but I couldn't hear the words. Then her look of gladness changed to one of horror as I moved forward, the dagger uplifted in my hand.

I strained to check the motion of my limbs, but Damal never loosened her control. Terrified, I understood what the end to my quest was to be, what my aid to Damal was. I was to kill the Grey Rose.

I curse you, Damal! I cried to the mind that held me prisoner.

The Dark Queen's laughter rang out through my lips.

Strike for me, precious Songweaver, she hissed. *Pluck for me a Grey Rose.*

I stepped closer, fighting the momentum of my body to no avail. From the corner of my eye, I spied Calman reaching out to stop me. Soundlessly, I thanked him. Brave Calman, I thought. He'd stop the dagger's thrust.

But the hand that held the dagger—my hand!—whipped about to strike him full on the brow with the hilt of the weapon. He fell, his forehead gashed, blood dripping into his eyes. Then I couldn't see him any longer, for Damal moved me closer to the Grey Rose, step by step. I wept for Calman. The Red Hounds *had* meant his death. But Damal controlled even my tears, and my eyes stayed dry.

My gaze rested on the Grey Rose, and I could see her terror. She knew. In my eyes she could see the two souls— Damal's and my own. I recalled that time in Yarac's tower, when I'd struck down the Waster who'd stolen the semblance of her flesh, and knew she was remembering as well. Now I'd kill her in truth.

Wave upon wave of horror filled me and gave me new strength. We fought for the control of my body, and for a moment I was stronger than Damal. I attempted to throw the dagger from me. It stuck to my fingers, and I succeeded only in throwing myself to the ground.

Damal had me standing erect immediately, stepping toward the flames. I flinched as they lapped my skin, but there was no heat. They were cold when I moved through them, searing cold, like the dagger in my hand, like the blast from the Red Hound's lance.

I couldn't give in!

The Grey Rose lifted her caryaln weapon and threatened me. Damal moved me another step closer. Then I was through the flames, upon the Grey Rose, the dagger ready for the strike.

Kill me! I pleaded to Meana.

The spear trembled in her hands. Then she lowered the weapon, and her lips shaped the words:

I cannot. . . .

Fiendish laughter tore through my skull as the dagger came down to strike between her breasts. I closed my mind to the dreadful sight and fought with all my strength in one last futile attempt to win free of Damal's control—

A clear, sweet sound rang through the air, trembling and frantic in its urgency. The dark hold on my mind loosened its grip for an instant, and I used that moment to twist aside, burrowing the evil dagger up to its hilt in solid stone. The jar of the blow numbed my arm. My mind reeled under the terrible impact of Damal's return.

Again the sweet sound shook the air. In front of me, Meana seemed to gather strength from some hidden reservoir. She traced a rune in the air that shimmered and held, shining so brightly that I thought my eyes would char from its glare. Damal's mind withdrew a touch from mine, and the gentle essence of the Grey Rose slipped inside me. She took what remained of my own strength and sent a blast of raw power at the other presence inside my body, inside my mind, and withered it under the sudden onslaught.

For a long moment I hovered on the brink of true insanity. I reeled as the two—Dark Queen and Bright—fought inside me. Then both presences were gone, and my body was mine again. Exhausted, I collapsed to the ground. The Grey Rose's rune dissolved, as did the flames about us, and utter darkness plunged over us. I felt Meana take me in her arms. We were spinning. Winds roared and howled, and the ground shifted under me as we whirled away. . . .

I opened my eyes to look upon the dusk falling over the Hills of the Dead. I lay in Meana's arms, my head against her shoulder, her face pressed against mine. By us lay the shadow-spear. I sat up slowly and saw Calman lying as if he was dead. I remembered the terrible blow I'd dealt him, and grief washed over me. Beside the dwarf was Galin, the small horn I'd found in Deepdelve set to his lips, his body frozen in the act of blowing it. His eyes were wide and stared sightlessly into mine without recognition. As I rose to step up to him, his body stiffened and crumpled to the ground.

The Red Hounds surrounded us. Through tear-filled eyes I saw their lances shatter in their hands, their mounts fade away from under them. Strange moanings filled the air as wisps of dark red mist escaped their armour. The armour fell to the ground before it, too, dissolved. The mists spiralled upward and were dispelled in the wind. A deathly silence fell over the hills.

CALMAN LIVED, BUT GALIN . . . THOUGH WE COULD SEE NO deathwound or even a mark on him, he was dead. Meana bent over him, her eyes closed, her face close to his, and remained so for a long time. At last she rose with a sigh, prying the horn from his stiff fingers.

"Damal," she said, "the Dark Queen . . . she dealt him his death-blow as she fled. His soul was caked with darkness and ice. All . . . all I could do was set it free. . . . "

I stared at his features, my eyes blurred with tears. I hoped that he was with Suara again, homesteading in whatever realm lay beyond life.

"I'll finish your satire," I whispered, "and I'll make you a song so that you'll never . . . be forgotten. . . ."

I stood with my head bowed for a long time, remembering the small things that had endeared him to me. Meana laid a hand on my arm after a while.

"This horn," she asked softly, "where did he get it?"

Briefly I told her of how I had found it in Deepdelve and how, when Galin blew into it, the roof had collapsed.

"I could see that happening," she said. "This is a horn of power, the like of which I've not seen for many years. How your comrade knew to use it, I fear we'll never learn. We can only be thankful that he did."

As she spoke, the horn crumbled in her hand, its pieces falling feather-like to the ground where they became dust.

"It will be used no more," she murmured.

We turned our attention to Calman, washing his wound and binding it with a strip of cloth torn from Meana's shift. She was tying a knot to keep it in place when he opened his eyes. They went round with wonder.

"Be this death?" he whispered. "There be fair company here, then."

"No, good dwarf," the Grey Rose said. "You live still. The thickness of your skull saved you."

Silence lay heavy on the hills as night hedged us in. Although the Dark Queen's presence was no longer in my mind and the Red Hounds were gone, the hill-gaunts that had attacked us earlier had taken up vantage spots around our camp. They crouched beyond bow shot range, waiting for the courage to attack us again.

I built a fire and brought Calman closer to it. Galin's body I brought closer in as well and covered with a blanket. The Grey Rose walked out a ways to set guard-spells against the hill-gaunts. When she joined us at the fire, she looked pale, her features drawn with weariness. The rose in her hair was wilted, and the edges of the petals were drying out.

"I am spent," she said simply. "My strength has fled me, I fear. Even such a simple magic as a warding-spell has exhausted me."

She glanced about as I readied some food over the fire, her gaze settling on the bag that held my harp. Her face lit up when she saw it.

"I had a dream," she said, "that the harp I gave you was lost, its strings broken, yet here I see it is still with us. This is a good thing. It renews my hope, for its power is great."

I looked up from the fire.

"Not so," I said sorrowfully. "Telynros is indeed lost— stolen and hanging in the rooms of Caradoc, the Masterharper of Wistlore. He broke the strings when he tried to play it. The one you see here is one that Calman . . ." I swallowed, sorrow welling up in me again. "One that Calman, Galin, and I made when the dwarwolves attacked us."

She looked puzzled, so over our simple meal, I told her of

all that had happened to me since we'd parted. Calman added a comment here and there when I went astray, but for the most part he sat silently, letting me tell it as I remembered. He was brooding, I knew, over Galin's death and how he'd misread the auguries told over him in his youth. Death *had* come when he'd met the Red Hounds—but it hadn't been his own.

I shared the guilt he felt at drawing Galin into this struggle. I knew his grief. But it lay heavier on him, for Galin had been a dear friend of his, whereas I hadn't known him for as long.

When I was done with the tale, Meana undid the bindings of the harp's bag and looked upon the instrument with a smile.

"This is a fair instrument," she said, "crafted as much from love as from need. The workmanship is rough, perhaps, but the hearts of its makers shine in the wood. It is a fit instrument for the best of Harpers, crafted by those whose skill is more than the simple work of the hand."

Calman, who was already somewhat in awe of her, reddened visibly at her words, the flush creeping steadily up from his collar. He mumbled something and shifted uncomfortably. I often had that feeling in Meana's presence, but I wasn't sure if it was lessened tonight because I'd seen so many marvels now or that her glamour had diminished with the waning of her magical strengths. The lessening of my awe changed nothing of my love for her. In fact, the simple companionability that lay between us now made me love her all the more.

"And what of you?" I asked.

"Ah, Cerin, it has been a time of trial and sorrow. I have been fleeing the minions of the Dark Queen from the time we parted in Banlore until this night. They have harried me ruthlessly—but let me begin at the beginning. You know that my father was the Hill Lord Wendweir and of Yarac's unkept bargain?"

She looked more to Calman than me. He nodded, for I'd related the tale to him months ago.

"Then my story begins in the Waster's tower in Banlore," she said. "When I knew of Damal's arrival in these mortal realms, I knew as well that it was in part my doing. There is a Covenant between those of the Tuathan—my people—and the Daketh. It stemmed from the wars of the elder days when both races walked these lands. We can die here in the mortal realm . . . and many did. So a pact was drawn up that neither Tuathan nor Daketh would walk Mid-wold again, lest those days return. But should one of either race come to walk here once more, a member of the opposing race is freed from the Covenant as well. In this way, the Balance is maintained.

"I was raised in the realm of the Tuathan, although my father was more mortal than fey. When the Wasters warred against the Hill Lords, many folk of both the elder races were present in Mid-wold. The once-born blood in my father called to me, so that I walked these lands once more. When I struck my bargain with Yarac, the remaining Tuathan and Daketh withdrew to their own realms, leaving Yarac and me alone in this world.

"In Banlore I learned that he'd recently summoned Damal from the darkness of the Daketh's realm; her power allowed him to capture me. But in so doing, he broke the Covenant. With his death the balance was restored, except that now Mid-wold is faced with the threat of Damal's power. Those of the Dark do not keep to the Covenant as truly as do my people. Once they have a foothold in a world, only a great power can shake them loose. I could withdraw, you see, but she would still remain, spreading her evil until one of the Tuathan rids the world of her.

"You have seen for yourselves how quickly her influence spreads. The blight of her presence already overshadows Wistlore. In time, it will spread over the land, fouling and tainting all that it contacts. Caradoc was never more than a grasping man. Now he has turned wholly evil—imprisoning Hickathrift, setting the dwarwolves upon you. The old shadows in Drarkun Wood stir, turning Wistlore into an armed camp and forcing the erlkin to arm and prepare for war. If this continues, the wars of the elder days will return, laying this world to waste. For when the old races make war, little survives, be it mortal or fey.

"When I left you outside Banlore, I returned to the realm of my people. I put my case before my mother Willoney."

I stared at her. I knew she was of the Tuathan, I *believed* it, but hearing it again from her own lips. . . .

"We light the May Fires for her on the West Downs," I said.

"And she watches you do so," the Grey Rose said with a smile.

My awe returned in a rush. My blood ran hot and cold in my veins, and I stared at her as if I expected her to sprout horns or wings or the lower torso of a raewin.

"Cerin," Meana said and laid her hand on my arm. "Do not look at me so. We are friends, no matter what blood runs in our veins."

"B-but . . ." I stammered.

"Think of the Tuathan as you do of the erls. We are an elder folk, that is all. The Kindreds named us gods. We did not take that title for ourselves at first, although I fear over the years we have let it slip from our tongues more than once. We are responsible for the worlds, for their well-being and for the Balance, but we did not create them."

"But Truil was our Stone-father," Calman protested uncertainly.

"He fathered the first dwarf," Meana said, "but he did not make the mountains themselves."

"Then . . . who. . . . ?" I asked.

Her shoulders lifted and fell helplessly.

"The answer to that riddle is the greatest of the Great Mysteries," she said. "My father's people, the Hillfolk, believed that the world was created by the Moon-mother and her consort, the Wild Lord."

"What do you believe?" I asked. "If your people were the first. . . ."

Again she shrugged. "There were beings that walked the worlds before ever the Tuathan and Daketh were born. I believe there is a power like the taw of the Wysling, a hidden silence like music that shaped the world.''

For a long time we said nothing. I looked to where Galin's body lay and thought that he alone of us would know what the living could only guess. At length, the Grey Rose continued her tale.

''I pleaded with my mother, but although she sympathized with me, she would not help me.

"This is thy own trial, child, she said. *The reason for your birthing—though when first I bore thee, I knew this not. This much I can tell thee: seek the strengths of thy father's people. They will cast thy foe back into her own realm. They could even slay her.*

''When she spoke, I knew what strengths she meant—none other than the shadow-weapons, the caryaln. They are what Damal fears. Not a simple exile into her own realm, but rather an ending to her very existence.

''I departed from the realms of the Tuathan and went to the barrows in the Trembling Lands where Yarac had told me the last of the caryaln was hidden. Do you remember? He mocked me with the knowledge, thinking it would do me no good. But despite all the barrows I searched, I met with no success. The weapon had been there once, but the barrows were empty and whatever treasures they had once held had been stolen long ago.

''It was there that the Red Hounds first caught my scent, as I strode from the Hill of Halgwer, the greatest of the Hill Lords—my hands empty, my mind bemused. Almost they had me, but I spied them first and fled before they could close in.

''For two months they dogged my trail, harrying me throughout the land. At length I came to the Southern Kingdoms. Passing through the hall of Lord Kassen in Twerlen, far to the south, I found what I sought. The shadow-spear lay in a shrine, revered by the folk as a relic of the old gods. I slipped into the shrine with the Hounds fast on my heel, grasped the spear, and made good my escape.

''Once I had the caryaln in my hand the hunt became yet

more earnest—or so it seemed to me. Damal realized that I now had the means of slaying her, and she threw her Hounds upon me with renewed force. All the roads to Wistlore were blocked by her magics—at least the freywen were, the spirit paths. There are only a few of those secret roads that I have the strength and knowledge to fare upon, and they would have sufficed, had there not been watchers and guards upon them all.

"So I tried faring by mortal roads, slow though they be. But there I was at the mercy of the Hounds, who were mounted. Back and forth I scurried, from freywen to mortal roads, the guards blocking me on the one, the Hounds harrying me on the other until I despaired.

"I took a desperate gamble then and fled into Dalker—the realm of the Daketh—where all is chaos and ruin. I hoped to travel swiftly and undiscovered and then quit that foul realm near Wistlore. Alas, no sooner was I in Dalker than two of the Hounds were upon me. I still had some strength, and I fought them, but they ringed me with soul-fire before I could make my escape.

"We were at an impasse then. I had the caryaln, so the Hounds could not draw too close to me, but they had me imprisoned. It was then that you and your companions arrived. My guess is that at first Damal meant to have you lead her to me, but when I snared myself in her realm she found another use for you, one well suited to her twisted mind."

"She said as much," I said, "before she forced me to attack you."

Meana laid her hand on my arm and squeezed it reassuringly.

"It was never your fault," she said, reading the guilt in my eyes. "I know you would never harm me."

I nodded uncomfortably, the memory still too real.

"What puzzles me," I said, "is that the Tuathan came to me in my dreams . . . and that I heard them in Deepdelve. They warned me then of the Hounds. If they had no intention of helping us. . . ."

"That was my mother, I think," the Grey Rose said. "She,

too, has seen the magics in you, Cerin. The blood of our fathers ties us together, and for the sake of that bond she gave you her warning."

"I have no magics," I said.

Her eyebrows lifted. "What of your mindspeaking, and the shield you raised against Damal's searching thoughts?"

"She was only toying with me. I can't manage even the simplest of harp spells."

"Ye lifted your mother's curse from me," Calman said.

"But what of the dwarwolves?" I replied. "It was the rose-harp that freed you of the curse, not I."

"Not so," Meana said. "Telynros merely focuses the strengths you already possess. Given time, you will be able to work harpspells on any instrument. That is something you must learn."

I nodded, and we fell silent again, following the paths of our own thoughts. I wondered how much of what she said she truly meant and how much was merely said to comfort me. I knew something stirred in me—my father's weren blood—but what use was its potential if it could never be realized?

"And now?" I asked, breaking the silence in the end.

"And now," she said, "we must fare to Wistlore."

"The way is beset with dangers," I said, "and we're ill prepared to face them."

I glanced from Galin's still form to where Calman was nursing his wound.

"I be strong enough to travel," he retorted when he caught my eye.

He stood shakily. Taking his axe from where it lay beside him, he walked to the Grey Rose and laid it at her feet.

"My axe I lay down in your service, O Child of the Tua-than."

Meana rose gracefully and bowed low to him.

"Your service is gratefully accepted, Calman Stonestream, Lord of Deepdelve."

Her words had a formal ring to them, and Calman lifted his head proudly to look up into her face.

"That I be," he said, "though my newfound realm lies in ruin. For now I can but give ye the weight of my axe arm, the strength of my heart."

"I thank you," the Grey Rose said. Her eyelashes were damp and sparkling in the firelight. "I only pray that I do not lead you to your death."

"How will we go to Wistlore?" I asked. "What road can we take?"

"I know not," she said, shaking her head. "The land stirs with evil as the creatures of the Dark rise to block our way."

"What of these . . . spirit paths you spoke of?"

"The freywen?"

"Couldn't we brave them, dealing with the guards as we meet them?"

I thought the idea forlorn but felt I might as well ask it.

"That would be a hard task," she replied, "one beyond our strengths. And it would warn Damal of our arrival. We must be stealthy and sly, catching her unawares, or she will raise such terrible defenses that we could never penetrate them. At the moment we are far from her, and she can relax until we draw near her or she has gained sufficient followers to send them out after us once more. But even now her strength far exceeds our own. Our route seems impassable, yet if we could creep into Wistlore and catch her unprepared in her own stronghold . . . we would have a glimmer of a chance."

"But how?" I voiced the impossible question.

Meana had no answer.

"I have not the strength at this time to take even myself by the freywen—even if they were not guarded—let alone all three of us. And all three will be needed once we have penetrated Wistlore. It seems hopeless. . . ." Her gaze strayed to the harp that lay near the fire. "Unless. . . ."

"Unless what?"

"There is another way," she said. "The harp could bring us."

I shook my head. "There's no magic in me for such a spell, no matter what you say. Just as there's no magic in that harp, except for the magic that calls forth a simple tune from lifeless strings.''

''You belittle yourself, Cerin, but in part you are right. There is no magic in this harp—but Telynros has magics. It is the roseharp that will bring us to Wistlore.''

''It's impossible!'' I said. ''How can we use Telynros when it hangs in the very heart of the enemy's stronghold?''

''This is the way,'' she said. Her eyes shone with a renewed hope that I did not feel. ''The roseharp, with its broken strings, has known your touch. It is sympathetic to you. If you can play this one,'' she nodded to the harp that we'd built in Calman's cabin, ''while you picture the other in your mind, it may be possible for you to build a bond between the two instruments that has enough power to take us to where Telynros hangs in Wistlore. See,'' she continued, seeing my blank look, ''do you but picture Telynros in your mind, cause it to sound, picture its surroundings, and then picture us there.''

''I've never been to Caradoc's chambers,'' I protested. ''And the roseharp's strings are broken—how could they sound?''

''Telynros is more than a physical construction, Cerin. For Caradoc the strings are broken—but for you. . . .''

I shook my head. ''This is beyond any knowledge or power that I might possess.''

But I remembered that I *had* seen the harp in Caradoc's chambers in a vision. Had it been a true-seeing?

''Cerin, Cerin,'' she beseeched. ''This is the only way. Can you not feel Damal clawing at us even now? Will you not even try?''

I looked from her to Calman, despair tying my stomach into knots. I longed to do as she asked, but I knew in advance that the venture was doomed to failure. Yet . . . I could at least try, couldn't I? For her sake and ours I could at least make the effort.

''I will try,'' I said.

I rose and took the harp onto my lap to tune it. The simple task seemed to take forever, and I knew that I was only buying time, trying to put off the moment of failure that loomed like a great terror in my heart. I remembered my failure in Calman's cot. This would be three times worse, for now I was in the presence of my beloved Grey Rose.

At last I could delay no longer. I was merely tuning strings that were already on key, fretting over the pegs aimlessly. I must try. I plucked a string, and the sound rang dully in the night air, echoing my own feelings of inadequacy.

The Grey Rose came to sit at my back. Her fingers massaged me, loosening the tight muscles in the nape of my neck as she whispered encouragement in my ear. Her hope only made the approaching failure all the more bitter for me. I'd felt useless before, a mere player in the schemes of other folk, and had longed to take my own destiny in hand, to set my own mark on my life. I had feared that my maid of the Grey Rose would have no more need of my help. But now she did—the moment was here. And I was too afraid, knowing I was out of my depth, knowing that my failure affected more that just myself.

At my back, her soft form pressed against me. It was distracting to be so close to her, but I savoured the feeling, knowing that when my impending failure was fact, there'd never be a moment like this again.

Not so.

I wasn't sure if it was her voice I heard in my mind, as if she was answering my fears, or if it was no more than the desire of my own heart speaking.

I took a deep breath and shook it all from me—the doubts and fears and thoughts of myself. I drew a strong melody from the harp, and the notes escaped the instrument, drifting off to lose themselves in the night air. My breathing was loud in my ears, as were the thumping of my pulse and the crackle of the fire in front of me. I stared at the harp in my hands, the play of the light on its wood and strings, the quicksilver motion of my fingers. Closing my eyes, I tried to picture Telynros. All I saw was darkness—a dark that seemed to spell the ever-growing power of the Dark Queen.

I strained to see the roseharp, but my mind remained as

blank as new parchment. Where was this magic that the Grey
Rose said was in me? Where now the stir of my father's blood
when it was so sorely needed?

I knew I had skill on my instrument, but I was self-taught
and so lacked some subtle essence—the harpmagics that the
Masterharpers were capable of. Was it something that could
only be learned in Wistlore under the guidance of the Harpers? Something that escaped any who didn't take their pren-
ticeship there?

My fingers played on, without my concentrating on what
tune they played, until I realized that I was playing an air as
unfamiliar to me as the harpmagic I sought was beyond my
grasp. The never-lessening darkness wore on my nerves,
draining me. I opened my eyes, but there was nothing before
them. Open or shut, I saw only darkness. Meana and Calman, the campfire in the hills, everything was gone, and I
floated in some place that held only darkness.

Then I heard the voices.

Aid him, brother. He has the need.

*This is not our struggle, sister. He must find the strength
within himself.*

But my child. . . .

Hazily, as if through gauze, I could see the speakers. Their
voices were the same as those I'd heard briefly in the judgment room in Deepdelve, and I recognized them immediately
as the tall, red-haired folk that I'd come to know as the Tuathan. Had I tapped into their realm once more?

*We cannot aid her. Would ye have the Daketh manifest
themselves as well? Would ye have the whole of this world
destroyed in our warring?*

Damal walks that world.

Aye, sister, but your own child . . . was she not there first?

But the youth. If he fails. . . .

Aye, if he fails, she will be no more. . . .

My heart shook at those words. All was darkness again.
The voices had stilled, but I could still hear that last phrase
ringing in my ears. It grew in intensity.

If he fails, she will be no more. . . .

The Grey Rose would be no more. By my failure, Meana would perish. The strength was in me, the man's voice had said. He seemed so sure. . . .

If he fails, she will be no more. . . .

How had the roseharp looked, when last I saw it? The judgment room in Wistlore swam into my sight. I remembered Caradoc fingering the roseharp's strings and saw the gleaming lengths snap, one by one, a terrible note of doom in each sundering.

If he fails, she will be no more. . . .

Telynros. The supports, just so. The carvings . . . a curlicue there, the ribbonwork along that side . . . here a face, there a fox's shape, his tail curling about a sleeping hare . . . and the grey rose, set in the head where the soundbox met the upper support. . . . The harp shimmered in my sight, complete for an instant, then slipped away.

If he fails, she will be no more. . . .

The strength was in me—I had to believe it. I had my father's weren blood. My mother had been a Harper. I was no longer the same boy who'd walked moonstruck over the West Downs. Had I learned nothing for all I'd gone through so far?

Again I forced the harp into view. It was clearer now, steadier, and came more readily. I began to picture which of its strings were broken, how each broken string curled. A room hovered, held fast, in my mind's eye, only to fade as the darkness fell once more.

If he fails, she will be no more. . . .

Whether they'd intended to or not, the Tuathan were aiding me. Unplanned it might have been—though I had an inkling now that it had been planned. Willoney was the Grey Rose's mother. She wanted her daughter to be safe. I was sure it was her doing that I'd overheard her conversation with the man who appeared to be a High Lord of the Tuathan. But, planned or not, that phrase, its awful truth, screamed in my mind, driving me to my limit.

I wouldn't fail, I told myself over and over again. I couldn't. I *had* the strength. Again I built the roseharp up in my mind, recognizing Damal's hand in the difficulty I had in summoning the image up. Her defenses were tightly woven about Wistlore. I worked slowly now to build up the picture of the harp, faring delicately, conscious always that I mustn't raise the alarm.

Again Telynros was in front of me, misty and glimmering. I forced my mind to encompass more of the harp's surroundings in the image. Like a great weight lifting from me, the tableau grew vivid in my mind, and I was looking on the roseharp as it hung in Caradoc's chambers.

One part of my mind concentrated on the harp that I played in the Hills of the Dead, while the other held the image of that room firm. A window I saw there, hung with rich crimson drapes or the same material as the covering on the bed. On the bed! There was Caradoc himself, startled and gazing about himself as if he suddenly sensed my presence.

Fare softly now, I told myself.

The tune I played gathered in volume, sharpened in intensity. When I looked to where Telynros hung, I saw the broken strings curling together, straightening, the severed ends reaching for each other. With bated breath I watched. The tune grew stronger still. Caradoc was staring at the harp on his wall, his eyes bulging with wonder. He rose from the bed and stepped close to it, a hand uplifted.

At that moment the strings came together, the broken ends merging with a gentle ringing that echoed harmoniously with the tune I played. Before the echoes had time to fade, the harp in Caradoc's chamber began to play as well.

Note for note, it was the same tune, as if my fingers plucked the strings of both harps simultaneously. Caradoc stepped back from the roseharp, gazing about his room. He must not give an alarm, I thought, and frantically pictured him frozen in place. His movements slowed until he stood stock still, like a statue. Now I worried that Damal would sense my intrusion.

How close to the Harperhall were Tamara's chambers? Surely the harp was sounding through the whole of Wistlore

as loudly as it roared in my own head? Was Damal, clothed
in Tamara's flesh, already raising the alarm?

As the two harps continued to play, I stole out of Caradoc's
chambers, drifting ghost-like through the walls, down the
corridor. I reached a junction with another hallway and saw
two erl maids conversing quietly. They gave no sign that they
noticed anything amiss, so I sped back to Caradoc's chambers. Inside the room the roseharp still played, and Caradoc
himself was still immobile, frozen where he stood. I gathered
the last of my strengths then.

I pictured the campfire in the Hills of the Dead. Slowly,
my vigour waning, I took it all in my mind: Galin's dead
body, Calman frowning with his axe in hand, the Grey Rose
behind me, holding me, her eyes closed in intense concentration. It was strange to see myself from outside my body.
We were a sight, soiled and dirty like a pack of bedraggled
beggars. My gaze drifted to the harp that my body played,
and I gasped. The strings were broken, exactly as the roseharp's strings had been. Cracks and seams ran up and down
the soundbox and supports, crisscrossing the wood. I knew
that if I didn't make my move quickly, it would be too late.

I gathered them all in my mind—even Galin, for though
he was dead, I wouldn't leave his corpse to the hill-gaunts
that lay in wait just beyond the Grey Rose's guard-spell.
Gathering them, I pictured us all in Caradoc's chambers. My
strength was quickly ebbing now. I forced myself to concentrate, using the harping as a focus, but nothing happened.

It was one thing to picture what was or what might be, I
realized, and quite another to change the reality of it. Cursing, I strove again.

If he fails, she will be no more. . . .

The Grey Rose would be no more, and all hope would be
lost. The words twisted like daggers through my heart. I cried
out as everything started to spin and whirl. It had to be now.
The tune I played seemed to fill the whole of the world.
Nothing existed except for it and the image I filled my mind
with: *we were in the room where the roseharp played.* Telynros drew us to the chamber. We were there—now!

Darkness hit me like a living thing, the music thundering through its blind reaches. Then shafts of myriad-hued lights tore at my mind. We were spinning, spinning—

And we were there.

For a moment the scene held like a freshly-crafted painting. Then I fell forward, dragging Meana with me. The wreck of my harp pushed against my chest. The music had stilled. Lifting my gaze, I saw Caradoc freed from its spell. He was in motion, eyes narrowed.

"You!" he cried.

He leapt for a sheathed sword that hung on the wall near his bed. At my side, Calman's arm lifted, and his axe flew through the air to imbed in the Masterharper's chest. He flew back under the impact of the blow and struck the wall. As he slid down to the floor, he plucked at the weapon, his blood staining his fingers. Then he crumpled. I turned from the ghastly scene, my stomach churning.

"It is done," Meana whispered in my ear. "O bless you, Cerin, you did it."

We rose from the tangle of our limbs. Before we had a moment to plan our next move, a knock came at the door. We exchanged fearful looks as the handle of the door turned. Then, from somewhere deep inside the keep, came the tolling of a bell.

THE DARK ROSE

> The interplay
> of Light and Dark
> can be as fierce as battle,
> as common as branch shadows
> in the bright sunlight,
> or as mysterious
> as the choices that
> confront each one of us.
> A lack of wisdom
> is as much the enemy
> as any foe.

—from the SONGWEAVER'S JOURNEYBOOK

I FROZE, HOLDING ONTO THE GREY ROSE'S ARM. WE WERE discovered. The thought burned in my mind as I looked for some hiding place. My gaze rested on Caradoc's corpse, his blood staining the pale blue rugs a deep crimson. No use in hiding—not with the Harpmaster so obviously slain and Galin's corpse lying in plain view as well.

Calman retrieved his axe, cleaning it on Caradoc's mantle, and came to stand in front of us as the door opened. Up went his strong right arm. The door creaked open to reveal Robin Marrow on its threshold. An erl stood behind him in the corridor.

His gaze raked us. Taking in the threat of Calman's axe, he gestured, fingers bent in crooked shapes, and the weapon burst into flame. Calman threw it to the ground, nursing his fingers. I saw the axe land on the floor, where it lay untouched by flames. An illusion, I thought, and edged my hand to the tinkerblade at my belt. Calman moved forward, the threat now in his bare hands. I could imagine the glare in his eyes.

Robin looked beseechingly at us.

"Stay your hands," the Grey Rose said quietly, and the dwarf stopped his advance.

Robin entered the room with the erl on his heels. He closed the door, then stood shaking his head at us.

"This is beyond belief," he said. "How did you get in here? And Caradoc. . . ."

Calman stood to one side, his fists clenched at his sides. I was more uncertain now, for I read no threat in the young Wysling's eyes, but I still wanted the tinkerblade bared in my hand. From outside the chambers, the deep tolling of the bell sounded again.

"You must be the maid of the Grey Rose," Robin continued. He inclined his head to her. "I welcome you to Wistlore, m'Lady, though I fear no other might. Save one, that is. . . ."

He made another gesture with his hand, this time directed at the erl who'd entered with him. The erl's form shimmered, and he changed, becoming—

"Hickathrift!" I cried, stepping forward.

Forgotten was any thought of a threat as hope rose in my heart once more.

None other, Cerin, he replied. *You are well met.* He nodded a greeting to the Grey Rose. *I looked to meet with you again . . . the more so in the months I languished in this keep. Our hope lies in your strengths.*

He was thin, I saw, having lost a great deal of weight since the last time I'd seen him. But the courage remained in his eyes, and there was still strength in them. He greeted Calman warmly, his gaze taking in the corpses of Galin and Caradoc. He didn't know Galin, but the Masterharper. . . .

So the slaying has begun, he said. *I pity Caradoc. He was so skilled, yet so misguided. . . .*

"Were a foe he was," Calman said brusquely. "What do ye in his chambers?"

I realized then that Hickathrift had lost some of Calman's trust by appearing in Robin's company. At the same time, the dwarf's question was well put. I wanted an answer as well.

"We came to question Caradoc," Robin replied. "There are a great many riddles that need answering—riddles we thought Caradoc could've unraveled for us with a little persuasion." There was a hard look in the Wysling's eyes. "In the cellars where Hickathrift was imprisoned, we found today the body of—"

The bell tolled yet again and broke into his speech. Robin started openly. The atmosphere of the keep had become overhung with a deeper pall of oppression and despair since last I was here. I could feel Damal's presence like a shadow that lay over everything. The bell added to the weight of our fears, tolling like a funeral dirge, as if ushering in the beginning of the Dark Queen's reign.

"I'd forgotten," Robin said. "The council meets. The bell calls the Masters to the judgment chambers." He looked to us. "Listen to me. You must trust me. There is a way to end this now, if you'll follow me. You have the caryaln," he glanced at the spear in Meana's hand, "so we need only a bit more time. Caradoc is expected in the judgment room. If he doesn't appear, they will come searching and find that." He nodded at the Masterharper's corpse. "And so find us as well. Cerin, will you take on his guise and appear at the council while we ready ourselves for our last effort?"

"I?"

I glanced about. How could I take Caradoc's place? I looked nothing like him. The Grey Rose touched my arm reassuringly.

"I'll throw an illusion over you," Robin said, "so that you'll appear to be him. Once inside, I'll have you play your harp . . . subtly. Some gentle spell to set them at their ease that they won't suspect what we're up to."

I hesitated, looking to Meana for advice. She nodded, so I agreed, though not willingly. This was not a part I thought I'd play well.

Be certain to disguise his scent as well, Hickathrift reminded. *The brecaln Kentigern has keener nostrils than those of erls or men.*

"I like it not," Calman muttered.

I liked it even less, but already Robin's hands were in motion, his crooked fingers shaping queer designs in the air between us. I felt a tingle run through me. I looked in the mirror by Caradoc's bed and took a step back at what I saw. The Masterharper lived again.

"Take your own harp," Robin said.

I nodded numbly and took Telynros from the wall, seeing that its seeming had been changed as well. It looked a twin to the instrument that lay by the door—Caradoc's harp. The bell tolled once more. Robin hurried me to the door, explaining what turns I was to take to reach the judgment chamber. I stepped over the threshold, fear stalking me for what I was about to do.

I looked back and saw Calman's scowl and Hickathrift nodding encouragingly to me.

"Luck go with you, Cerin," Meana said.

I turned, hearing Robin's businesslike voice follow me as I left.

"We must make haste," he said. "First we'll. . . ."

I lost the rest of it as I turned a corner and walked alone in the halls of Wistlore, faring for the judgment chamber.

My fear grew so much that by the time I reached its doors— after two false turns—I was certain that the thumping of my heart and the trembling of my limbs would give me away, even if Robin's spell held. The guards regarded me intently, and my fear was such that I was sure they suspected my disguise. Nevertheless they opened the doors and stood back courteously as I entered. Perhaps they stared because they wondered that I was so late in answering the summons.

I stepped inside, and the doors closed behind me. The room was unchanged from the time that Hickathrift and I had stood before the council. All the chairs were filled with the same folk, except Caradoc's. It was empty, and I quickly made my way to it.

"You are late," William Marrow said.

"My pardon," I replied, starting when the voice came out as Caradoc's.

I sat down, feeling the weight of their gazes upon me. I had little faith in Robin's spells at that moment. These folks were Wyslings, erls, and Loremasters. And here as well, disguised as I was, sat Damal. Surely I reeked of magic—surely they could see through this flimsy disguise? I soon found that they had more pressing matters on their minds.

"I have called this council," William Marrow said when I was seated, "for strange tidings have been brought to my attention. I will let the folk concerned speak of these things themselves before we take council on them. Selwyn?"

The erl lord straightened in his chair.

"The old evils are stirring in Drakrun Wood," he reported, leaning forward as he spoke. "It is as if a great army is gathering in its depths. My scouts report similar stirrings for leagues in all directions, as if the land itself rises against us. Dwarwolves and worse have been seen on the edges of Drakrun, spying on us. The ice on Lanesse has cracks from which strange mutterings issue forth. Many dark and foul creatures have been glimpsed, even from the walls of the keep. So far they have not engaged our patrols, but they grow in number with each passing day. I fear an attack on the keep itself . . . and that soon."

"Mayhap," Tamara said at William Marrow's side, "the Dark Rose is hosting her army to come north, and these are its outriders. She must know that we are aware of her presence in this world and that we will stand against her while there is breath in our bodies."

She seemed so sincere as she spoke. But there were mysteries and secrets in her deep, dark eyes, and I knew the truth her false sincerity hid. There was no Dark Rose. There was only Damal, the Dark Queen, and she posed as Tamara herself. Were they all blind? Why, for all their wisdom, couldn't they see this for themselves?

"What luck have you had in far-seeking this Dark Rose?" Merla asked. "She was in the Kingdoms, last you told us."

I looked at her, surprised at her words. But then I realized that she mustn't let on that she knew the truth, or Damal would have her slain on one pretext or another.

"She was," Tamara replied. "The image was clear and strong in the seeing-glass. I saw her with her companions in the Hills of the Dead, mostly lately. The youth that escaped our halls was there, along with a dwarf and a man's corpse. The man was from the Kingdoms, I would guess from his garb. The boy and the dwarf sat huddled about a fire, while just beyond their camp—held back by guard-spells, I wager— were a pack of the hill-gaunts that have lately left the Waste and infested those hills.

"The image was clear, as I have said, but then—and this was when I called the Lord," she nodded to William Marrow, "of a sudden, the glass went dark. When it cleared, they were gone. I have been unable to find them since, though I've cast my search far into the Kingdoms."

"I can feel them," the Wysling Lord said. "They are close to us . . . very close."

I trembled at his words. We were close—how close he hadn't guessed yet, but when he did. . . . I prayed that whatever plan it was that Robin and Hickathrift had concocted would be set into motion before we were discovered.

I had another worry that rose unbidden in me no matter how I tried to put it from me. I loved Hickathrift as a true friend, but I still knew nothing of Robin Marrow. He was the Lord's son, after all. He might have beguiled Hickathrift. He could be tricking us all.

Could they be in Drarkun Wood? Kentigern asked.

I glanced at the hill cat sitting beside me, then turned away from his sudden scrutiny.

"Perhaps," Tamara replied. "I have been concentrating my search farther from Wistlore than that, but it's a thought well worth considering. Have your scouts any recent news, Selwyn?"

As the erl shook his head, I remembered what Robin had told me. Whatever doubts I had about the young Wysling's trustworthiness, I still had to play out this role that had been thrust upon me. The only other choice was revealing myself to the council and surrendering. Hesitantly, I lifted my harp to my lap and ran my fingers along the strings. I'd been too sudden, though, for all eyes turned to me. Fear scudded in my heart when William Marrow spoke.

"You are quiet, Caradoc. Do you let your instrument speak for you? I fear we are not so skilled in reading a meaning within music as you are."

"I seek only to think upon some clearer course of action," I replied. "The music soothes me."

I ran my fingers down the strings once more, following a minor scale and trying to keep my nervousness from the music.

"Would you rather I was still?" I added.

"No, play on," he said. "I find it soothing myself. And you are correct. We need a clear strategy." He mopped his brow with the end of his sleeve. "Sometimes I feel there is a mist hanging over all—it makes it hard to think. What can we do?" he asked his council. "Must we sit here like rats in a hole, waiting for the ferrets to sniff us out? What of the men we sent to find the Dark Rose? And of the ones that sought the caryaln? Is there no word from them yet?"

"They are dead, my Lord," Tamara replied. She seemed puzzled by the questions. "I told you of what befell them when last you were in my chambers—how I saw them in the seeing-glass, slain by horned riders clad all in red and mounted on terrible steeds."

"Aye, aye," the Lord mumbled irritably. "I remember now."

She was a bold foe, this Damal. I doubted that she'd even sent the men. But if she had, her minions had slain them, and she spoke of the deed now as if it were another's, as if she knew nothing of the Red Hounds.

"Let me take our host into Drarkun," Selwyn said. "Those under my command fret and tire of patrolling the keep. Let us sally forth to strike a blow ourselves."

"Mayhap. . . ." William Marrow began.

A confusion at the doorway interrupted him, and he broke off. All heads turned in its direction as the door opened. Two

erls strode inside, armed with spears. One balanced the shaft
of his weapon in the crook of his arm and carried the body
of a dead man . . . Galin's body.

"Sire," he said. "We found this man dead in the east
halls. There was no one about him—no wound on him, no
sign of struggle. And not one guard saw him gain entrance
to the keep."

One voice broke the deadly silence that followed his report.

"That is the man I saw in the company of the Dark Rose
in the Hills of the Dead."

Tamara spoke. My fingers faltered on the strings. What
was Galin's body doing here—and where were my companions? I gazed fearfully about, sure that I was about to be
discovered.

"You are sure?" William Marrow boomed. I lost the thread
of my tune and set Telynros aside as he continued. "Have
others penetrated the keep?"

I stared at Tamara, searching for fear but finding none.
Anger was in her eyes, and ever those hidden secrets. At the
far end of the room, Merla stood up.

"Where there is one, there will be more!" she cried. "We
must find them, and quickly!"

Selwyn was already out of his seat, approaching Galin's
still form. I gripped the arms of my chair, ready to hurl myself at Tamara should she rise from hers. The erls who'd
brought in Galin's body held their spears ready, flanking the
door. The one nearest me called out:

"What goes there?"

He pointed with his spear to the drapes behind Kentigern's
chair. All gazes followed his spear's point except for mine,
for from the corner of my eye, I saw the other erl jerk back
his arm to cast his spear at Merla.

"No!" I shouted, but I saw the spear shimmer in the air
and turn into a shadow-weapon. I was too late. The caryaln
plunged between Merla's breasts, skewering her to the back
of her chair. She shrieked horribly, moaning as she writhed
along its length trying to free herself.

Selwyn drew a long silver sword from the sheath at his belt and held the erl who'd cast the spear at bay. The erl stood as still as silence itself while William Marrow rose from his seat, his eyes blazing, his arms upraised. There was death in the magefire that crackled between his fingers as he began his spell, and I knew that this magic would be no illusion.

I sat numbed in my chair, unable to move. Then the erl's form shimmered, as Hickathrift's had done in Caradoc's chambers. Before us stood the maid of the Grey Rose. My gaze froze on her, shifted to Tamara who sat staring at the maid, then returned to Meana. How could she have done this?

"You?" the Wysling Lord roared. He seemed to gain in stature as his voice filled the chamber with his rage. His eyes were wild and his face flushed. "You would dare strike at us in our very halls?"

Golden magefire grew in intensity in his hands. I longed to rush forward, to place myself between his wrath and the Grey Rose, but I couldn't move. I was dumbfounded. I felt cheated, betrayed. All our struggling had been to no avail.

"Hold!" a voice cried from near me.

Robin Marrow's shape grew from the form of the erl who'd distracted us.

"Hold?" his father said, his voice deathly calm now. "Are you my son, or are you some sending of the Daketh in his guise? No matter. Either way, you are leagued against us and will pay for this hideous crime. I am the Lord of this holding . . . I am the Lord of Wistlore. My word is law."

Not so!

This was from Kentigern. He launched himself from his seat to pad in front of the Wysling Lord, his eyes narrowed to slits, the end of his tail flicking.

A veil has been lifted from my eyes, he said. *You are not the Lord of Wistlore . . . there is no such creature. We have no need for such. I will bow to no man, I will call none my Lord. My respect I will give, but I will not bow to another's will.* His gaze raked the council. *Can you not see the lie of that veil?*

"It was the veil of madness," the Grey Rose said.

Robin strode to her side. From the doorway came the sound of a small skirmish. Hickathrift entered then, followed by Calman. Still fighting the length of spear that impaled her to her chair, Merla writhed and screamed curses. I stared at her, and her features swam in my sight. Smoke smoldered from her flesh where the caryaln touched her.

"Look closely," Robin said. He pointed at the woman who mouthed obscenities in Merla's form. "That is your Dark Rose . . . that is Damal, the Dark Queen."

Merla's form twisted horribly as he spoke the dread name. She shifted and spun in my eyes until I recognized the horrific aspect of the Dark Queen. Her skin was alabaster, the blue veins protruding as she strained and struggled to escape the trap. The eyes were those of an insane beast. Jagged teeth showed through the slavering foam that covered her mouth.

I rose to my feet as it all became clear to me. It'd been Merla, or rather Damal in her form, who'd freed me from Wistlore, given me the dagger, and set me on the trail of the Grey Rose so that I'd almost killed her. I had been her only way of striking at the one person who truly threatened her. She'd blinded everyone else—myself included. Only the Grey Rose could recognize her, so only the Grey Rose knew who the shadow-death must strike. Even if I'd taken the spear, I'd have tried to kill Tamara with it, not Merla.

"No!" William Marrow bellowed, his voice cracking. "This is treason! This is madness!"

The lightning erupted from his hands. I leapt for him before he could strike Meana, but Tamara was quicker. She had a goblet in her hand, and with it she struck the Wysling Lord on the nape of his neck. He fell forward, the magefire blasting the wall, and sprawled senselessly across the floor. Tamara looked down at the goblet in her hand, then at the still form that lay beside her.

"So this is the way of things," she said, passing a hand over her brow. "Indeed a veil has been lifted. How could we have been so blind?"

The Grey Rose walked to where Damal fought the caryaln. She took the spear in her hands and twisted it, crying:

"Begone! Your power is no more!"

As her hands touched the weapon, an amber glow surrounded her and ran down the length of the spear's shaft. Where it touched Damal, the Dark Queen burned. She wailed, thrashing about in an attempt to win free.

"Yaln ser brena!" Meana cried.

Damal's wild motions ceased, and she lay very still. The amber glow encompassed her. Her mad eyes were stark with fear.

"You were summoned," the Grey Rose said, "and you came. So was the Balance sundered. Death is your reward."

The amber glow exploded blindingly and filled the room. A hideous cry ripped the air. When the light faded, only the Grey Rose stood by the empty chair. Damal was gone. Meana's form seemed diminished, her head bowed with weariness. The shadow-spear smoldered darkly in her hands for a moment longer; then it, too, was gone.

"It is done," Meana whispered.

I hastened to her side, catching her as she fell, utterly spent.

ᴛᴡɪʟɪɢʜᴛ's Sᴏɴɢᴡᴇᴀᴠᴇʀ

> *Which is more secret:*
> *the moon in the sky*
> *or her silver light*
> *reflected in the waters below?*
> *Some riddles have no answer*
> *save that which is hidden*
> *in the hazel grove*
> *where a horned wind plays*
> *the twig-strings of the trees*
> *and the grey-eyed Harpers*
> *listen.*
>
> —"The Mysteries"
> from the Sᴏɴɢᴡᴇᴀᴠᴇʀ's Jᴏᴜʀɴᴇʏʙᴏᴏᴋ

A Wʏsʟɪɴɢ ɴᴀᴍᴇᴅ Oʀɪᴏɴ Sᴛᴀʀʙʀᴇᴀᴛʜ ᴛᴏᴏᴋ Wɪʟʟɪᴀᴍ Marrow's place in the council. When Robin refused to take his father's position, Orion was summoned from the Amberwood where he was biding.

"I'll not take a seat on the council," Robin said, "until my own studies are completed."

When the old Wysling Lord regained consciousness, his powers were stripped from him in some dread Wysling ceremony. He was treated kindly and not exiled, for all knew that he'd been under Damal's influence. Although the taint could not be removed from his spirit, once his powers were removed he was nothing more than a helpless, slightly mad, old man.

The erl commander Selwyn led his warriors against those of the Dark who'd been hosting around Wistlore. Merla had been his sister and very dear to him. It had been her body that Hickathrift and Robin had found in the cellars.

Selwyn's revenge was awful and grim. In a month's time he'd slain or driven off the evil creatures that had been gathering against Wistlore for a distance of more than thirty leagues. Only Drarkun Wood remained untamed, but its sentience faded back into slumber with the death of the Dark Queen. At length, sickened of the warring, Selwyn took his leave from Wistlore. His task was done, and there was too much within its walls to remind him of his grief.

Caradoc, we discovered, hadn't been in league with Damal at all. His journal was filled with page upon page of irrational suspicions and rantings. Few mourned his death, for he'd been a selfish, grasping man and had treated many others as he had my mother. It was ironic that it'd been Calman's hand that slew him, for Caradoc had been the instrumental force in my mother's exile. Calman had taken her revenge for her.

Eoin Fairling took up the mantle of Masterharper. Hickathrift had always spoken fairly of him, and he and I got along well. He treated me with respect and loved to tell me tales of my mother's youth, for they'd known each other when they were young. He vowed that, should I be willing, he'd indeed have me study under him.

Calman left. Unable to abide the acclamation heaped upon us by the folk of Wistlore, he departed for Maelholme where he planned to gather those of his folk who were willing to rebuild Deepdelve with him. He bade me a gruff farewell early one morning, not wanting to hear my thanks, just extracting a promise from me that I'd come to visit him when the ruined halls were an underground kingdom once again.

Galin was laid in state in the crypts of Wistlore amongst the tombs of the wise and the venerated of the ages. Calman took his guilt for Galin's death with him and wouldn't let it rest. I knew that same guilt, and when the dwarf left, I watched him go sadly, knowing too well the sorrow that lived in his heart.

THE TWO MONTHS FOLLOWING DAMAL'S FALL WERE MORE OF a joy to me than even that summer when I fared almost daily to the Grey Rose's cottage in the Golden Wood. Meana was weak from her long trials—no matter that the Tuathan were her kin. Her mother might be Willoney, but her father was a Hill Lord with as much mortal blood in him as weren.

I cared for her during those days. The folk of Wistlore weren't easy to sway from the honours they wished to bestow on us—honours that only embarrassed us—so we remained closeted in her chambers. Sometimes Hickathrift sat with us, but more often she lay abed, propped against the headboard with a mountain of pillows while I played Telynros for her and we told each other stories as we'd done before the troubles began.

The days were a much needed joy, for our nights were grim. Time and again, she awakened from terrifying nightmares, and I sat with her through the dark hours, comforting her as I could. In time, though, the rose in her hair began to bloom once more, and I knew her strength was returning.

I was happy for her, but almost I feared her growing well too quickly. It was a mean thought, but I knew that when she was whole again she'd leave me. I couldn't abide the thought. Life without her would be an endless grieving, her departure a pall upon all my days. She knew I loved her, I'd told her as much before, but now that we were alone, without the strife hanging between us, I found it impossible to voice the words again. They caught in my throat, and I played sad airs on the roseharp in place of them.

I knew she was aware of what went on inside me. I'd find her looking sorrowfully at me at such times. Then as soon as I caught her eye, the sorrow would slip away and she'd smile brightly.

When she was stronger, we took to sitting in the great hall of Wistlore—the hall where Hickathrift and I had first come when we entered this holding. Sometimes he'd sit with us, relating strange lost lore that he'd delved up from somewhere and arguing points of it with Meana when she had an opposing view. Other times he'd listen to my harping, an accompaniment rumbling deep in his chest. He'd regained his lost weight and spent more and more time out of doors, haunting the borders of Drarkun Wood for a glimpse of the raewin.

Others spent time with us—Calman before he departed, Robin, and Eoin Fairling—but mostly we sat alone, talking softly of many things until one day I took my heart in my hand and laid it before her. She sighed as I spoke, taking my hands in her own to clasp them tightly.

"Ah, Cerin," she said. "Would that it could be. There is love for you in my heart as well. It runs deep and true—I can't deny it. But it can't be. The Balance has tipped my way now—I am the one who upsets it. I must return to the realms of my people before the Daketh send another troubling."

"Couldn't I come with you?"

"It can't be. That would upset the Balance more gravely than if I remained here. And see, Cerin . . . I am old as you count years. Although you will have a long life—this much your weren blood gives you—you will be grey and withered when I am still young as you see me now. And when at last you do fare beyond this world, what then of me? What would I do, young in seeming, ever yearning for you? It would not be good. As you grew old, bitterness would enter you. Your heart would sour toward me, and that I could never abide."

"Better that we take what joy we can where we can find it. You promise me long life, but what good would it be . . . only endless years to long for you."

"Do not be bitter," she said. "There will come other maids in your life—don't frown so—and you will yet find joy. I must return to the realms of the Tuathan, and you must remain here in Mid-wold, and we each must eke out of our lives what peace we can. I would not have us part with hard words between us."

"But what will I do?" Despair washed heavily over me.

"Become a Harper, Cerin. Be my Songweaver. Has not Eoin already asked you to study under him?"

"He has," I mumbled.

"Well then. This is what you yearned for, long before you met me. Now your moment has come, now you can become a Harper—the greatest of Harpers—and set your true worth before the world. Be strong, Cerin. Take the threads of your life into your own hands and weave a tapestry of them that I may point to and say: 'This man I knew. This is the man I loved. Though his life be short and sweet as the leaves of the wood, see what he has wrought. See how his songs sing forever, when he has long passed into other seemings.'

"That would comfort me as the years speed by, Cerin. Telynros will guide you, but without the learnings of the Harpers, you would soon come up against walls that you cannot breach without help. Be a Harper, Cerin. Give to the world the magic of the songs that lie waiting for life inside you. And although we part soon, remember that we dwell forever in each other's heart.

"Once you told me that you had raised a fane for me in your heart. There is one for you now in mine. Let us keep them sacred, each for the other. Will you do this for me, Cerin, my Songweaver?"

ONE DAY, A WEEK BEFORE MY STUDIES UNDER THE MASTERHARPer were to begin, the Grey Rose met me in the great hall. I was sitting with Hickathrift, and we were talking of the days to come. I'd promised him that, when my studies were done, I'd take him to where I'd met Gwenya in Drarkun Wood and that I'd go north with him to the Woods of Auldwen as well.

And a fair journey we'll make of it, he replied. *There's a—*

He broke off when we saw Meana approaching. She took me by the hand, and I stood up beside her. Looking down into her face, I saw the glisten on her eyelashes and knew that the time for her leaving had come. Rising on her toe-tips she kissed me, her lips fierce upon mine.

"Farewell, Songweaver," she whispered.

She wasn't so tall as she'd once seemed, but the sweet heady scent of autumn still seemed to drift about her. She nodded to Hickathrift, then disengaged our fingers for, when she'd taken my hand, I held fast, not wanting to let her go.

"Fare . . . well. . . ." I said, the word catching in my throat.

I watched her walk down the aisle. She paused at the tall doorway and looked back, her arm raised in a last farewell. Then a shimmer came over the threshold and she was gone, faring the freywen, the spirit paths, back to the home of her mighty kin.

Tears stung my cheek as I sat down beside Hickathrift again. He put a broad paw comfortingly upon my leg, and we sat there all that day until the night fell solemnly outside the walls of Wistlore. I went to the courtyard and stood there, gazing at the starlit clouds, thinking of Tess in the West Downs and Calman in Deepdelve and Meana in whatever place it was that the Tuathan dwelt.

I thought of the bloom in her hair that twinned the one in the roseharp. I remembered Robin telling me that the little people of the hills named her Twilight. Where did the twilight go when night was come? Where did she sleep in the day?

Words came to my mind, soft-stepping an air that came from the fey blood of my father that stirred deep inside me.

> *Twilight is a dusky lady,*
> *her sweet breath like the wind;*
> *her eyes are dark with secret turnings,*
> *brimmed with fancy's wings.*
>
> *Her hair of many autumn colours*
> *o'er slim shoulders falls;*
> *day's end, moon-lit, on the hills,*
> *she has me e'er enthralled. . . .*

I'd polish it, I thought, breathe a fuller life into it. The Hare Moon rose high in the sky as I stood there—a horned moon, newborn. As its light touched the clouds, I thought I saw them shift, shaping the image of a rose, grey in the sky . . . full-blooming and wondrous with wild magics.

"Dursona," I whispered and wiped the misting tears from my eyes. "Farewell. . . ."

Only the wind breathed a reply.

Glossary

Note: (S) indicates Sennayeth words.

a-meir (S)—"well-met"
ar moorlig (S)—"blessed be"
Avenal—the Tuathan Lady of Earth and Moon

balance, the—*see* Covenant
Ballan, the—the Tuathan Lord of the Travelling Folk
brecaln (S)—a hill cat
bren ser meir (S)—"you be well" (literal translation)

caryaln (S)—literally, "shadow-death"; refers to weaponry that can destroy Wasters and others of the Daketh
Celeste—the Tuathan Lady of Dreams
col-neh (S)—"my thanks"
Covenant, the—an ancient agreement between the Tuathan and Daketh (that some say was forced on them by the Grey Gods) that states, in part, that they may no longer walk in Mid-wold. If one of either does come to the middle realm that lies between their own, a ranking member of the opposite gods is permitted to come as well, to maintain the balance that was broken in the Chaos Time, resulting in the destruction of Avenveres which was the First World.

Daketh, the—the Dark Gods
dalin (S)—globe-shaped lights made by dwarves
Dalker (S)—the realm of the Dark Gods
Damal—the Dark Queen, daughter of Yurlogh Tyrrbane
dursona (S)—"godspeed"
dwarwolves—creatures bred by the Daketh in the elder days; they have a dwarf's upper torso and a wolf's lower body.

erlkin (S)—an elfish folk; divided into high erlkin, who were the First Born of the Tuathan's children, and the low erlkin, who were the Second. High erls are a tall, golden folk, not bound to any one place. Low erls are much like their cousins the weren, or Wild Folk, and are usually bound to their forests, if they are wooderls; to their hills, if they are hillerls, and so on.

Freya—the Tuathan Keeper of the Winds *(see also* Weaywd)
freywen (S)—spirit paths utilized by the Tuathan to take them quickly from one place in Mid-wold to another.

galsa (S)—a small hardy plant that grows in moorlands and foothills; the roots are good for eating.
Greymin—the Tuathan Lord of the Sky
Grey Rose, the—*see* Meana
gwandryas (S)—a nomadic people of the Grassfields and the Great Waste

heartstone—a jewel that, when worn long enough by one of the Tuathan, takes on a part of their essence
Heartsure—a plant with tiny bell-like gold flowers that has healing properties
het ser meir (S)—"it is well" (literal translation)
Hillfolk—the ancestors of the gwandryas who settled in the hilllands; they were mortals but were related to the weren.
Hill Lords—the highborn of the Hillfolk
Hoof and Horn—*see* ren Carn ha Corn
Horned Lord—a weren god; consort of the Moonmother; called variously Cernunnos, WerenArl or Wild Lord, and Pan the Piper

Jaalmar—the Tuathan Lord of Secrets and Quiet Walking
Jarl—the Tuathan Lord of the Sea

Kindreds, the—*see* Seven Kindreds
knar (S)—a board game
kwessen (S)—"friend"

Meana—the Tuathan Lady of the Twilight; also called the Grey Rose

melyonen (S)—a gold flower found in late summer and early autumn

Middle Kingdom—often used incorrectly to describe the realms of the erlkin and others of the Kindreds; it is in fact the realm of the weren, but as the years have gone by the usage has blurred to refer to either.

Mid-wold—a term used to describe the lands that lie between the realms of the Tuathan and the Daketh

Moonmother—the weren goddess of the Earth and Moon; has three aspects, those of maiden, mother, and crone; also called Anann, Arn, or simply Mother or Moon

muryan (S)—weren moorfolk

mys-hudol (S)—talking beasts

quen (S)—"come"

raewin—beings with the upper torso of a human and the lower torso of a deer

Red Hounds, the—minions of the Daketh's High Born, such as Damal

ren Carn ha Corn—"by Hoof and Horn" (refers to the Wild Lord); an exclamation

root-ways—a mys-hudol term for old knowledge and lore

Seven Kindreds—the children of the Tuathan, in order: the high erls, the low erls, the mys-hudol or talking beasts, the cawran or giants, the dwarves, the kemys-folk or halflings (beings such as the raewin), and mankind. The Tuathan make no claim to the last, however, and they are cited as one of the Great Mysteries.

taw (S)—inner strength; usually that which is used for spell-working

Telynros (S)—literally "rose-harp"; the name of the instrument that Meana gave to the Songweaver

Truil—the Tuathan Lord of Stone and Father of the Dwarves

Tyrr Stormbringer—the High Lord of the Tuathan

Waster—the First Born of the Daketh
Weaywd—the Tuathan Keeper of the Winds (*see also* Freya)
weren (S)—the Wild Folk
Wild Lord—*see* Horned Lord
Willoney—the Tuathan Lady of Flame and Fertility
wooderl—low erlkin, usually bound to a particular tree or forest

yargs (S)—base-born minions of the Daketh
Young Innes—the Tuathan Lord of Wild Roses and Harpers
Yurlogh Tyrrbane—the High Lord of the Daketh